What the critics are saying...

ॐ

All Knight Long

4 1/2 Stars "Devlin has written a very sexy, fun story" ~ *Romantic Time BookClub Magazine*

"Vampires, werewolves, and babies—oh, my! ALL KNIGHT LONG is a sensual and thrilling ride into the world of the paranormal" ~ *Romance Reviews Today*

5 Angels "I loved the latest book in the My Immortal Knight series...very entertaining, very sensual and highly recommended...When you combine her excellent characters with the great plot, this story becomes a must read" ~ *Fallen Angels Reviews*

Relentless

5 Blue Ribbons "The unexpected plot twists in My Immortal Knight: Relentless left me in awe as to Delilah's mastery of her craft" ~ *Romance Junkies*

Also 5 Stars from *Just Erotic Romance*; *5 Hearts* from *Love Romances*; *5 Stars* from *eCataRomance*; *5 Angels* from *Fallen Angels Reviews*; *5 Unicorns* from *Enchanted in Romance*

Also by Delilah Devlin

ℰℴ

Contents

ALL KNIGHT LONG

Dedication

ಌ

To Lena Austin for her expert advice for the Tarot reading, and to my sister, Myla Jackson, for her imagination and loving partnership.

Chapter One

ဢ

The small sign in the café window read: Welcome Vampires and Sanguinarians! *(No blood products provided — none permitted on premises! The Management).*

Joe Garcia snorted. Every human in the place was a walking, breathing blood product — a portable soda fountain for the Fanged Ones.

He pushed through the glass door and tried to dampen the hope that rose in his chest, causing his heart to beat faster and his hands to sweat. Thus far, he'd met only disappointment in his long search. This might be just another dead end — the last one he could afford before his cash ran out and his credit card was maxed.

Professor Carlson was his last hope.

Inside the cafe, enticing aromas assailed him. The smell of roasted coffee beans, which had been his life's blood in another existence, was overlaid with the tangy scent of the real thing — the warm, viscous red stuff. The latter reminded him he hadn't fed this evening, and hunger gnawed at his belly, making him edgy and irritable.

And something else enticed him. Something dark and sensual perfumed by a female musk with a tincture so unique it immediately sent a curl of heat to his groin.

He walked past the coffee bar without acknowledging the barrista's greeting and wound his way through the tables, ignoring the human appetizers. His gaze was fixed on a menu board at the entrance of a roped-off area in the back, that read "Vampire Survey Here". An arrow pointed down to a table laden with a stack of pamphlets.

He brushed past the table, searching the back of the restaurant for his quarry.

"Sir, are you here 'bout da survey Professor Carlson is conductin'?"

Joe turned toward the voice flavored with a deep Louisianan accent. A pleasant-faced girl with black corkscrew curls all around her head sat at a table near the cordoned entrance.

He bit back the rude retort that immediately came to mind and answered, "Yes. I need to speak with her."

"Well, you'll have to complete a screenin' survey first," she said pleasantly but firmly, holding up a stapled document.

Joe sighed and accepted the papers. What the hell? Five more minutes wouldn't kill him.

"Do you have a pencil?" she asked. When he shook his head, she gave him a superior smile and extended a short, sharpened pencil.

Joe didn't like her attitude one bit, so he reached for her hand, running his fingers over her palm before taking it.

Her smile slipped and Joe could well imagine her thoughts. Another vampire wannabe was hitting on her. He smiled and let her see his teeth.

Her eyes narrowed and a single brow rose. She wasn't impressed.

That actually gave Joe hope he was in the right place after all. His sharp fangs hadn't fazed her.

"You can take a seat with the other guy," she said, indicating the first booth along the back wall.

Joe walked over and slid across the vinyl seat opposite a young man dressed in black leather and sporting no less than five facial piercings. The piercings glittered like tinsel in the dim light and Joe wondered how the kid could stand leather in May—New Orleans was already sweltering, even at night.

Turning over the top page of his survey, Joe quickly scanned the questions. He hoped like hell they were only meant to screen out the weirdoes and pretenders. Otherwise, he was screwed.

He wet the tip of his pencil on his tongue and read the first question.

"Do you consider yourself a Vampire or a Sanguinarian?"

Since he had no clue what a Sanguinarian was, he checked, "Vampire."

"If you checked 'Vampire', skip to question 6."

Maybe this wouldn't take so long after all.

In the middle of the page, he found 6. "How often do you have the urge to drink blood?"

He checked the block beside, "More than three times a day." *Three times a night would be more accurate.*

"How often do you drink blood?"

"Once a day."

"Do you drink your own blood?"

"What would be the point?" he muttered, and checked "No."

When he reached the question, "Do you drink blood during sexual encounters?" he'd had enough.

He tossed the survey to the table and started to rise.

"She won't see you unless you finish the survey," Metal Boy said, without looking up from his form.

"She'll see me."

The young man's mouth twisted into a sneer. "You'll have to wait your turn. I was here first."

Joe lifted his lips and showed him his fangs.

Metal Boy smirked and then lifted his lips, displaying a whole row of sharpened teeth.

Joe took a quick glance around the café to make sure no one was near, and then leaned over the table and shook his head. He let the change come over him, reveling for once in the wildness that surged in his veins as the bones in his forehead and brow shifted, and his skin stretched tightly.

The boy's eyes widened until the whites symmetrically framed his irises. "I-I've just thought of somewhere else I need to be," he said, and quickly scooted off the seat and ran for the exit.

Satisfied that vamping was good for at least scaring the shit out of punks, Joe took a deep breath and relaxed, feeling his face reform to his human mask. Then he headed back to the girl with the wild hair.

"I'll see her now," Joe said, not even trying to conceal his impatience.

"Have you finished dat survey?" she asked, her nose buried in her Cosmo magazine. When he didn't respond, she raised her eyes.

Something in his expression made her hesitate. "I'll see if she's free."

Joe smiled grimly. "You do that."

She was back in a moment. "Professor Carlson'll see you now. You left your survey on the table, but I gave it to her."

He followed her to the farthest corner of the café, toward another booth. A green lamp suspended over the table lent the corner a warm glow. When he drew alongside the green vinyl seat, the girl indicated he should sit and promptly left. Joe turned his gaze to the figure seated on the opposite bench.

His research had told him the professor was considered an expert in vampire lore. She'd written papers, magazine articles, and books, and even been consulted by more than one movie producer. When he'd typed "vampire expert" in the Internet search engine, her name had popped up everywhere.

All his research told him she might hold the answer, but it hadn't said anything about how young or *drinkable* she was. Her hair was neither blonde nor brown, but the warm color of whiskey. Her eyes, hidden behind a pair of wire-framed glasses, glinted cognac. Her lips were a pale rosé.

The hunter within him woke.

Realizing he'd been staring, he cleared his throat. "You're Professor Lily Carlson? The author of 'Vampires: Myth and Reality'?"

Her gaze swept over him. An action so swift, he thought he might have imagined it. "And you are?" she asked, leaning over the table to extend her hand.

Joe froze. That indefinable scent was all over her. He had the urge to rub on her like a kitten in catnip. He eyed her small hand, afraid to touch it and feel the blood humming below the surface of her creamy, white skin. He was *that* close to jumping her. "I thought the survey was anonymous."

"Oh, it is," she replied quickly, withdrawing her hand. "You're responding to the ad, then?" At his nod, she looked vaguely disappointed. "Well, I suppose I should review your answers. Please have a seat," she said, waving him toward the bench seat opposite hers. "Thank you for taking the time to help me with my research."

Bemused, Joe slid onto the seat. He knew he should get straight to the point, but he stalled. For just a few minutes, he wanted to be with a woman while she looked at him as if he was just like any other man. Well, perhaps like he was a man with a serious mental disorder. But at least, she wasn't recoiling in horror or inspecting him like the Bearded Lady at a freak show.

Not that she was a great beauty, nor even as strong and fierce as his ex-partner Darcy. Dressed in a boring-beige suit, her whiskey-colored hair piled in a loose knot on top of her head, and her glasses sliding down her shiny nose, she looked like the schoolmarm she was. But while all the beige and brown should have made her look muddy, she glowed golden in the lamplight. And her scent—richly textured with something wild and animalistic—was extraordinary.

The woman opened his survey and glanced at his answers, then flipped the page. Her lips pursed for a moment, drawing his gaze to her full lower lip. "There are a few more questions I need answered. Do you mind if I learn a little more about you?" she asked, glancing up at him from beneath her gold-tipped lashes.

The surge of heat that centered in his groin was way out of proportion to her innocent question. Afraid he'd stutter over a tongue that suddenly felt too large for his mouth, he merely nodded.

"You understand the questions I'm about to ask you are part of a sociological study I'm conducting about our vampire subculture?"

Again, he nodded.

"All information you provide," she recited as if from rote, "will be completely confidential. I hope you will answer me honestly," she gave him a doubtful stare, "or to the best of your ability."

She looked expectantly at him, so he nodded again.

Her gaze returned to his survey and she cleared her throat. "You…are a vampire?"

"Yes." This was the first time he'd admitted that fact out loud, and he knew how ridiculous it sounded.

"So, are you a Psy or a Sang?"

"There's more than one kind?" Joe asked.

"A Psychic vampire feeds on a human's energy; a Sanguinarian is a blood-drinker."

"I guess I'm a Sang."

"You drink blood once a day?" she asked, her head still bent over the paper.

He shrugged, hoping she'd glance up at him again so he could see whether her eyes really were a warm, golden-brown. "More or less."

She scribbled something in the margin of his survey. "Well, which is it?"

"Sometimes more."

"Do you drink human blood?"

Joe wished she'd end this line of questioning, or he'd be drooling shortly. Her scent had every appetite revving into high gear. "Yes."

She glanced up from the survey. "How long have you had the urge to drink blood?"

"Since I woke up, tonight."

She blinked. "No, I meant…since ever."

"Last winter."

"Did you by chance suffer some sort of emotional trauma?"

Joe stiffened. If you consider I died, and the woman I loved had her boyfriend turn me, then hell yes! "Yes."

"Was the trauma centered around a love relationship?"

He drew a deep breath. The professor was determined to hit every sensitive nerve he owned. "Yes."

"A woman?"

He glowered at her and didn't respond.

She did another of those little sweeps of her eyelashes that left him feeling confused. "Woman," she said softly and annotated his answer. "Was it a sexual relationship?"

Every muscle in his body contracted. The memory of the last time he'd seen Darcy, the last time he'd been inside her, had his cock straining inside his jeans.

"Was it?" she insisted.

Joe nodded, feeling his face harden, knowing he looked as dour as the Grim Reaper right about now.

"You say, you drink blood during sex."

He felt like howling. "Sometimes."

She looked up, her head canting to the side. "Why?"

"To give myself and my host greater pleasure. The orgasms are worth dying for," he said, hoping to give her a taste of his discomfort.

"Oh." Her face suffused in pink, and she cleared her throat. "Do you use lancets to bleed your host?"

He didn't understand her question and stared.

"Do you use something sharp to pierce your host's skin?"

"My teeth. I bite them." He lifted his lips and let her see the teeth he couldn't convince to recede into his gums—he was just too damn hungry.

"Oh." Her expression remained professionally frozen, but Joe had the feeling she wanted to roll her eyes. She reached into her handbag and pulled out a silver cross, and then held it in front of him. "Do you get a burning sensation when you see this object?"

"No."

"Does this produce any sensation at all?" She touched his hand with it.

Air hissed between his teeth at the first touch of her hand. He was on fire. His hand curled beneath hers, curving into a fist.

Her eyebrows lifted and she quickly scribbled something else on his survey. "Do you believe in Satan?"

"Yeah, if he's the evil that lurks in a man's heart."

"Do you worship Satan?"

"Uh, no."

She reached into her purse again and pulled out a tiny bottle of water and a sharpened stick.

Joe stared at the items she stacked neatly in a row in front of him and his blood began to boil. Silver crosses, holy water, and a fucking stake. Shit! The woman had studied *Buffy 101*. She was a fraud. She didn't know the first thing about vampires— hell, she didn't believe they existed. "I don't suppose, Professor, that in all your research you've ever actually met a vampire?"

She blinked and pushed her glasses up her nose. "I'm the one asking the questions here."

"And I'm finished answering," Joe said, his eyes narrowing. "Have you ever met a real vampire?"

The little Professor sniffed and raised her chin. "No, I haven't."

Joe slumped in the booth. His last hope dashed.

"Are you all right?" she asked, eyeing him with suspicion.

"Just pissed and hungry." He let his gaze fall to her neck. "Want to know what it feels like?"

"What?" she asked, her eyes wide.

"To be sucked by a vampire."

The Professor's cheeks turned a fiery red. "Certainly not." But her words lacked true outrage.

Joe's mouth stretched into a smile. The lady had a dirty mind. Although, now that she had him thinking about it, the idea took root. She might not be able to give him the information he needed, but she could certainly share a little blood in exchange for the sweet release he'd give her.

"Can I come home with you?" He hadn't meant to blurt it out quite like that, but she was too delectable to pass up—and she owed him. He'd come halfway across the country just to speak to her.

Now, she looked truly alarmed. "I-I think that's all the questions. Thank you for coming."

Joe smiled and settled his back against the seat, stretching his arms across the top of the bench. He knew the action pulled his T-shirt taut across his chest—a well-developed chest, or so he'd been told.

Her next nervous sweep indicated she'd noticed.

"Don't you want to complete your research? Don't you want to know what it's like to feel a vampire's kiss?"

Her chin came up. "I think if there was truly any merit to the legends, I'd have discovered that by now," she said primly, her hands clenched on the table. "Stop playing with me."

He dropped his voice to a purr. "Don't you want it to be true?"

She stared at him, her face growing solemn and her gaze haunted. "I've wanted that more than you could ever know."

Joe tired of baiting her. He reached across the table and grabbed her hand.

She tugged it back, but he turned her hand and brought her wrist to his nose. He inhaled deeply. "Not perfume. You." He licked her delicate wrist, his breath deepening when he felt her heart rate increase.

"What are you doing? Unhand me!"

"I'm going to give you a kiss," he said, never letting his gaze leave hers. "Here." He slid his lips on her wrist. "I'll show you what a vampire can do without ever being inside you."

Her mouth fell open and her cheeks paled. She drew her hand back, again.

"Just a taste," he whispered, not letting go.

"You're going to bite me?" she asked, her tone incredulous. "What about shots? Blood tests? There's a pamphlet on the table that describes safe bloodletting techniques—*biting isn't one of them!* Christ, think of the bacteria!"

Joe's eyes narrowed and he sank his teeth into a vein that trembled just under her skin.

"Ow!" she gasped, her eyes rounding.

Then he sucked, and she gasped again, only this time her body fell back against the upholstered seat. Her eyes closed for a moment and her lips formed around an astonished 'O'. "That's...incredible!" she moaned, her back arching.

He mouthed her skin while he continued to feed, drawing her rich blood across his tongue, down his throat, pulling her scent into his nostrils—as overcome with sensation and rising passion as his shocked little host-*ess*.

"Please," she said, her voice quavering. "Please, stop."

Joe withdrew his teeth immediately, though it damn near killed him. His body was wound tight as a spring. Then he looked at her. Her eyes were wary and wide, like a doe's caught in the crosshairs. Wild color flooded her cheeks.

The poor Professor had enjoyed her lesson a little too much!

Satisfied he'd planted a seed of sensual curiosity, he dropped his gaze to her wrist and the blood dotting her pale skin. He licked her until the small wounds closed, and then he laid her hand on the table. "Do you see now?" he asked softly, feeling not the least ashamed he'd used his persuasive "powers" to excite her.

She drew a long shaky breath. "I see that my research needs to be expanded. I should make a point to appeal to the Sanguinarians for input. Of course," she said, looking at her wrist under the lamplight and frowning, "I should probably make sure my tetanus is up to date, first."

Joe stared at her, wondering what it was going to take to prove he was a vampire. Morphing wasn't an option—it tended to kill his victim's sexual interest. "Jesus, you still don't get it!"

Surprise at his outburst caused her face to pale. "What's to get? Other than you think you're a vampire?"

Joe stood, and then leaned over the table, crowding the professor into the corner of the booth. "Lady, you wouldn't know a vampire if he bit you in the ass!"

"I beg your pardon," she said, a frown drawing her eyebrows together.

"You don't know a damn thing about vampires. Hell, you can't even tell when one's fed off you!"

"Now look here, I've studied all the texts, from every country with vampire traditions—China to Transylvania." She folded her arms over her chest. "I've also read quite a bit about blood-drinking behavioral disorders and blood fetishists."

"Tell me you didn't feel it, too." His gaze fell to her tweed-covered chest. "Did your studies tell you that a vampire's bloodlust is linked to sexual lust?"

"Th-there is an erotic allure to vampirism," she said, reaching to tuck a strand of hair into her bun. "After all, blood is the source of life and passion—which is what I'm assuming you're experiencing now. The clinical term is haematodipsia—a sexual thirst for blood."

"You're babbling," Joe said, leaning close enough now that he could look into the cleavage at the top of her beige blouse and draw in her heated scent. "Tell me why your pulse is elevated and you're perspiring."

Her hand fluttered on her chest, and she closed the collar of her shirt. "There's no doubt a term. I just can't think—"

"Well, I'm not talking about sexual disorders. I'm talking about lust that grows in proportion to the amount of blood shared by a host."

She blinked. "That happens?"

"You don't know a lot of things, do you?" He drew back and glowered. "You don't know how fast a vampire can drain a human dry. And do you have any clue how dangerous this is?" He raised the survey and crushed it into a ball, unaccountably angry with her. "You could have drawn a bloodthirsty bastard with a nasty sense of humor. Someone who wouldn't have a qualm about taking your head off to get at your blood."

Her small pointed chin lifted. "I took precautions against being accosted by unhinged characters," she said, glaring pointedly at him. "I'm in a public place with people around me."

"Do you know a vampire's strength and speed is many times that of a man? You wouldn't stand a chance against one."

"I'll concede that—*if*—you were a vampire," she said her voice rising, "I might indeed be in trouble."

He leaned closer, his hands clutching the table and the top of the bench seat. "Don't you want to know for sure, Professor?"

"Short of you taking a bite out of my neck—yes! But biting me with capped teeth won't prove a thing. Hell, I have a mirror here somewhere—" she dug into her purse again, "we'll just check your reflection."

Joe shook his head. The woman watched way too much *Buffy*. "If I'm telling you the truth, will you take me home? Feed me?"

Her breath hitched, and she licked her lips. "If you're telling the truth, shouldn't I be afraid of you?"

"Lady, you haven't a thing to fear from me. I need you."

"To feed from?"

"No. To make me human."

Chapter Two

∽

"Y-you want to be human?" Lily stammered. Again. Something about this obnoxious man made her witless. Something besides all the muscles and the dark, brooding looks—oh, and the delusional behavior.

"Yes," he said, the word clipped.

"Well, I'm not sure I can help you there." She had a hard time concentrating when he loomed so close. Her unfortunate *condition* made it impossible not to notice how masculine he was. How large his chest and thighs were. Or how well he filled out the front of his jeans...

Her pussy pulsed. *Damn! Not again.* "I've only ever seen it depicted on television—Dark Shadows re-runs, I think." Inwardly, she cringed at the nonsense spouting out of her mouth. But his testosterone-packed "package" was making it hard for her to concentrate. "Of course, Spike and Angel regained their souls, but no, I've never read anything about vampires transforming into humans. I think once you're 'awakened', you're st—"

"Doomed." His mouth thinned into a straight line.

Her gaze followed the unhappy curve of his lips, and she caught herself just before she leaned forward to drag his masculine scent into her nostrils.

Enough of his hovering. He made her so sexually aware she'd sunk to blathering. She scooted toward the end of her seat, forcing him to step back to let her stand. Unfortunately that didn't diminish his dangerous appeal. His size intimidated while at the same time sending her heart skipping. Even in her heels, the top of her head only reached his collarbone. His endless chest clothed in a tight, black T-shirt was lip-level. If she took one deep breath her boobs would graze those rock-hard abs. She cringed at the thought. Her nipples were so damn sensitive these days.

And caveman that he was, he didn't seem inclined to budge another inch. She heard him sniff. His nose was next to her hair.

Oh, yeah! Now, I don't feel so intimidated. She had to get rid of him. "Well, I'm sorry I couldn't be of more help...with your problem, that is. If you'll excuse me..." He didn't take the hint. Lily looked past his broad shoulder to Cissy and tilted her head toward Tall, Dark and Toothsome.

Cissy's warm brown eyes widened and she hurried over.

With reinforcements coming, Lily gave him a challenging stare.

The man took a deep breath and stepped aside, looking as though the weight of the world had settled on his shoulders. Poor man. He was just confused—damaged by the woman who had scorned him.

Lily felt a moment's compassion for him—until she realized he was staring at her neck again. And worse, this close proximity with the dark angel was playing havoc with *her* hormones. She moved away from the table then turned to face him. "Sir, you'll need to move along, now. I have work to do here."

A muscle in his jaw clenched and his intense, black stare pinned her to the spot. "Take me home with you."

Her body throbbed beneath his gaze. She shook her head, afraid to say anything. The only word in her one-word dictionary at the moment was *yes!*

"Professor, do you want help packin' up the materials?" Cissy's voice broke in.

Relief made her knees weak. Someone else stood between her and her wavering willpower. "Yes! I'm finished here tonight. Good evening, sir." Then she turned her back on him and walked away.

With Cissy's help, she quickly gathered the pamphlets remaining on the table and stacked them in a cardboard box to take home, carefully keeping her back to the man.

"He's still here!" Cissy hissed from the opposite side of the table, her gaze trained on a spot behind Lily's shoulder.

"You'd better call me a cab," Lily whispered.

"I'll make sure one of the guys walks you out. He seems kinda intense."

Lily shivered. That kind of intensity could be devastating when turned full force on a woman. Too bad he was deranged. "I'm sure he's harmless, but why take a chance? Go call me that cab."

* * * * *

It had taken Joe half an hour and a quarter pint of blood to find her apartment in the long, white two-story stucco building in the center of the French Quarter. The super led him straight to the door, then walked off, his eyes glazed under the influence of Joe's suggestion he give his wife a tumble.

It took another half an hour to feed from the man who lived in the apartment next to the professor's until he slept, just so Joe could climb out on his ironwork balcony and make the leap to hers.

Finally, he stood hidden in the shadows while he watched her through lacy curtains, her French doors opened to the sultry night air. With only light from the streetlamp outside to chase away the darkness, Joe could discern every detail of her bedroom. She lay not five feet from him atop pale pink sheets. *Naked.* Her knees bent, her creamy thighs splayed. So close he could smell her ripening scent.

She was pleasuring herself.

Joe's cock stirred and unfurled, lengthening by the second as he watched her.

A fan pulsed from the ceiling above her, lifting the gold-brown hair curving over her breasts to tangle with the fingers tugging at her nipples. When her hands moved down her rounded belly, his gaze clung hungrily to the turgid points surrounded by their pale rose circles. His mouth watered, imagining the velvet-soft flesh surrendering to his kisses. Succulent morsels yielding the sweetest gift—her blood from the heart of her femininity.

She truly sealed her fate when one hand glided past the fur at her mons to cup her sex. Joe's cock pressed insistently against his jeans, tightening when her fingers stroked between her outer labia to caress the thin folds within. Moisture glistened as she rubbed it over her lips, long sliding strokes that dipped inside and swirled outward.

Then her other hand entered the play, and her fingers parted the swollen labia, pulling them back to expose her engorged clitoris. She touched the shiny nub once and shivered as though the spot were too sensitive, and then her fingers glided away.

She circled the mouth of her vagina, dipping her fingertips into the well and spreading her juice. Liquid seeped to coat her hand, and she brought her fingers to her mouth and licked the tips clean. Soft appreciative groans broke from her throat.

Joe sweated. He'd never seen a woman enjoy her own essence like this one. His body was gripped with the need to shove his cock deep inside her cream-filled channel.

Instead, he braced an arm against the window casing and his other hand went to the hard bulge at the front of his jeans. Desperate to take the edge off his need, he flicked open the button on his waistband and eased the zipper down, shoving his briefs beneath his balls, enjoying the way the elastic constricted. His hot flesh escaped its prison, filling his hand. He encircled his shaft and stroked it, letting urgency fill his loins as he watched her.

Her hand slid beneath her pillow and pulled out a long, flesh-tone object that she caressed like a man's cock. She sucked the head of the dildo, wetting it with her spit, closing her eyes. Did she imagine a man shafting into her mouth?

Joe did. His cock pulsed and a pearl of pre-cum beaded at the tiny opening atop the crown of his sex. He rubbed the moisture around the tip with his thumb.

She fingered the base of her symmetrical shaft and it hummed, just like his body, triggered by her sexy moan at the first touch of her vibrator to the tips of her breasts. Her mouth opened in a gasp.

Joe's breath drew in sharply, imagining her taking his cock into her mouth. He squeezed himself, gliding the skin stretched tight as a rubber band over his cock, back and forth, faster.

She circled the dildo on one tit while her free hand massaged the other, the nipple winking between her fingertips. Then she placed it between her generous breasts and squeezed them around the dildo as her body writhed on the bed, her hips lifting, pulsing in the air.

Joe's hips answered, pushing his cock through his clenched fist, faster now, building heat and friction. He dropped spit onto his shaft and worked it with his fist, gliding easily, imagining the woman's undulating body convulsing along his cock.

Abruptly, the woman rolled onto her stomach and came to her knees, planting them wide apart on the bed, letting her chest fall to the mattress. Reaching between her legs, she spread her lips and coaxed the vibrator into her pussy, working it inside her, inch by inch, twisting it in her cream to lubricate its length and push deeper.

Joe's grip nearly strangled his cock. The sight of her pale cheeks quivering in the air, the dildo clutched in her fist pumping in and out, pushed him over the edge. He felt the pressure build in his balls.

Her chest rubbed on the sheets and her hips circled on her hand-held cock, until she cried out and shoved the dildo deep, cramming it inside as far as it could reach with the flat of her palm. She moaned and bucked, her soft whimpers carried on the air. When the pulsing of her hips stopped, she sobbed and fell to the blanket, turning to her back, her legs askew, her hair a tangled cloud on her pillow.

Looking at her quivering belly and the dildo that peeked from inside her body, Joe groaned and spent his seed in a hot stream on the floor of her balcony.

Too late, he realized he'd cried aloud.

"Is someone there?"

Lily clutched the edge of the sheet and pulled it over her body. She'd heard a groan. A man's guttural moan.

Someone had watched while she masturbated. A shadow shifted on her balcony and a large figure stepped through her door. Ashamed and frightened out of her life, Lily knew she didn't have time to reach for the telephone. Besides, her throat was closing around her terror—making it impossible to scream for help.

She dropped the sheet and rolled off the bed, landing on her feet. The dildo dropped to the floor with a dull thud. She'd almost reached her bedroom door, when a weight slammed into her back and forced her forward. She expected pain, but at the last minute the man's hands steadied her and eased her to the wall, his weight pressing against her naked flesh.

"Remember me?" a deep, resonant voice drawled.

Lily shuddered and bit her lip. Did she remember? Tall, Dark, and Tawny as a cat? She'd come, fucking a dildo, while this man's voice purred inside her head.

Something stirred against her buttocks and she grew cold, realizing his naked cock poked at her. It was substantially larger than her dildo. Finding her voice at last, she asked, "Are you going to rape me?" She was proud her voice didn't tremble.

Suddenly, she was released. Afraid to turn, she hugged the wall for a moment and listened to the rustling behind her to determine what he was doing. She heard the rasp of a zipper and his footsteps walking toward her bed.

Just as she'd decided to make another go at the door, something warm and nubby was dropped around her shoulders. Her robe. She stuck her arms inside and quickly belted the waist before turning to face her intruder, glad for the flimsy protection of a garment.

Shadows mottled his face, but she saw enough to note the tension that made a muscle jump in his jaw and the ones in his shoulders bunch. His fists were clenched tightly at his sides.

Lily took heart in the fact that he appeared unarmed — and that he'd tucked his substantial cock away. Perhaps, she could talk him out of whatever he planned. She took a deep breath. "Do you mind if I turn on the light? I can't see your face."

She walked slowly toward her bed, keeping her eyes on him, and switched on the bedside lamp. Golden light spilled into the room, but didn't lessen her fear. Her heart leapt faster. He appeared even larger in the light. His shoulders seemed to fill the room, his height stretched toward the ceiling.

Maybe she just needed to get a grip.

"Why are you here?" She replayed what little she knew about him. *Appeal to his delusion.* "And weren't you supposed to wait for my invitation?"

The man shrugged. A smile tugged at the corners of his lips. "You refused mine. So I followed you home."

"I didn't think you guys could just come inside someone's home unless invited."

He shook his head. "I don't know what you're talking about."

"You. Vampires. You can't come inside without an invitation."

"Can it," he said, his mouth twisting. "You don't believe in that stuff. You're patronizing me. Trying your psycho-bullshit to talk me out of what I have to do."

Lily lifted her chin and tightened her lips to keep them from trembling. "And what is that?"

The little half smile did nothing to soften his expression. His eyes grew heavy-lidded and he took a step closer. "First, I need to fuck you…"

He said it so matter-of-factly his meaning took a moment to sink in. Then Lily gasped and stepped back. "I'm not—you're not—" Even as her heart raced in alarm, liquid heat pooled between her thighs.

He took another step. "I need to feed from you…"

Her knees met the edge of the mattress. Another step and he'd be on top of her. Why that thought didn't make her scream mystified her. Instead, she held her ground, lifting her chin defiantly. She ignored the fact her belly shivered with excitement.

He leaned down, his lips hovering just above hers. "Then I'm going to get some questions answered."

She drew in a ragged little breath, drinking in his musky-male scent. "And after that?"

He stared at her mouth. "If you ask me real pretty, I'll fuck you again."

Her traitorous body responded, her knees growing wobbly, her pussy throbbing in time with her pounding heart. She lifted her hands to push him back, but they fluttered on his chest before settling there. "And after?" Her voice shook now, but not from fear.

His head lowered and he nuzzled her ear. "You think I'm going to kill you, don't you?" he whispered and kissed her neck. "I don't do that, lady. I'll leave you well satisfied."

Lily cursed her weakness, the heat that curled in her belly and perfumed the air with her arousal. She wanted to be stronger.

Her hands fisted in his black T-shirt and she glowered, cursing him silently for tempting her—then she shoved up his shirt.

His eyes widened and he held himself very still.

Lily looked up from beneath her lashes, knowing she blushed with mortification, but she couldn't help herself. She needed his nipples in her mouth, his cock inside her cunt. *Now.* Her arousal was full-blown and trickling down her thighs.

The bastard hadn't given her the space she needed to control her urges. Now the hormones waging war with her analytical mind ruled her. Her breath caught on a sob and she pushed his shirt higher, baring his flat, brown nipples. She nuzzled his chest, lapping at the fur dusting the wide expanse, until she found his tiny beaded nipple. Sobbing again, she drew a ragged breath and fluttered her tongue on the nub before latching onto it to suck.

His hands closed on either side of her cheeks and he pushed her away. He sighed. "Professor, wait. I didn't mean to frighten you."

She shoved him back, and this time he allowed it, his hands falling away from her face. "Lily, dammit!" she shouted. "If you're going to fuck me, at least call me by my name."

His face darkened. "Professor, I frightened you. And while I'm no Eagle Scout, I prefer my women crying *after* I've taken them. Not before." He held up his hands and retreated further away. "Stop crying. I won't touch you."

She scraped at the tears she hadn't even realized were there. His offer came too late. She'd die if she didn't have him, now. Her hands shook as they went to the belt at her waist and she untied it, letting the sides of her robe part.

Still, he resisted, shaking his head. But she could see the heat flare in his cheeks, see the rise and fall of his chest as his breaths grew shorter. He was as ensnared as she was by her need to mate.

A shrug of her shoulders, and the robe puddled at her feet. She stared at it, feeling as though another woman, a wanton woman, had stepped into her skin. Then she raised her head to eye him warily.

His beautiful dark eyes narrowed. Like a panther, his nostrils flared and he inhaled, his gaze sharpening when he caught her scent.

Lily raised the stakes and lifted her hair from one shoulder, baring the side of her neck. "Whatever kink you want to explore is fine with me," she said, not recognizing her husky voice, "so long as you fuck me, now." She dared another glance and saw his jaw clench. Stubborn man. "What were you doing out there on my balcony?" she goaded him. "Were you watching me? Did you like what you saw?"

"Yes," he replied, his voice tight and grating. "I jerked myself off watching you fuck yourself."

Her gaze fell to his groin. His cock bulged against the front of his jeans.

She lifted an eyebrow. "Doesn't look like it to me."

"I recover fast."

"So do I," she whispered. She raised her hands to her breasts and lifted them, offering them for his enjoyment.

"I'm trying real hard to do the right thing now." He planted his fists on his hips and glared. "You're not helping."

Lily liked that she'd turned the tables on him. She was the pursuer now. Her fingers closed on her nipples and she rolled them, plucking them to rigid attention.

His avid gaze fell to her chest, and his cock stirred in his pants.

"Fuck me, vampire," she said, caressing her breasts, letting him see her rising passion.

"Shit! Just remember. I offered you an out." He caught the hem of his T-shirt and drew it over his head, baring his wide, brown chest. "Well, which way do you want it?" he asked, his tone curt and driven.

She trembled beneath his heated stare. "Hmmm?" She shook her head. She hadn't understood a word he'd said. All that creamy, cocoa skin and the dark hair that marked him male turned her mind into mush. Her breasts strained against her hands.

"In your cunt, your mouth, or your ass?" He sounded angry, which excited her all the more. Most importantly, his hands unbuckled his belt, flicking open the button at his taut waist.

She licked her lips, staring at the widening gap that revealed the black arrow of hair disappearing beneath his briefs. "Do I have to choose?"

He cursed softly. "Do you want it standing or on the bed-"

"On the bed," she said quickly, relieved she knew one answer. Her knees were ready to collapse.

"Then get there. Now," his voice rasped. He shoved down his jeans, his stark white briefs with them, and toed off his shoes, leaving the last of his clothing in a pile on the floor.

Lily's gaze was glued to his cock. It sprouted like an oak from a nest of wiry black hair, thicker than her wrist, darker brown than the skin of his belly. It was huge and heavy, the tip a plump, purple spearhead. Her body shuddered at the thought of his enormous cock stabbing into her cunt. She sat on the edge of the bed and scooted back, knowing she left a moist trail on the sheet and opened her legs to show him she was more than ready.

He approached, his cock waving between his thickly muscled thighs. "Is this how you want it?"

"What do you prefer?" she asked, anxious for him to get on with it.

His knees came down on the mattress between her legs and he planted his hands on either side of her shoulders. He leaned over her, his mouth hovering above her breast, and then he looked up at her face. "Me, inside you. Deep as I can get."

Lily swallowed, excitement making her mouth dry as the desert. "Do it."

"Jesus." He rested his forehead on her shoulder and released a short bark of laughter. He reared back and stared at her. "How old are you, Professor?"

Why was he pulling away? She needed his flesh against hers! "Twenty-eight, and dammit — it's Lily!"

"How many lovers have you had, *Lily*?"

Her cheeks burned with embarrassment. "A few."

"Did any of them jump on you and fuck you without any preliminaries?"

"No!"

"Then what makes you think I'll do that?"

Her hands reached for his cock and she wrapped them around his hot flesh, tugging him to her center. "Because I want you, now. You can do…preliminaries later," she said, her body rigid with need. "Fuck me! I'll suck you off, let you fuck every orifice I have — just *please* come inside me, now!"

His face hardened, and he leaned over her again, resting on his forearms. "Take me inside you, then. This has to be your choice."

Lily guided his cock into her pussy, groaning as he pressed past her swollen lips, his shaft sliding inside her like a knife into butter. He was even thicker than her Magna-Cock, but she didn't flinch. Her inner flesh clutched him, drawing him deeper. But he kept coming.

He groaned and flexed his hips, driving deeper. She lifted her legs to encircle his waist, not giving him any space to withdraw. Not letting her vagina adjust to his size. She reveled in the power of his immense cock, burying itself deep inside her body.

He flexed again, pushing deeper. His slow intrusion was killing her by inches. When he was fully seated, Lily shuddered so strongly she shook his body.

"Easy, baby," he whispered, holding himself rigid above her, sweat breaking out on his skin.

Lily shivered again and felt her vagina constrict along his shaft. Readying itself to milk his cock.

"Christ! Hold still," he said, desperation tinged his voice. "I don't want to lose it now."

Lily's arms crept around his body, pulling his torso flush with hers. "It's okay," she said, looking up into his straining face. "Lose it. Take me." She pulsed her hips to encourage him to move.

His eyes closed and he withdrew partway, his thick shaft rubbing inside her tightly grasping vagina, and then he pushed forward, cramming himself back inside.

Her eyes widened, and she screamed. "Now! I'm coming now!"

Chapter Three

❦

Joe felt the woman come apart in his arms, trembling like a leaf from head to foot while her tight cunt pulsed around him. She'd come faster than a freight train.

Still, he didn't surrender to the darkness inside him. He had to protect her from himself. He pumped gently within her, reveling in the sensation of the creamy flesh that clutched him like a hot glove while he drew out her orgasm.

She wasn't making it easy for him to restrain himself. Her nails scraped his back and her hips pumped wildly beneath him. And the aroma of her arousal wound around him like a natural aphrodisiac, tempting him to let his monster loose on her. *Not yet.*

When she quieted at last, Joe waited for her to come back to awareness. He needed to see what lurked in her gaze the moment she came to realization—to see the naked truth in her eyes. For whatever reason the woman had been out of her mind with passion, even before he'd entered her bedroom. However painful, he wouldn't allow himself to take his pleasure until he was sure of her knowing consent.

Lily moaned softly beneath him and he braced himself on his elbows to watch as her eyelids fluttered open.

Her cheeks flooded with rosy color as she stared up at him. "I'm afraid…"she began, and Joe's heart sank, "…that I don't know your name. My research has gone beyond anonymous, don't you think?"

He blew out a relieved breath. "It's Joe. Joe Garcia." Joe felt a little embarrassed introducing himself while buried in her cunt.

Her lips stretched into a shy grin. "Bet you've never had a first date quite like this one, huh?"

"This isn't a date," he said softly.

Her smile disappeared, and he was sorry he'd chased it away.

"I suppose you're wondering why I attacked you," she said, a little frown wrinkling her brow. "It's kind of embarrassing."

"More embarrassing than my leaving cum on your balcony?" he murmured.

She wrinkled her nose. "Put that way, maybe not." She bit the corner of her pink mouth and looked at him, reluctance in her gaze. "I suffer from a sexual disorder."

"You mean, something worse than haematodipsia?" he said with a grimace of a smile.

"You remembered?" She looked at him curiously. "Who are you?"

"No changing the subject. You were telling me about *your* sexual disorder." Despite his acute hard-on, he was enjoying this odd conversation. And she was relaxing beneath him, her body adjusting to his size. He needed her loose and cooperative before he fed.

She drew in a deep breath and her eyes filled. "I'm a sex addict."

He really tried not to laugh, but his belly shook, giving him away. "I'm sorry. You think that's a problem? From where I'm lying, it's a very nice affliction."

"But you see where it led me? To sex with a man whose name I didn't even know!"

For some reason, her confession rankled. "Do you do this often?"

"No! But only because I guard myself constantly. I never get too close to a man, your scent drives me nuts. It makes me want to rub myself all over you."

"Me, in particular?"

"No! Well, at the moment, yes!" He grew worried when she looked ready to cry. "The thing is, I want sex all the time. It's like, I walk past a barbershop pole and I wet my panties. And forget the produce section of a grocery store—cucumbers and carrots make me shake like an epileptic! And have you ever noticed the shape of a gearshift? I had to trade in my car for an automatic!"

Joe found himself smiling. "How did you get through high school with all the horny boys around you?"

"That's just it," she said, her brows drawing together in confusion. "I wasn't like that, then. I scarcely noticed boys. I was more into my studies. My *affliction* started last fall."

"Did you by chance suffer some sort of emotional trauma?" he echoed the words she'd asked him during his interview.

Her body grew still. She barely breathed. Then she nodded. "But I don't know why it would have manifested itself this way. Why after so many years?" she whispered.

Joe pushed her hair behind her ears, soothing her with little touches. "Tell me."

She shook her head. "No. It doesn't make sense. It's probably a hormonal imbalance."

Joe traced her lower lip with his thumb. Now was not the time to tell her that just the thought of her pink mouth closing around his cock had him gritting his teeth. "Have you seen a doctor?"

"I'm too embarrassed." She was growing tense beneath him, her body tightening around his shaft. "What would I say? I'm horny day and night? I have to change my underwear several times a day?"

"Yes. That would get his attention, all right." He shifted his lower body, stretching his legs on either side of hers, squeezing her thighs closed to bring her back to sensual awareness.

Her lips pouted like two plump pillows. "I'm not ready to consult with anyone, just yet."

"Then it looks like you need to stay in bed. Play this thing out." He lifted an eyebrow. "I can help." He circled his hips, enjoying the tug of her clamped thighs.

"You're a bastard," she said, spoiling the epithet with a sexy little moan and a roll of her hips.

"Yeah. But I have the equipment you need," he reminded her with a slide of his cock. He dropped his voice to a purr. "And I'm the one planted inside you."

Her breaths came faster. "Yeah, you are." Her face softened with reawakened passion, glowing golden in the lamplight. "Do you think you could kiss me?"

Never slow to help a woman in need, Joe's head came down. It wasn't a tentative kiss. Their tongues met before their lips touched, lapping, fluttering, until Joe grew impatient for a deeper penetration. He closed his lips over hers and slid his tongue inside, swirling over the roof of her mouth, reaching to stroke her tongue.

Lily's mouth suctioned, pulling him deeper, a moan rising in the back of her throat. Her fingers dug into his back, squeezing, massaging his spine. Then slipped lower to cup his buttocks.

Joe broke the kiss and drew a deep, jagged breath. His body trembled with the need to drive into her. "Are you sore?" he asked, desperation making his voice tight and graveled.

Lily shook her head, her eyes glittering with renewed excitement. Her arousal gushed, coating his cock with fresh lubricant.

The muscles of his thighs bunched, and the pressure building in his already rock-hard balls threatened to overtake him. He hadn't learned to fully leash the monster, still being too new at this vampire thing. "I need you on your knees."

"Yes!"

He held himself rigid, trying to still the tremors in his thighs and belly.

"You'll have to let me up," she reminded him.

Christ! That meant he had to withdraw, had to bear the rub of his cock against her inner walls.

He pulled away, gritting his teeth, trying to ignore her wide-eyed gaze and the eager way she shoved to get him to move faster.

Finally free, he knelt, his cock straight as a pole and glistening with her arousal, throbbing in time with his racing heart.

She didn't move fast enough to suit him. Her fascinated gaze clung to his penis and she licked her lips.

He couldn't wait a second longer. He reached for her, flipping her onto her stomach, only vaguely aware of her yelp of surprise. She scrambled to raise herself on her arms and knees, but his hands were already on her bottom, pulling her into position, centering her ass and cunt on his cock. His knees roughly shoved her legs apart and his hands spread her cheeks. Her sex was wide open—pink and quivering.

Do I have to choose?

Joe remembered how Lily had stood before him, a blush painting her face and delectable breasts bright rose, her face misty with confusion when he'd offered her the choice of how he would take her.

At that moment he wished he had two dicks he could plunge into her.

Joe slid his thumb down the sensitive crease of her ass, and Lily turned her head to look at him, alarm in her gaze.

He circled the tiny opening. "Have you ever been fucked in the ass, Lily?" he asked, softly.

"Yes," came her swift reply. "But never by someone of your…proportions."

Indeed, she didn't look so much worried as embarrassed. Her body quivered with excitement.

"Later," he said, and continued his exploration downward to the full, flushed lips of her pussy. He pressed his thumb into her deep, dark channel and was gratified to find her dripping with honey. Bringing his thumb to his mouth, he tasted her for the first time, his eyes closing, savoring the salty, slightly astringent glaze and the flavor of her unusual musk.

With his body screaming for him to plunge into her, he still took a moment to spit into his palm and rub it over the head of his dick. Control was all in the pacing. "This isn't going to be finessed," he warned. "I'm too far gone."

"I'm ready," she said, her voice quavering.

He sincerely doubted it, but he guided his cock to her cunt, circled her opening once, then spread her with his fingers and pushed himself inside. In one long, inexorable glide he crammed his cock into her, ignoring her cries, ignoring her body's natural resistance to his intrusion. He had to be inside—all the way inside. *Now!*

When his balls finally rubbed her bush, he gasped and lay over her, curving his belly to her back, pressing his face to her shoulder. Sucking air into his starved lungs, he reached deep inside himself for something to anchor him. He didn't want to hurt her, but feared he'd waited too long. He wrapped his arms around her and groped for her breasts, molding them in his palms.

Lily whimpered and her cunt clutched and pulsed around him. "Move," she pleaded. "God please, move! Fuck me, Joe."

Though he fought it, he could feel the change coming over him, filling him with thick, tensile strength, bulging his muscles outward. He turned his head and found himself staring at their reflection in the mirror above her bureau. "Shit!" Too late, he'd forgotten to protect her. "Keep your eyes closed," he said, panting.

Then all thought receded, supplanted by the monster reforming the bones in his face to a grisly mask of protruding bone across his forehead and brow. His gums tingled as his teeth slid down from the roof of his mouth. All his being was focused on the elemental need to conquer her with his sex, drink her life from her blood-filled body.

He flung back his head and roared. Then he unleashed the monster.

Lily was enthralled with Joe's rough mastery. When he'd flipped her over and arranged her body to his liking, she'd felt an odd moment of recognition—that this was what sex was supposed to be. Being mounted, being mastered by a male.

When he'd shoved inside her, pressing deeper, harder than any man had before, she'd thrilled at his power even as her body winced in protest to his harsh intrusion. When his hands had clumsily groped her breasts, she reveled in the fact she caused him to lose control.

Then he roared and all hell broke loose.

His body hardened around her, his cock growing impossibly thicker, until she thought a tree trunk filled her channel. Then he began to move and she whimpered, wondering if she was woman enough to take all of him. She squeezed her eyes tightly shut, concentrating on the glide and jerk of his powerful cock.

Then her inner tissues gave, moistening further, caressing his shaft. Her hips circled, encouraging him to screw himself inside her, until he moved easily, stretching her to suit his massive cock.

He straightened away from her back and his hands sought her rump, a bruising grip that held her still while he pounded at her pussy.

Lily moaned and grunted harshly at the end of each of his powerful strokes, feeling the heavy, jackhammer thrusts pushing so deep inside her, she swore he stroked her heart.

His voice changed, no words uttered, just harsh, guttural groans that incited her to claw higher toward the peak. Then she was soaring, coming outside herself, splintering into a thousand shards of brittle glass. She screamed, and then screamed again when he hauled her up into his arms. He roughly nuzzled through the hair clinging to the perspiration on her neck until he found her skin.

The sharp sting of his bite pierced the sensual haze and her eyes flew open. She saw them in the mirror, kneeling on the bed, her knees spread open across his thighs, his hands working her hips up and down on his cock while he fed.

Thought, crisp coherence, was impossible at the cool rush of blood flowing out of her body, pulled from her head and extremities to feed his voracious hunger. She grew faint, pinpoints of black clouding her vision, and then she saw his face, bent over her flesh. Not Joe's face at all. A vampire's!

Her last thought as she was pulled into the void was she'd finally found one.

* * * * *

The vampire savored the rich, hot blood that flowed over his tongue, quenching the thirst that raged in his soul. He crashed his hips upward, impaling the woman on his hard shaft, tunneling endlessly. Growling, his hands gripped her hips, bouncing her buttocks on his lap, then sliding her forward and back as his fevered motions brought him to release.

His cock exploded and he disengaged his teeth from her neck to howl, his cum bursting from his loins in a raw, hot torrent. Jetting into the woman—*his woman.*

Finally, the wildness inside him quieted, and he let his head fall back on his shoulders to draw deep, cleansing breaths of air. As his body reformed, a niggling awareness grew that something wasn't right.

Joe opened his eyes. The sheen of perspiration dried on his skin, making him shiver beneath the oscillating blades above him. Lily lay inside his embrace, her head lolling on her neck, her body limp.

Horrified, Joe pressed her head to the side and looked at the twin rivulets of blood that trickled down her neck onto her breast. Like obscene red scars. Had he taken too much? He'd been so out of control, he'd passed all human consciousness when he'd taken her. He couldn't be sure.

Sick at heart, he opened his lips around the wounds and licked her skin to close them, then turned her in his arms to lay her on the bed. Leaning over her, he cleansed away the trail of blood, stroking her flesh with his tongue.

She stirred and he leaned back, kneeling on the bed beside her. Her lids fluttered open and she smiled sleepily at him.

"Wow!" she said softly.

"How do you feel?" he asked, anxious to know whether he'd harmed her.

"Mmmm. Sore." She wrinkled her nose. "Deliciously so." She took a deep breath and closed her eyes.

"Lily." Joe didn't want her going to sleep, not if he needed to get her to a hospital.

Lily's eyes blinked. "Are we doing this, again?" she asked, a grin breaking across her face. "Because if we are, I'm afraid you're going to have to do all the work. I'm limp as a noodle."

"Are you sure you're all right? Are you feeling dizzy? Try sitting up." He lifted her shoulders off the bed.

Her arms snaked around his neck and she hugged him tightly, and then her lips brushed the edge of his jaw and slid down to nuzzle the corner of his neck. "Did I tell you how much I love your smell?" she murmured.

At that point, Joe figured Lily was just fine with no symptoms worse than a sore pussy and fatigue from his energetic attentions. He relaxed then felt a grin stretch his mouth. She'd been overcome with passion. His passion. *Hot damn!*

Joe closed his arms around her and carried her to the bed, rolling her beneath him. "Do you need to sleep?"

Her lips parted and her eyes widened. "Like I said, I'm a little sore there."

Joe gave her a heavy-lidded stare. "Care to make another choice?"

She winced, her face heating. "Do I have to say it?"

"Mmm-hmm." He liked her lady like reticence. He liked it even better when she forgot her manners and screamed what she wanted.

"Why? You're a guy. Don't you just do what you want, anyway?"

"Last time I looked, there were two of us in this bed. I had mine. It's your turn to choose."

She huffed. "I suppose we'll just lie here like this all night unless I tell you, won't we?"

"Yup."

"I want…" Her gaze dropped to his chin. "I want you to…give it to me in the ass." She said the last in a rush, and then looked back into his eyes.

Joe pressed his lips together to smother a grin. Her embarrassment was adorable—pink chagrin and pearly white indecision biting her lips. "So do you want preliminaries this time?"

She scowled at him now. "You're making fun of me. I don't know if I like that."

"Let me make amends," he whispered. "Please? For being rough before."

"But I liked it," she said softly.

Joe searched her gaze until he was satisfied she told the truth. "I don't like to lose control like that. You don't have to be afraid. It won't happen again."

She opened her mouth to protest, but Joe pressed a finger to her lip. "You don't have to say it. I know I wasn't gentle. It was just…" He hated baring his soul, but she deserved the words. "You were so damn sexy. So hot. I couldn't keep it together."

"You mean, because I acted like a whore?"

"No!" If he hadn't seen the vulnerability beneath her steady stare he would have shaken her. "You were naked. Not just your body. Your desire. I've never been so turned on. It was beautiful. You're beautiful."

Her eyes filled and she turned her head. When she looked back at him, her gaze was curious. "So tell me more about these…preliminaries."

Joe felt uneasy, knocked off-center by the depth of passion he'd found with the professor. He'd loved Darcy—loved his old partner still, but the woman beneath him intrigued him from her sweetly rounded curves to her shy, inquisitive stare. If he weren't careful, she'd creep into his heart. It was a good thing he'd be out of there soon. In the meantime, he'd better keep things light.

"Well, I haven't tasted these little berries yet," he said, his gaze dipping to her chest. "And while I've probed the depths of your pretty pussy, I haven't tasted the well water…thoroughly."

Lily's breath gusted on a laugh. "What about me?" She circled her mouth with her tongue. "Although as large as you are, it may take me all night to explore every inch of your cock."

Joe felt his proud flesh respond to her compliment, growing to nudge her inner thigh. "So we're agreed? I get to order the breast pâté for the appetizer, followed by the soup—"

"Soup!" She slapped his shoulder. "Don't you dare say it!"

"Du Pussy."

She let out a shriek of laughter. "What do I get? The leg of mutton?"

He winced. "Doesn't quite have the same connotation. How about a spicy burrito!"

She wrinkled her nose. "Beans."

"A foot-long…"

She appeared to ponder it for a moment, and then shook her head. "Too obvious."

Joe waggled his eyebrows. "Filet of love muscle?"

She gave a very unladylike snort. "I can't believe we're talking like this."

Joe stroked her lower lip with his thumb. "Why? Because it's silly?"

"No, because I'm dying to ask you to do one thing for me," she said, her voice so soft he had to lean close to hear her.

"Baby, my body is yours to command," he whispered.

"Let me watch you while you change."

Chapter Four

ဢ

Lily held her breath as she waited for him to respond. How she'd kept it light since waking from her vampire's "kiss" she'd never figure out. She wanted to burst, to crow, to fling open her windows and scream it to the world, *Vampires do exist!*

Of course, her very first thought when she'd woken to find him hovering over her was whether he was going to drain her dry, but the guilty concern he'd shown as she'd tried to recover her wits had pretty much told her Joe wouldn't harm her.

The ominous stare he gave her now, however, had him inching back up the creepy scale.

"Talk to me," she said, nervously licking her lips. "Are you wondering what gave you away?"

One eyebrow lifted, but he didn't answer.

She took it as a cue to continue. "My first clue was when I touched you with the cross. You hissed like it burned." She gave him an impish grin. "Of course, every Dracula in any Psych ward would do the same, but you looked embarrassed."

Still, he didn't speak. But his incredulous expression had her wondering if he'd even noted he'd given her that little clue. She didn't have to remind herself a broody, unsmiling vampire lay draped across her body. Her nerves jumped and her mind raced on, her tongue following close behind. "Then of course there's the whole thing on my balcony. Not the shooting cum on the floor thing—the flying up to get there. Mind you, I had thought the bat-thing was pure Hollywood."

"And no one has a cock like yours, besides John Holmes— although I've never actually seen any of his films, so for all I know it's a really bad comparison. The fact is, I knew vampires had an odd erotic reputation, but I didn't know how they earned it."

"But the real clincher was the blood drinking. I've given blood before. Pints to the Red Cross, in fact. But never once did I nearly orgasm from my donation. If that was the normal affect, blood banks wouldn't have to hold drives." She finally ran out of nervous steam. "Talk to me. You're awfully quiet."

"You saw me in the mirror," he said flatly.

She nodded slowly, feeling his weight press her into the mattress. "Guess that whole mirror thing's a myth, huh?"

"You weren't freaked?"

"No!" she rushed to assure him. "It's incredible! I've been searching for evidence for years. If I'd known all I had to do was place an ad—"

"Stop it."

Lily's euphoria dissipated. Joe's expression was dark as a thundercloud. She made a note to tread lightly until she understood what put the kink in his underwear. Then she remembered, how vampires were made. If that piece of the lore was true, he'd likely nearly died to complete the transformation.

"All right," she said. "I'm sorry about my...enthusiasm. I've annoyed you and acted terribly rude." She caressed him from his shoulder to his fine, round buttocks, relieved when his muscles clenched in response to her shivery touch. "How did it happen?" she asked softly.

"Leave it. We're not talking about that," he said, his tone flat and remote. He shifted off her. "We've gotten off topic. I have questions I need answering."

Disturbed by his sudden change of mood, she rolled to follow him, not willing to lose the intimacy of their skin-to-skin connection. "Wait a second. You promised me preliminaries."

"I promised another go. *After* my questions are answered."

She spread her legs over his hips and snuggled her pussy onto his semi-erect cock. "Maybe I won't be in the mood."

He raised one dark eyebrow. "Lady, according to you, you're always in the mood."

He had her there. Lily felt a chill and resisted the urge to cover her body. If he wanted answers he'd just have to get them from her naked and pressed to the heart of his masculinity. If it was a quarter as difficult for him to think as it was for her while she oozed all over him, *then tough*!

"This has to do with what you told me at the coffee shop," she said, curving her back to rub her cleft along his length. "You want to be human again."

He inhaled sharply, flaring his nostrils. His heavy hand landed on her backside, halting her movements. "Have you ever read anything that says how this condition can be reversed?"

Lily slid her lips across his collarbone. "No. Like I said before, I've only seen it depicted on TV."

Joe pushed her off his body and turned to sit on the side of the bed, his back to her. "Give me something—a name, somewhere to look," he said, his voice ragged.

Lily reached to caress him, but her hand hovered in the air. The rigid set of his shoulders warned her away. "I can't think of anything. One of my sources, a woman who delves in voodoo and pagan spiritualism might know someone. I can't make any promises, but—"

"You'll take me to her." He glanced back at her.

She couldn't have said no if she'd wanted to. His look of desperation cut straight to her soul. "Yeah. I'll call her in the morning."

He nodded and exhaled. "So now that you know, how will you sleep? Won't you be afraid?"

Lily smiled. "I plan to keep you too busy to think of your stomach for the rest of the night. You guys do rest during the day, don't you?"

"Like the dead," he replied dryly.

"I'll make the call tomorrow. But it being a Saturday, I won't have to leave in the morning. I'll sleep with you." She knelt behind him and kissed his shoulder. "So we really do have the rest of the night to make love."

"Fuck. We're fucking, Professor."

"All right." She blushed at his blunt words, but he was right. She'd allowed a stranger to enter her bedroom — one she'd considered slightly deranged. And she'd begged him to take her. That fact didn't speak too highly for her moral fiber. If he thought she was a whore, it was only to be expected. Still it stung.

"I don't mean to embarrass you, but I don't want to give you false expectations about what's happening here," he said, drawing a deep breath. "I need information and to scratch an itch. When I get what I came for, I'm out of here."

Lily swallowed and nodded that she understood. She couldn't have gotten the words past her tongue to save her life. Her disappointment was too keen. Here was proof of her lifelong obsession and the most incredible lover she'd ever had. But their time together was limited.

She cleared her throat. "Well, since that clock is ticking, don't you think it's time you made good on your promise?"

Lily squealed when he twisted, his arms grasping her waist. He took her down to the bed. Lily found herself once more lying beneath his long, hard body. She told herself to remember every detail, every touch, every scent, and every whispered moan. Because she knew she'd never experience the likes of Joe Garcia again.

As his head lowered, she committed his handsome face to memory.

"You're thinking too much," he said, his mouth hovering centimeters from hers.

"Will I get a chance to ask questions, too?"

His mouth thinned for a moment, and then he nodded curtly. "I guess that's fair."

She raised her head to glide her lips over his, and then settled back on the pillow again. "So tell me…"

He groaned. "Now?"

She laughed softly and squeezed her thighs together to trap his cock. "Were you this big when you were human?"

Joe's mouth curved into a feral grin. "Not quite."

"Hmmm. So along with pointy teeth, I should be looking for gargantuan cocks. Guess I'll have to add a few more questions to my survey."

"Think any guy's going to tell the truth?"

She traced the outer shell of his ear with her fingertip and grinned. "Looks like I'll have to bring a ruler."

Joe's eyes narrowed, but Lily knew from his rapidly hardening flesh nudging her portal that he wasn't going to pull away this time. "What you're doing is dangerous, you know."

"Who's to say the next vamp who walks in won't be as 'honorable' as you?"

"Exactly my point."

She lifted her chin. "What will it matter? You won't be around."

"True. But I'd hate for anything to happen to you."

"Well, it won't be any of your business." Lily wriggled her hips so his thick head was glazed with her passion. "Are you trying to weasel out of our deal?"

"A promise is a promise." He scooted down the bed until his face was poised above one breast. "Preliminaries…mmmm." His tongue darted out to flicker at her nipple.

Lily arched her back to push her nipple into his mouth. His teeth closed over the tip and he bit it. Then he sucked it into his mouth, pulling hard, his tongue swirling around her areola.

"Oh God!" Her fingers clutched the back of his head and she held him close. No way was he going anywhere. Her thighs widened around his chest and she slid her calves along his sides, writhing under and around him while he tortured her breast.

Already she could feel the tension build deep within her belly, curling tightly, readying her vagina with a soft slow convulsion that spilled fluid from her pussy. The sharp scent of her arousal filled the air.

Joe released her breast and lapped at the tender underside. He pulled down one of her hands from where it had curled around his ears and pressed it to the breast he'd tormented. "Play with this, while I see to her twin."

Lily moaned and cupped herself, squeezing hard when he turned his attention to her other straining breast. The hard pebble beneath her palm and the nipple he suctioned shot electrical charges straight to her loins.

Her hips curved and she rubbed her slick pussy against his abdomen.

Joe lifted his head. His lips were blurred and rosy from his efforts.

"Please," she begged. "I need more."

Abruptly, he scooted lower until his shoulders pressed against her inner thighs. His hands curled under her knees and he lifted her legs, pressing them high and wide.

As his face hovered above her pussy, Lily's breath suspended. His dark, avid stare at her core had her squirming and self-conscious. She'd never seen herself down there... "Like what you see?"

Joe's gaze lifted to hers. Heat stained his cheeks and his eyes glittered darkly. "I like pretty, pink cunts."

More hot liquid gushed to bathe her channel. Lily's hands reached for his head, her fingers spearing into his hair to drag his mouth down to her aching mound. "Eat me."

Joe's tongue snaked out to lap at the center of her heat. "Mmmm. Honey."

Lily gasped and her thighs tensed. His tongue was hot and raspy, like fine sandpaper—like nothing she'd ever felt there before. His wicked mouth teased her, sucking on her swollen outer lips, then his tongue tunneled between in all too brief forays.

Before too long, Lily's hips bucked uncontrollably. "Joe. Please, my clit. Suck my clit," she begged.

"You said I should take it slow." He turned his head to nip her thigh.

"No! You're driving me insane." Her head thrashed on her pillow. "Pay attention! My clit!"

The wicked vamp spread her lips with his thumbs and lapped her tender entrance in wide circles, letting the scrape of his beard graze her, but he didn't approach the small, sensitive pearl.

Desperate, Lily reached between her legs, until her finger slid over the distended button at the top of her pussy.

Joe's hand clamped around her wrist. "No cheating."

"Then do something."

Joe fluttered his tongue once against the kernel and Lily's hips jerked.

She moaned. "It's too much!" she cried.

"And I don't want this over until I have my fill." He sucked both of her outer lips, rhythmically tugging. Then he licked lower, approaching her asshole.

She held her breath, embarrassed and painfully aroused at the same time. He wouldn't—

Christ, he did! His tongue swirled over her tender nether mouth, circling again and again, until Lily's body shuddered with delight. At the first stab of his tongue at her tight, hot center Lily keened loudly, her back arching off the bed.

"Make your choice."

What the hell was he talking about? "Choice?" Lily barely recognized her hoarse voice.

"Your ass or your cunt?"

The man was a sadist. "Don't make me say it again."

His tongue speared into her ass and fluttered, then withdrew. "Say it, Professor." His teeth grazed her thigh.

"My ass! Fuck my as—" Lily shrieked when she was flipped to her stomach.

"Give me your pillows," his voice grated.

Lily reached and tossed them over her shoulder. An arm encircled her waist and raised her, and the two pillows were stuffed beneath her hips. Suddenly, Lily discovered she was entirely at his mercy, her bottom in the air, unable to lever herself up on her knees due to the awkward position. Cool air from the fan bathed her moist, hot pussy, reminding her that her most intimate parts were exposed to his gaze.

His hands grasped a cheek each and he spread them. A heavy drop of moisture fell into the crease between her buttocks.

"Wait!" She wasn't at all sure she was ready for this. With her heart racing like a bunny on Viagra, she was sure she'd expire at the first probe of his thick cock.

"Too late. You're right where I want you."

A finger slid along the crease, smearing the moisture in its path until he reached her tight anus. He circled it once.

Lily shuddered, her body tensing in anticipation.

His finger pressed inside, twisting in, then pulling out.

She moaned and wadded the bedding in her fists.

Again, he pushed inside, deeper this time. And she felt his warm wet mouth slide over the globe of one cheek.

She forgot all about her modesty and opened her legs wider, inviting him to forge deeper into her body.

A second finger worked its way inside, stretching her uncomfortably.

"Relax, baby, we're taking this slowly. These are just my fingers. I need you to loosen up before I stuff my cock inside."

Lily thrilled to his coarse language. But she didn't want him to take it slow. Her ass was burning—the pain only intensifying the heat curling in her belly. "There's a tube of K-Y in my nightstand."

He nipped her ass and withdrew his fingers.

She pressed her hot face against the cool sheets while he rummaged through the drawer, knowing he saw her array of toys.

"Tsk. Tsk. *Professor*."

"Shut up, vamp. The gel's in the back."

"Got it."

The mattress dipped behind her again and a moment later his fingers were pressing inside again, this time well lubed. More fingers pressed past her sphincter. Three, she guessed, and her ass trembled with wicked delight.

"Better. Almost there. Christ, you're tight!" His fingers screwed in and out, stretching her further.

Lily's thighs strained to raise her buttocks higher, to force him deeper. "Joe. Please. More." She rubbed her beaded nipples on the fabric and wriggled her behind.

He pulled out entirely and pressed hot kisses to her cheeks. Long, interminable moments of silence followed. He was lubing himself, she guessed. God, she hoped so!

Then his hands were on her again, gripping her hips to raise her a little higher. A moment later, she felt his fingers pressing her opening, and suddenly, something large and blunt pushed against her tender asshole.

Pain—searing, yet impossibly arousing—forced a groan from her throat. "Oh please! Please, please—"

"I won't stop now," Joe said, his voice hoarse with strain. He pushed his hips forward, trying to be gentle, but her ass resisted his invasion, the rosy lips holding firm beneath his assault. He grasped her cheeks and spread them, pressing his thumbs around her nether mouth to ease it open while he kept up the pressure from his cock.

Gradually, her muscles relaxed and he dipped inside a fraction of an inch.

Lily's back dipped and she groaned again, her knuckles turning white as they gripped the bedding.

Joe pumped with shallow pulses, adding a slight side-to-side motion to work his cock slowly past her tight muscles. His steady, unrelenting force finally allowed him to ease inside another inch.

With a kitten-like whimper, Lily rose on her elbows. "I don't know if I can take it."

Every muscle in Joe's body grew rigid and he broke out in sweat. His buttocks trembled with the need to slam inside her. Her body clenched around his cock like a tight, hot glove. He couldn't stop now.

Reaching beneath her he fondled her clit, relieved when Lily sank back to the bed at his touch. She moaned and twisted her upper torso, careful not to move her hips, but seemingly unable to resist his clever ministrations.

Joe held his cock still inside her and plied her dripping pussy with firm, deep strokes of his fingers, fucking her slowly at first then faster, rubbing, swirling, tunneling, until he felt an almost imperceptible wriggle of her hips.

He flexed his buttocks and drove a little deeper.

"Joe!"

He held his breath, wondering if he was strong enough to pull out before he caused her true pain, the urge to bury himself inside her so strong he gritted his teeth to fight it. She'd entrusted him with her body—and he never wanted to betray a trust with a woman again.

Lily groaned and widened her stance atop the pillows, her ass tilting higher, taking him deeper inside.

Relieved, Joe pulled partway out and stroked back inside, and then did it again, this time noting a slackening of her inner muscles. He began to pump, gradually stroking deeper with each inward glide, until finally his strokes were full, hard and coming faster.

Rising on her arms, she took it, jerking back to meet his strokes. His hand left her clit and he gripped her backside to hold her steady, moving faster and harder until he pounded into her ass, driving the breath from her lungs in harsh gasps.

She keened, a thin sound from between clenched teeth, pitched higher, longer, until she sobbed loudly, wildly. "Don't stop. Oh God, oh God!"

Joe felt the change take him, so fast his back arched—his body thickening from one moment to the next.

Lily shrieked, a jarring sound ripped from her throat and she bucked, her ass shuddering as she convulsed, the ring of her opening clamping around his shaft like a cock ring, further building the blood and pressure in his dick.

His hands forced her buttocks sharply forward and back to increase the violence of his strokes. He pummeled her soft buttocks, his cock shafting deep inside her, his balls slapping her juicy cunt.

Yet even as his intellect faded, he recognized one important fact. She took it. She took every goddamned inch of his monster cock.

Though he fought it, his teeth slid past his gums and his face stretched. Then a powerful shudder wracked his own body, stiffening his thighs, compressing his balls until they exploded, shooting cum into her ass.

When the constrictions of her inner passage milked the last of his cum, he collapsed onto her back, forcing Lily to the mattress, his body shuddering and pulsing to expend every last drop of his passion.

Lily quieted, her breaths softening, pale whimpers turning to sighs. With his cock still impaling her sweet ass, Joe swept his hands along her arms, reaching to entwine his fingers with hers. She gripped him tightly.

"So, Joe," Lily said, sounding breathless, "it looks like I'm running out of choices."

Chapter Five

❧

Lily listened to the sound of running water as Joe availed himself of the bathroom. She made a mental note—*Vampires pee like anyone else.*

She knew she ought to move. Her bottom after all was still high in the air, but she didn't have a bone left in her body. The ache in her nether region was a delicious throb. No doubt, she'd be sitting sideways in the morning.

The water stopped, and the pad of Joe's footsteps as he neared her bed revved the throb to full throttle. *Sheesh!* She'd been righteously fucked, but her body already hummed with anticipation of his touch.

Something warm and wet glided between her legs and she moaned. He didn't say a word as he washed streaks of drying cum from between her legs. The nubby fabric of the washcloth at the same time soothed and excited her. While he cleansed her intimate parts, she relaxed, feeling the ache ease beneath the heat and his tender care.

He left her again, but soon returned and the mattress dipped beside her. His large, rough hands slid over her rump and gently massaged. "If you stay like that much longer, I'm going to take it as an invitation."

"Can't move," she said, groaning when his fingers trailed between her legs to stroke her inflamed labia.

He stretched across the mattress, lying on his side, his head supported on one hand as he continued to pet her with the other.

Lily snuggled her cheek on top of her folded hands and stared at him. "This is just an interlude, right?"

His fingers prodded her vagina and she drew in a deep hissing breath. She doubted she could take another round of his lovemaking right now—even for the sake of science.

"You can't take any more tonight, Lily."

She stifled a yawn. "You didn't drink this last time," she said. "And you weren't as rough or out of control."

"That's because I'd fed. I was desperate before."

"Well, you still owe me." This time a yawn caught her by surprise, stretching her jaw wide.

"How's that? Because we haven't explored your third choice?"

"Uh-huh. Because I didn't get to watch you change."

"There's still tomorrow night," he reminded her, his voice a sexy rumble.

"Hmmm."

From one moment to the next, Lily fell sound asleep. Joe smiled. Her hands were curled beneath her cheek like a child's, but her ass was still hiked on the stack of pillows. Innocence and carnal temptation all rolled in one delectable little package. Lily was quite a woman. If he were looking for a mate…

Joe tugged a pillow from beneath her hips and tucked it under his head. He rolled to his back and stared at the ceiling, trying to block out the aroma of sex, which hung like a pungent cloud above his head. Already his cock stirred on his thigh, unfurling inch by inch.

The memory of her tight ass clasping his flesh aroused and unsettled him, reminding him of the last time he'd loved Darcy. Only it hadn't been love—he'd touched her, taken her with only thoughts of revenge fueling his actions. He'd tunneled into his partner's ass, his mouth sipping from her neck, while she'd burrowed into the comfort of Quentin's arms. Quentin—his sire.

Darcy hadn't looked at Joe once. Her choice clearly written in the way she'd taken comfort from her vampire lover. When

Joe had finished, he'd left the bed and her house—and he hadn't been back since.

He'd blown any chance he'd ever had with Darcy, when he'd blasted her for asking Quentin to turn him. And worse, when he'd nearly raped her.

It didn't really matter that she was responsible for his current state—he had no excuse for how he'd behaved after he was turned. Her only thought had been to preserve his life after he'd been shot. Instead of understanding, he'd taken her like an animal.

His anger had exploded, fed by his newborn vampire's hunger. Yet Darcy had bravely faced him, accepting his abuse, even offering her own blood for his first meal. However, the deal he'd entered with her vampire lover, Quentin, ensured he would never know her heat again.

Now he faced an eternity of loneliness. An eternity of guilt.

Separated from the rest of the Special Unit by his new "status", Joe was determined to find a way to reverse the transformation that had made him a monster. He'd seen how much pain and destruction vampires left in their wake—understood the dark hungers that ruled his body. He wanted to be human again to protect the world from himself.

Lily murmured sleepily beside him and rolled away from the pillow, settling on her back with a sigh. Joe reached for the lamp and flicked the switch to extinguish the light. He'd let her sleep despite the urgency building between his thighs. Perhaps he could appease another appetite with a little early morning snack. He rose from the bed and searched for his clothing on the floor.

All dressed, he slipped from the bedroom. Her keys lay on the kitchen counter and he shoved them in his pocket. The next time he entered her apartment it would be through the front door.

Outside, he turned to the right and headed back down the narrow street, his ears and nose alert to the scent of a meal. It had rained. Just enough so the glare of the streetlamps reflected off the pavement and the faint stench of sewage clung to the moist air.

A movement in the alley next to the apartment building drew his attention. A rustling, too loud for a dog or cat, was followed by the sound of a low, menacing growl. Joe's predatory instinct raised the hair on the back of his neck like hackles. Then he caught a scent he didn't recognize.

A heavy musk—like a man's, but also like the smell of wet dog—drifted from the alleyway. Every vamp-born instinct screamed for caution. Joe hastened the descent of his canines with a grinding of his teeth.

A blur of motion seen from the corner of his eye was all the warning Joe got before something heavy slammed into his chest, taking him down. Its heavy body weighted Joe's limbs, pinning him to the cement. He had a glimpse of a wolf-like face with flat, reflective gold disks for eyes, thick fur, and a long, dark snout. The black nose poised above Joe's face and the creature inhaled deeply. Sentient intelligence gleamed darkly in its gaze, then it lifted its head and howled—a sound unlike any canine howl he'd ever heard.

For a long moment, Joe lay beneath it, unresisting and unbelieving. The beast was another kind of monster—one he'd thought a figment of folk tales and Hollywood. Kind of like vampires, before he'd learned different during his years on the force. If what his gut told him was true, werewolves did exist! And this one looked pissed.

It sniffed Joe like a dog savoring the smell of its next meal. The animal's hackles rose, and the longer it scented, the louder its rumbling growl grew, until it reverberated within its chest.

The werewolf opened its mouth and long, serrated teeth sank into Joe's shoulder. The creature straddling his body shook its head, tearing at his flesh.

Joe roared, his lips drawing back in a feral snarl. Adrenaline screamed through his veins, pumping into his muscles, firing the rage in his inner beast. His arms strained against the creatures weight until the change slammed through his body, adding strength to his human frame.

With a powerful surge, he lifted the beast and rolled with it, smashing the back of its head to the pavement. Then thought became impossible. Rage, and the struggle to live, supplanted his growing horror. The beast within him warred with the werewolf, their primal cries a din of growls and grunts and fierce bellows.

Joe's hands pried the wolf's mouth from his shoulder and he pushed its neck back until bones crackled and the creature made a strangling sound. The wolf's haunches strained, forcing Joe to roll again, but this time he raised his knee, slamming between the creature's legs. It screamed and drew back. Joe planted his foot into the beast's belly, shoving it farther away, and then he scrambled to his feet.

On all fours the werewolf hunched its shoulders, its head low to ground as it circled Joe. Beneath the thick pelt, muscle rippled as it poised to attack. The wolf's unblinking gaze locked with Joe's.

"What the hell?" A voice from the end of the alley shouted. "You there, need help?"

Joe raised his arm and turned his face away from a bright light that blinded him momentarily. He heard the patter of feet and realized the beast had run to the opposite end of the alley. Forcing his face to reform, he drew in a deep breath and reined in his inner monster.

"Mister!" The voice was closer now. "Looks like you need an ambulance."

Joe made out the shiny badge and the blue uniform of an NOPD cop.

The large, barrel-chested officer continued to flash his light in Joe's face. "What the hell kind of dog was that? Animal Control's gonna need one big mother-fuckin' cage."

As the man drew closer, Joe's human perception sharpened. He realized the last thing he needed was a cop nosing around this little mystery. "It wasn't like any Rottweiler I ever saw," Joe murmured.

The officer shined his flashlight on his shoulder, then up again at Joe's face. "Do you mind me askin' what you were doin' in this alley?"

Joe shrugged. A few months ago he would just have whipped out his badge and traded cop talk. Instead, he said, "I heard a sound."

The officer snorted. "Do you make it a habit to investigate odd sounds in dark alleys? It's a wonder you're still breathin'. Looks like he took a chunk out of you — you're bleedin'. If you'll come with me, we'll get that seen to." He reached for the radio strapped to his shoulder.

With a twinge of regret, Joe lunged, his arm snaking around the cop's shoulders to draw him close to his body.

The officer struggled, his foot stomping on Joe's instep, his elbow slamming back into his ribcage. Joe opened his mouth and bit into the man's neck.

The officer continued his fight for a moment, and then his body grew slack.

Joe fed for several minutes then lifted his head to whisper in the officer's ear. "You heard a noise in the alley and investigated, but you found nothing. Spoke to no one. Now go back to your squad car." He let the man go and shoved him toward the street.

Without looking back, the officer walked away, shaking his head. "Just a damn dog."

Joe watched until he turned the corner, and then walked to the opposite end of the alley where he'd seen the werewolf escape. He sniffed the air, but only faint traces of the creature's scent remained. He retraced his steps, wondering what it had been doing in the alley in the first place. Near the entrance were large trash bins, which served the apartment building. The side door of one was open and a shredded bag of trash laid half-in-half-out of the bin.

As Joe stepped closer, he saw a piece of paper flutter to the ground. It was a phone bill with the name "Lily Carlson" printed at the top. Heedless of the acrid smell from the bin, he reached for the remnants of the one demolished bag and dumped its contents. Tissues and feminine articles littered the ground. Lily's fragrant musk permeated the items.

What interest would a werewolf have in scenting on Lily's trash? Joe's instincts, his cop instincts, knew this wasn't a random act. The wolf had targeted Lily's bag among all the others in the bin.

He hurried back to the apartment building. Until he knew what all this meant, Lily wasn't going anywhere without him.

* * * * *

"You snore."

Lily lifted one eyelid and glowered at Joe. Only the light from the open bathroom door shone on his features; he'd covered the French door with a blanket. He was lying on his side, his head propped on his elbow — watching her.

She hoped she hadn't also been drooling.

"I do not snore," she enunciated.

A grin turned up the corners of his mouth. "How do you know?"

"I've never heard it."

"Ahhh…so you only believe what you see or hear for yourself?"

She twisted to look at the digital display of her alarm clock. It was 3:30 in the morning! What right did he have to look this good and expect her to engage in an intelligent conversation? She drew a deep breath and lowered her eyebrows to show her displeasure.

His gaze went straight to her breasts and she realized she was still naked as a newborn while he was fully dressed. She pretended unconcern with the disparity and tilted her chin. "Any good scientist bases her conclusions on empirical evidence."

"Yet you believe I fly only because I entered your room from your balcony."

"Are you telling me I came to an erroneous conclusion?"

"No, I'm telling you that you jump to conclusions like the rest of us. Sometimes, you trust a kernel of evidence and believe what you want to believe."

Lily opened her mouth to give him a rebuttal, but he pressed his finger over her lips.

"Sometimes, you have to forget about the survey data, or even what your own eyes tell you, and just trust your gut."

Lily knew he was talking about more than her snoring. "I can trust," she grumbled.

"Is there anyone you trust fully now? If he said, 'I've seen the Loch Ness monster in Lake Ponchartrain', would you trust it was true?"

Lily thought hard. The Loch Ness Monster?

"Is there anyone you'd believe?"

Lily felt her frown deepen and didn't care her forehead probably looked as wrinkly as a Shar-pei's. "So I snore."

"That's better," he said, his expression too intent for this conversation to be over.

She wasn't ready to hear what he had to say, especially if he was going to say he was leaving. "It's not very gentlemanly of you to mention it."

"I thought you'd like to know. And I never said I was a gentleman."

A yawn caught her unawares and her jaw stretched wide. She wished he'd stop staring. She knew her hair was likely squashed on all sides so that she looked like her head was really,

really long and that her face looked like a roadmap from all the pink sleep creases. While he looked so damn unrumpled she knew he'd never slept.

But he had showered. She sniffed. He smelled powder fresh while she was as ripe as the inside of a gym bag. "I must have fallen asleep. Do you have this effect on all your women?"

"Would you trust me, Lily?"

She wanted to—she really did. Instead of a direct answer, she demurred. "Did you wake me for a reason?"

She'd disappointed him. It was as if a veil swept over his face, wiping the intensity from his expression, leaving a pinched, wary look in gaze. "What can you tell me about werewolves?"

"That they have hairier chests than yours?"

He didn't appear to appreciate her attempt at wit. "Besides that."

"You're serious, right?" At his curt nod, she sat up and reached for her robe. She didn't know how he could concentrate with her naked beside him—she couldn't concentrate while one part of her brain wanted him to caress her breast or glide his lips over hers.

When she'd arranged the fabric to cover her, she sat cross-legged on the mattress. "Well, there's pretty much an international tradition of folk tales describing shape-shifters. Of humans who could transform into animals—often into animals people considered their foes like wolves, bears, and lions. Of course, there's the Hollywood version of werewolves—they can only be killed with silver bullets, they change to wolves during the full moon—"

"Is it?"

"Is it what?"

"A full moon?"

"I can check my calendar. Why?" Lily realized something was wrong. His change of clothing, the difference in his mood since she'd fallen asleep... "You've been out. What happened?"

Joe's face darkened and his gaze swung back to nail her, accusation in his dark eyes. "Why would a werewolf be nosing around you, Lily? What aren't you telling me?"

Lily shook her head. Werewolves? It was as unlikely as having a vampire in her bedroom. "Are you sure?"

Joe shoved up the sleeve of his fresh T-shirt to expose his shoulder. Long, angry red gashes, already scabbing over, marred his skin.

She gasped and her gaze returned to his face. "A…wolf did this? You couldn't have mistaken a German shepherd or some other large dog for a wolf?"

"It smelled like a human," he said, his voice flat and hard. His gaze was so intent she feared he could read every thought that flashed through her jumbled brain.

Then her mind slowed to embrace a single clarifying thought. He wanted her trust. No, he needed it. Whatever had happened to him before, he'd lost trust somewhere.

Without a single shred of proof, she relaxed and accepted that she wanted to love him. She'd give him her trust, even if that was the only thing he ever wanted from her. Without wavering, she looked into his eyes. "All right, you met a werewolf tonight. Have you ever seen one before?"

He drew in a deep breath. "I didn't know they existed."

"You're sure he targeted me?"

"Yes. And I think it has something to do with your scent."

She grimaced. "I'll take a bath."

"No, your woman's musk is very distinctive. I noted it right away."

Not sure that was a flattering remark or not, she said, "What brought you to the conclusion he was interested in my…musk."

"He pulled your trash bag out of the bin—the one with your feminine items."

Lily blushed and toyed with the belt of her robe. "You mean, my panty liners, right? I told you I have…a problem."

Joe's hand settled over hers, and he squeezed. "I don't mean to embarrass you, but I think your problem is more significant than just a hormonal imbalance."

Lily nodded, but she did not want to discuss her feminine hygiene any further. "Those scabs look like they're over a week old."

"Vampires heal fast."

"I should be taking notes."

"You know you won't be believed if you publish your findings."

Lily gave him a lopsided smile. "My colleagues already think I'm a bit wacky because of my area of specialization." She wrinkled her nose. "They only tolerate me because I'm multi-published."

"So why *did* you choose vampires?"

Lily looked away. He didn't know it, but she'd promised him her trust. Trust bled both ways. "I never knew my mother, but my father was my whole world. We moved a lot when I was growing up. I didn't know why. One night we came home and someone was in our house." Lily took a deep breath, trying not to let the horror of that night get to her like it always did.

Joe's palm cupped her cheek.

She leaned her face into it for a moment and then straightened. "My father attacked him. Killed him. Afterward, Daddy didn't call the police, even though he was hurt. We didn't pack our things—we just left." She blinked to dry tears filling her eyes. "I didn't know how bad he was hurt. Before he died, he said I should be wary. That the man was a vampire." She looked into Joe's troubled gaze. "He said vampires are my mortal enemies."

"So why would you seek other vampires?"

Lily shrugged and felt the tears spill onto her cheeks. "I had to know he wasn't crazy. That he hadn't died for nothing." She sniffed. "That he hadn't murdered for nothing."

His thumbs rubbed her tears away. "You saw him kill the vampire?" Joe asked softly.

She nodded and blinked again. "He fell behind the couch in our living room—so I never saw his body."

"If I'm your mortal enemy, why aren't you afraid of me?"

"I was."

"What changed your mind?"

His directness made her squirm. He deserved no less from her. "The fact you offered me an out, when it was obvious you were dying…to fuck me."

His eyes glinted dangerously.

She recognized that look now and her body responded, her nipples constricting into hard, erect points. Lily nodded toward her French door. "You covered the glass."

"It'll be daylight soon."

"Oh." Worried for him, and yet morbidly curious, she asked, "Will you disintegrate in the sunlight?"

His lips pursed around a smile. "I'll melt into a puddle of goo."

Lily suppressed a smile at his teasing and licked her lips. "I can *so* relate to that."

"Take off your robe," his voice purred.

She shook her head and clutched the collar of her robe. "You first."

His eyes narrowed, but he reached for the hem of his T-shirt and drew it over his head. Then he reached for the button at the waist of his jeans.

Lily's gaze ate up every inch of flesh revealed. Despite the angry wound on his shoulder, his broad frame gleamed with masculine power. His happy trail of black hair drew her gaze downward. Her mouth watered.

Joe shucked off his jeans and his sex sprang from its dark nest of curly hair, alert and potent.

Instant, intense arousal pulsed deep within her pussy. She shrugged out of her robe and lay down, opening her arms.

Before his body covered hers, his fingers went straight for her moist cleft, sliding between her pouty lips, his thumbnail flicking the hood covering her clitoris.

Lily moaned and widened her legs, making room for him to settle between them. Her hands drew his shoulders down, scraping his back, urging him to take her with her sighs and eager caresses.

Joe's breath, already shorter, fell hot upon her cheeks, and then his mouth closed over hers and she was lost. Their tongues warred, their chests met, his fingers rubbed moisture around her opening, and then he was pressing his cock inside, crowding the tender tissues, groaning into her mouth.

Lily slid her calves around his thighs and higher, pressing his hips closer, pleading with her body for him to tunnel deeper.

Joe's thrusts were shallow, just deep enough to excite her inner walls into releasing more cream to coat his thick cock. He rocked inside the cradle of her thighs, ending each thrust with a little jerk.

With her legs closing around his buttocks, she lifted her hips off the mattress, squeezing, forcing him to drive deeper.

Then she was shattering, climaxing so strongly, she moaned and writhed beneath him.

His mouth ate at hers, sucking on her tongue, biting her lips, nuzzling under her chin—drinking her moans and giving them back with his own deep, rumbling groans.

Then he planted his hands on the bed and pushed up. His eyes glittered in the dim light, the skin tautening over his flushed cheeks. Beneath her heels she felt the flex of muscles in his buttocks as he rocked forward, gliding his cock inside her so deep he rammed her cervix. Another flex and he pulled out, then in, and out...

Lily's fingernails dug into his back, as she strained upward, trying to meet each thrust—but he was too fast, too hard.

And his face was changing. She watched in fascinated horror as the bones of his forehead pushed outward, stretching his skin into a frightening mask. His lips curled up to bare his teeth, which slid downward. They gleamed white and menacing in the dark.

Impossibly, she felt a second dark wave wash over her and she held up her wrist to his mouth. "Drink! I want it all."

He bit into her wrist and her breath hissed on an indrawn breath. He mouthed her flesh and sucked, his buttocks turning to steel, his body and cock thickening. His powerful thrusts pushed her up the bed until her head banged against the headboard. She reached with her free hand to brace herself against it, and then all thought stopped.

Only sensation registered in her brain—flames licked at her loins, curling inside her belly, drawing breath and blood to her core like a cold-hot ball of tension that curved her toes, pulled her legs higher, and arched her back off the bed.

As if from a distance, she heard a long, thready scream and color burst like a fireball behind her closed lids.

She came back to herself slowly, hearing her jagged breaths loud inside her ears. Sweat cooled on her face beneath the strokes of the blades above her, and a large weight pressed her body deep into the mattress.

Lily raised a shaking hand to stroke the short, wet curls at the back of Joe's head. His face nuzzled her breast and his hot mouth latched onto her nipple. Lily's heart squeezed. In the most elemental way, he sought comfort from her body.

He stirred, but she held him within the circle of her thighs, reluctant to let him leave her. He plied her breast with glides of his tongue then kissed the crest of her nipple and raised his head. "You make me forget why I came here in the first place."

Lily smiled, feeling tired and a little sad. She didn't need reminding he was here only because he sought a "cure" for his condition.

"You'll call your voodoo priestess, today?" he asked.

She nodded.

"We have two questions for her, now."

Lily was suddenly too sleepy to ask him what the second question was.

"Lily?"

"Yes?" she murmured sleepily.

"Don't go out alone today."

Chapter Six

ಕಾ

Lily woke with a start. Sunlight winked from the edges of the blanket covering the door on her balcony. She reached out and felt along the surface of her nightstand for her alarm clock and held it in front of her face, waiting for her eyes to adjust to the bright readout. It was mid-afternoon.

Turning on her side she found Joe, lying on his back, his chest barely moving. Alarmed, she leaned over him and pressed her ear to his chest. His heart beat—albeit slowly. He hadn't been kidding when he said he slept like the dead.

Lily brushed his chest with a kiss and cuddled close to his side, her arm stretched over his belly. It had been such a long time since she'd woken up with a man in her bed. She drew in a deep breath and closed her eyes to savor his man-smell—the tangy fragrance of sweat, a trace of spicy aftershave, the lingering aroma of sex.

His face, softened by sleep, was beautiful. Something she hadn't really noticed when his dark, sensual gaze burned away all other observations. His eyelashes, thick and curly, were dark crescents, his nose a sharp blade, his mouth a wicked curve, even in his sleep.

Her gaze drifted down, across his latte-colored chest and belly. A light furring of black hair led her gaze downward to the edge of the sheet. It dipped between his legs and molded the hummock of his sex.

She wondered whether he dreamed—and whether she figured in his dreams.

Her hand idly caressed his chest, traced the quickly healing wounds on his shoulder, and drifted downward to circle his taut belly. She had maybe one or two more nights with her vampire—not nearly enough time to pump him for information she needed to feed her research. Not nearly enough time for all the loving she wanted.

Her fingers nudged the sheet draping his hips.

Stick to the research! She wondered how vulnerable this deep sleep left a vampire and whether he would respond to external stimuli. She rose up on her knees. "Joe," she whispered.

No response. Not a flutter of an eyelash. No change to his breathing pattern.

Lily extended a finger and tickled his ribs.

Again, no response.

Feeling bolder, she poked him hard with her finger. Still he didn't move.

"Hmmm…" Lily slowly peeled down the sheet to expose his penis. It lay curved along his thigh. Sleeping, it hardly appeared the fearsome sword he'd wielded the night before.

She bit her lip and pondered the ethics of examining a man's private parts while he slept. She traced his length with her fingernail and glanced up guiltily to see whether he'd moved.

Nothing.

She reached for her glasses in the top drawer of her nightstand and slid them over her nose.

Then she reached for his cock and straightened it along his thigh to measure it with her palm and fingertips. It was one hand plus the length of just her fingertips long when relaxed. She laid it gently on his belly and cupped his balls. They were heavy, about the size and weight of a couple of tangerines.

She gently squeezed and tugged his sac noting his cock expanded and lengthened. Could he be fully aroused in his present hibernating state? She wanted to know, although she didn't have a clue where she could publish such a finding.

Stripping the sheet away to bare his legs and toes, she came to a quick decision. She had a duty to explore every attribute of her subject—in the name of science, of course.

On her knees, she stepped over his leg and gently pushed his thighs wider to make room for herself. She knelt between them and bent to take his balls into her mouth.

Joe fought his way through layers of dreams where monsters with golden eyes and savage fangs chased him through damp, dark, cobblestone streets. He ran on, the sound of his heart beating and the searing breaths squeezing from his lungs, louder than the impact of his booted heels.

His limbs grew more leaden the farther he ran. He'd been here before, knew what the outcome of this encounter would be, and knew he was powerless to change his course. The sounds from his pursuers were closer now. He didn't dare take his gaze from the uneven road in front of him to look over his shoulder, but he could hear the scrape of their claws just behind his heels and smell their foul breath as they closed in on him.

This is a dream! No more. And yet he knew he'd lived these minutes. Every detail was too clear, the scents and sights too crisp for imagination.

With dread weighing down his shoulders he waited for them to pounce and tear at his flesh. He almost wished they'd go ahead and end it. For then he'd awaken—as he always did.

Instead, this time the sounds of the wolves grew faint and the damp, dark street faded. His sluggish heart beat faster. He was waking this time before they killed him.

Joe felt the pleasant tug of something warm and lusciously wet on his balls. His eyes opened only a slit to peer down at the woman mouthing his sac. *Lily!* She'd chased his nightmare away.

A shaft of light reflecting off the mirror above her bureau struck her hair, igniting the golden strands in her hair like a halo and glinting off the wire surrounding her glasses. The odd sight of her naked body bobbing above his groin and her glasses slowly fogging had him suppressing a smile.

She tugged again, her tongue swirling over first one ball then the other, and he noted that one hand rested lightly on the end of his dick. He wished for a stronger grip, but guessed she was gauging his growth by the way her hand squeezed first one side, then the other, and then her finger measured the distance from the tip of his dick to his belly button.

His professor certainly took her research seriously.

So did his cock. He felt the blood rushing to his loins, filling his staff with steely ardor.

Regrettably, she released his balls. "Oh my!" Lily slid her glasses down her nose to peer at him above her misty lenses.

Joe carefully regulated the rise and fall of his chest and kept his eyes slitted to see what she'd do next.

Lily measured him from root to tip, using both hands, palm to fingertip, palm to fingertip. When she finished, her lips pursed around a silent whistle.

"I suppose you'll want to slip a scale beneath him next," he murmured.

Lily screeched and rested her hand on her heaving chest. Color flooded her stricken cheeks. "You could have told me you were awake."

"And cut short the investigation? I did promise to answer your questions."

She scowled at him above her glasses. "Shouldn't you be asleep?"

"Shouldn't you be up and about?"

"I-I will be. I have plenty to keep me busy today—notes to take, *measurements* to document."

Joe's eyes narrowed. "You aren't really thinking of measuring more vampires' cocks, are you?"

"A single measurement does not a finding make," she said with a haughty tilt of her chin.

"You know the only way you'll get more statistics will be by bringing them here, to your bedroom. Would you really take that kind of risk?"

"I did with you."

Joe shook his head, fighting fatigue. They needed to get a few points straight. Lily was heading down a road for disaster. "What if they want to take more than a bite from you? What if they kill you?"

She shrugged. "Then I'd be resurrected as a vampire and continue my research."

"You don't really want that, Lily. Besides, your vamp may not be interested in turning you. He could just leave you looking like hamburger."

Lily grimaced, but her chin tilted higher. "Shouldn't you be sleeping?"

"You woke me up—how do you expect me to go back to sleep with this hard-on?"

Lily licked her lips. "Since I'm responsible, I should take care of it." Her nonchalant tone didn't fool him for a minute. A vein at the base of her throat pulsed. "What would you like?" she asked as casually as she might ask him how he liked his steak.

Every red corpuscle roared toward his cock. He lifted his hand toward her, palm up. "Climb aboard."

A shiver shook her breasts and her face tightened. Lily laid her hand inside his and crawled over his hips, her slick cleft leaving a trail of moisture along his rigid shaft.

"Are you sore?"

She blushed a fiery red. "I wish you'd quit asking me that."

He ignored her embarrassment and reached down to slip a finger inside her, noting the heat of her swollen lips and inner tissues—and the liquid that drenched her channel. Lily had worked herself into a state of high arousal as she'd conducted her "investigation".

He swirled his finger around, watching her face for signs of pain, but Lily closed her eyes and sighed. Her areolas dimpled. Her nipples constricted and elongated. Joe's mouth watered. "I think you can take me," he whispered.

"Damn right." She rose on her knees and grasped his cock in her fist.

With his thumbs pressing her lips apart, Joe did his part to ensure her comfort, reducing the friction between his cock and her plump labia.

Lily centered her entrance over his fleshy head. Then she sank, taking him inches inside her. Her indrawn breath expanded her chest and his gaze zeroed in on her luscious, pouting nipples. She rose and sank deeper.

Her breath quickened and Lily leaned forward to brace her hands against his chest. With a determined cant of her chin, she lowered herself, taking nearly half his length inside.

His jaw hard as granite, he bit out, "Faster." He released the folds of her cunt and glided his hands up to her breasts, squeezing them in his palms. "Faster, baby."

Lily's face was mottled red, her lips trembling—inches from her orgasm. She snuggled her knees closer to his hips and bounced tentatively on his cock, a moan tearing from her throat.

The lenses of her glasses misted over and he pulled them from her nose, setting them on the nightstand. He leaned up to kiss her shoulder, and her back arched, bringing her breast to his lips. He latched onto one tight nipple and sucked hard.

She cried out, gliding her hot cunt all the way down his cock. Joe's head nearly exploded. His hands circled her back and reached for her buttocks, gripping her hard, shoving her hips down, then sliding them forward and back to grind his short hairs against her clit.

"Joe! I can't move. Can't—" Her voice broke on a groan.

He bit her nipple gently, sucking the tender tip between his teeth then swirling his rough tongue to increase the pleasure.

Lily's hips jerked and her thighs shuddered over his hips. He could sense her orgasm building sweet tension in her body. With his hands gripping her round bottom he raised her, then slammed her down as he thrust his hips upward, stabbing deep into her core.

She screamed. Her fingernails dug crescents into his shoulders. Her eyes closed and a wash of fiery color spread over her breasts and cheeks.

Joe felt his own climax rising from his thighs, slamming though his balls and dick to shoot a geyser of cum inside her body.

He held her hips flush to his for several long moments, circling her body on his cock, prolonging her orgasm until the convulsions milking his sex grew fainter. Finally, Lily collapsed over his chest, nuzzling her face into the corner of his shoulder.

Joe caressed her back, soothing her while her jagged breaths grew even and her racing heart calmed. Finally, his own heart slowed and he receded below the layers of his dreams. This time he watched through misted glass as a girl with whiskey-colored hair pleasured herself.

Lily sang while she showered, confident the vamp wouldn't wake again to hear her off-key warbling. Her fingers itched to start putting some of what she'd learned into her computer, but first things first.

She had to make an appointment with Madame Leveque and shop for a dinner suitable for a vampire. He'd asked her not to go out alone, but it was still daylight. Weren't werewolves nocturnal creatures as well?

As she stood before her mirror, she suffered long moments of indecision. Hair, up or down? Makeup, her usual careless swipe of pale pink lipstick or a full face?

She wrinkled her nose at her reflection and decided not to take special pains with her appearance. Who was she kidding? Femme fatale, she wasn't. She quickly wound her hair into a knot and secured it with pins, but she glazed her lips with a deep rose.

Hurrying to the kitchen counter, she found her planner and flipped to the address section. She punched the numbers into her cordless handset and tucked it between her shoulder and ear while she gathered her planner and keys and dropped them in her purse. She was quickly running out of daylight.

"Madame Leveque's."

"Cissy? This is Lily Carlson."

"Professor, you manage to slip past that weirdo last night?" Cissy asked, wry humor in her tone.

Lily felt a blush rise all the way from her toes. "Not exactly."

"He give you any trouble?"

"Ah no." She quickly steered the conversation back. "Look, I'm calling because I need to see your grandmother tonight."

"Oooh, I don't know. Grandmere's been here since early this mornin'. She may be too tired. Can you come this afternoon?"

"No. That wouldn't be possible." Lily hated imposing on her friendship, but this might be her only shot at finding an answer to Joe's dilemma. "Would you ask her? It's very important I see her tonight."

"Sure." Cissy's voice reflected curiosity, but she didn't press for a reason. "I'll be right back."

Lily didn't have long to wait. "Professor, Grandmere says she's been expectin' your call. Come after dark, she said."

"Tell Madame, I'll be bringing a friend."

Relieved she'd accomplished one thing on her list, she let herself out of her apartment. At the front steps she met Mimi Comeaux, the superintendent's wife. She wielded a deck brush, applying it vigorously to the concrete steps—and she humming, an unusual occurrence for the normally pinch-faced woman.

"Good afternoon, Mimi," Lily said as she passed her.

"Mornin'," the woman trilled.

Lily gave her a second glance. "You seem chipper this morning."

The woman actually blushed. "It's a pretty day."

Lily eyed the overcast sky and raised an eyebrow. "Do you mind my asking what you are doing?"

"Some poor dog left bloody paw prints all over the front steps. I'm tryin' to bleach them out."

Lily looked at the smeared prints the woman hadn't yet reached with her brush. They were enormous. "You're sure those belong to a dog?"

"Sure. A very big dog. He must have cut a foot."

Lily remembered Joe's account of the werewolf and wondered if the woman was washing away paw prints from a primordial creature. Despite the heat, she felt a shiver creep up her spine. *Joe would have my ass if he found out I left the house.* But werewolves were said to be nocturnal creatures, she repeated to herself. Lily shrugged, bid Madame Comeaux *adieu*, and headed for her car.

As she unlocked the door, she heard an engine fire and glanced down the street. Nothing out the usual. She was just jumpy. Nevertheless, she locked the doors as soon as she slipped inside.

The local grocer was only a block away. She parked next to the door and quickly made her way inside the store. Heading straight for the meat section, she wondered how she'd word her request. Bluntly: Do you carry pig's blood? What else could a vampire consume? All she knew was what she'd gleaned from TV and movies—human blood and flesh as the main entrée, rats and pig blood in a pinch.

The butcher smiled as she approached.

"How are you, professor? Would you like shrimp fresh from the Gulf this morning?"

"Um, by chance do you carry pig's blood? I'm thinking of making…an old family recipe…for uh…gravy."

The portly butcher eyed her quizzically. "I'm sorry. If you would like to special order—"

Never comfortable telling a lie, Lily demurred. "No that's okay. Do you have something especially…juicy?" She knew her cheeks burned a fiery red.

Both eyebrows rose, like black beetles perched on his brow. "I have inch and half steaks—plenty fresh and dripping with blood, if that's what you really want."

Why hadn't she thought to go to another shop? He knew her preference for white meats and seafood. Her sudden taste for blood-soaked red meat had to be raising a question in his mind.

"Professor," he grinned broadly. "Are you by chance *enceinte*?"

That was one plausible explanation she hadn't considered. Lily felt her already hot face burn. "The steaks will be fine. Two of them please."

"Two?" His beetle-eyebrows waggled. "I won't be a moment," he said, and disappeared into a back room.

Lily took a deep breath and looked around, ticking off the other items she would need when she noted a tall, broadly built man just down the aisle from her. He was turned away, but she had the sneaking suspicion he had been watching her. Somehow, he looked out of place standing in front of a rack full of baby diapers.

Any other day and she would have given him a second and third considering look. He was handsome—his features spare, harshly etched. Manly. If Joe hadn't already awakened her appreciation for dangerously sensual men, she might have lingered to discover whether he really had been checking her out.

Instead, a shiver of unease raised the hair on the back of her neck. His build radiated power. His dark slacks molded thickly muscled thighs. His loosely fitted cotton shirt didn't disguise the sinew of his back and shoulders. How easily he could overpower a woman if that were his intent.

He reached for a package from the row of diapers and she noted a white bandage wrapped around his palm. He looked over his shoulder and his gaze met hers. The intensity in his light-colored eyes and the hard, chiseled features caused her heart to trip. Some instinct she would have said she didn't possess told her that yes, he had been watching her.

"Professor, your steaks?"

Lily blinked and turned to the butcher, smiling her thanks automatically. She was done shopping. She needed to get home quickly.

Lily paid for her package and walked swiftly to her car.

"Miss! Your change!"

He'd followed her out of the store. She didn't dare pause to answer. She opened her door with the remote, tossed the package on the passenger seat, and slid the key into the ignition with a shaking hand.

A shadow fell across her and she knew he stood outside her door. She shifted into reverse and hit the gas. As she pulled away, she finally looked at him. A feral smile stretched the man's hard mouth.

Chapter Seven

ဆာ

Joe heard the scrape of a key turning in the lock, then the clank of keys dropping to the tiled floor, followed by a mumbled oath. He let go of the worry he'd experienced over the past hour when he'd risen beyond his dreams to find Lily had gone.

Now anger swept through him, fast and blinding. He opened the door ready to tear into Lily for her carelessness, but the look on her face pulled him up short.

"Oh my God!" She launched herself into his arms.

All his anger and worry disappeared in an instant as he held her trembling body. He glanced up and down the hallway. Seeing no menace lurking in the shadows, he pulled her into the apartment and shut the door, turning the bolt to lock them inside. He leaned back against it, pulling her body flush with his and waited for Lily's explanation.

"Oh my God!" she repeated. "He followed me. In the store." Her breaths were as choppy as her words.

Joe's body tightened with outrage. A man stalked her? That Lily, normally so guileless and oblivious to her appeal, had noticed the man's actions gave immediate credence to her claim. He fought his resurfacing anger to rub soothing circles on her back. "Take a deep breath," he said from between clenched teeth, "and tell me."

Lily leaned away and looked into his face. The fear in her gaze and her trembling mouth had him wishing the man were here now so he could take his head off. "His hand—" she gasped, "he was standing by the diapers—but I knew!"

He pressed her face against his chest. By her jittery, incoherent explanation, he knew it might be a while before he pieced together the story. His rage boiled like an ulcer in his belly—but she didn't need his anger. She needed his comfort now. "Shhh. Take it easy, baby. I've got you now."

A shudder shook her frame and her arms tightened around him. "There was a car down the street. I was nervous." She sniffed against his chest.

Joe smiled, wondering if she realized she'd just wiped her nose on his T-shirt.

"Then the butcher thought I was pregnant."

He shook his head at that last thought. She was so rattled she wasn't making any sense. He smoothed the hair from her forehead and she raised her face. Grabbing her chin, he lowered his mouth to kiss her—something he'd wanted to do the moment he'd seen her again.

She drew back again. "But—"

His hand grabbed a fist of her hair and tilted her head. He sealed his lips over hers.

She murmured a protest, her hands pushing at his shoulders.

He kept kissing her, sucking on her lower lip, enticing her to open her mouth and let him in.

Finally she relaxed, her arms creeping up to encircle his neck.

By the time he pulled away, his heart galloped and his body had grown hard as a rock. He was a bastard, but all he could think of doing was taking her—right here. *Now!*

He pulled her blouse from her slacks and reached beneath to palm her breasts through her lacy bra.

Lily's lips, blurred and reddened by his kisses, formed a passionate moue. Then she blinked. "No! You have to listen."

Joe let his head fall back to the door with a bang and dragged air into his lungs. She was driving him nuts.

"I th—think your werewolf followed me," Lily said breathlessly. "I went to the grocery store down the block. Had to get something for dinner—for you."

He rubbed her back again, the motion soothing his own racing heartbeat. "How do you know it was him?"

The little frown that wrinkled her brow indicated she'd switched to analytic mode. "There was blood on the sidewalk. Bloody paw prints from a very large dog—*your wolf.*"

The way her mind leapt from one disjointed thought to the next left him dizzy. "Why did the paw prints make you think the man was the wolf?"

"He followed me. I heard a car start as I was getting into mine." At his dubious frown, she scowled. "I know it was him, and he was watching me in the store. He had a bandage on his hand. I left my change at the register and he followed me out."

"He couldn't have just been a good Samaritan?"

"No! It was his eyes. His stare was so intent." She looked at him, apology in her expression. "Just like yours. He was *smelling* me!"

Joe quirked an eyebrow. "You don't think any man would love the way you smell?"

"He looked like he wanted to eat me!"

A rueful smile lifted the corner of his lips. "So do I."

Lily shoved at his chest. "You don't believe me."

All humor fled. "I didn't say that. I think we should be very cautious. What I want to know is why you went out alone, after I specifically told you not to."

She huffed. "You are not the boss of me." Her arms came up between them and she struggled against his hard embrace. "Besides, there's no vampire food in the fridge."

"Vampire food?" His head was starting to hurt. Her leaps from subject to subject were hard to follow when his brain had fled so far south.

"Well, I wasn't sure what your diet consists of besides human blood, but somehow I didn't think chicken breasts and Rocky Road ice cream would appease you."

He sighed. "So what did you get?"

"Well, I asked for pig's blood, but the butcher said I'd have to special order it. So I bought steaks."

"Steak will do. I woke up hungry as hell." He gave her a heavy-lidded once-over. "You worked up my appetite."

"Oh." She blushed and smoothed a strand of hair behind her ear. "Oh!" Her eyes widened. "I left the steaks in the car—and my purse. I have to go get them."

"No you don't! It's dusk, give it a few minutes and I'll get them."

Lily took a deep breath and bit her lower lip.

Her telltale clue said she wanted to ask him another question. He caressed her buttocks and pulled her against his arousal. "Out with it."

Her glasses had slid toward the end of her nose and she glanced up at him from beneath her golden lashes. "What's so special about the way I smell?"

Joe felt the throb in his cock begin a slow drum roll. "You smell horny—all woman-spice and musk, and a little wild."

"I smell gamey?" She looked appalled.

"No. Primitive. Feminine. Your scent grabs a man by the balls."

"Yuck! I should have bought strawberry douche!"

The look on her face made Joe's shoulders shake with laughter. "Baby, you can't improve on nature. It's the first thing I noticed—even before I met you. I just followed your scent."

Color leeched from her face. "So did the werewolf," she whispered.

He leaned down and kissed her lips. "Yeah, he did." He took a deep breath. As much as he'd prefer to take her straight to bed, Lily's safety was at risk. "When do we see your voodoo queen?"

"She's not a voodoo queen—she's a spiritualist." Lily snuggled her hips against his. "She'll see us just after dark." She looked over her shoulder at the shrouded window. "Now."

Joe pulled her into his arms and gave her one last hard kiss. "Let's go. I'll eat in the car."

* * * * *

Madame Leveque's shop was just off Bourbon Street. An orange neon sign advertising "Tarot/Voodoo" gleamed brightly above the small doorway of a narrow, white stucco building that adjoined a row of shops. A bell tinkled above the door as Joe hustled Lily through the entrance with a hand to the small of her back. He gave a final look up and down the street before following her inside.

The narrow shop was small and dark; the shelves filled with cheesy Voodoo amulets and dolls, T-shirts with skeletal jazz bands, New Orleans key chains, and stuffed toy alligators.

Lily headed straight to the back of the shop, past the counter where the girl with the corkscrew curls nodded to a curtained doorway. Her eyes widened at the sight of him and Joe grinned evilly. As he passed, her eyes narrowed in a warning he couldn't miss.

Lily pulled back the drapery and he followed her into a cozy little sitting area with a sofa along the wall and a small wooden table in the center flanked by two chairs. The air smelled like cooking spices and Joe spotted incense burning from a small brass bowl.

A door opened from beyond the table and a short, wizened black woman stepped through. "Miss Lily."

"Madam Leveque," Lily said, shaking the old woman's hand. "I hope you don't mind that I've brought a friend."

Large, dark eyes gazed up at him for a long moment, and then a slow smile brightened her face. "Vampire," she said softly, and raised her hand.

Shaken by her immediate recognition and acceptance, Joe reached for her hand and turned it, bringing it to his lips to press a kiss to the crepe-paper skin. "Madame, I'm Joe Garcia."

She smiled with delight and motioned toward the table. "One of you may sit on the sofa. As you can see, I am accustomed to seein' only one person at a time," she said, her voice low and melodic. "Lily, you must have a very interestin' tale to explain how you come to be in the company of dis handsome man."

Joe pulled out one of the chairs for the old woman and she slowly sat down, smiling her thanks.

"Madame," Joe interrupted. "We have questions."

She held up her hand, "Don' tell me now." She softened the command with a smile and pointed toward a cupboard in the corner. "Bring me the candle and my cards, please."

Fighting his impatience, Joe found a stubby candle in a wax-encrusted dish, matches, and a worn deck of cards bound with a rubber band.

Madame reached for the matches and lit the candle. "Miss Lily, would you turn off the light? The switch is beside the door." She smiled at Joe conspiratorially. "I work best in the dark. As I imagine you do, too."

When the overhead lamp flickered off, the glow from the candle cast the old woman's face into relief, lending her a look of ageless wisdom. "I would like you to shuffle the deck for me, please."

Joe glanced at Lily, feeling a frown settle between his eyes, but she only nodded her encouragement and motioned him toward the chair.

As the old woman lit the candle and set it to her left, Joe removed the rubber band and carefully shuffled the age-softened cards. The design on the backs of the cards was of some celestial body. The faces were unlike any deck of cards he'd ever played poker with. He knew he was about to have his fortune read.

He sighed, resigning himself to the fact he would have to humor the woman in hopes she'd let him ask his questions in good time. When he'd finished, he handed her the deck.

"This won' take long," she said, humor crinkling the corners of her eyes.

Joe felt heat creep across his cheeks and gave her his attention while she laid three cards facedown on the table.

"Let's see what the cards can tell me about you, boy. Dis is called the 'Holy Trinity' — only three cards," she assured him with a wink. Her gnarled fingers turned over the first card. A grin creased her face and she looked from Joe to Lily, a wicked gleam in her eyes.

Joe looked down at the card and saw the figure of a man, wearing a robe of fiery colors and holding a beautiful golden wand.

"The King of Wands," she said, tapping the card. "This card tells me you're a man of passion. Handsome, conscientious, noble, and strong..." she looked up at him with a coquettish tilt of her head, "...and a good lover." She laughed at Lily's telltale blush.

Her hand hovered over the next card. She flipped it over and gave a small gasp. When she looked up, all humor was wiped from her face. Joe squirmed beneath her look of pity. "The Ten of Swords," she whispered.

This card depicted a body covered in blood. Ten swords pierced the torso. Despite his cynicism of the whole ritual, a chill crept up Joe's spine.

The old woman closed her eyes for a long moment. "Misfortune, ruin, loss, failure, desolation beyond tears. You have suffered." She was still so long, Joe thought she might have nodded off, then she sighed. "Ah..." When her eyes opened her gaze held warmth. "But all is not lost. The evil is nearly over."

Joe heard the distant sound of a bell tinkling and the curtain stirred. The candlelight wavered, nearly extinguishing, then fluttered and burned brighter. Madame turned the last card. "The Blessed Virgin sends a message." She raised her gaze to him.

The third card drew a gasp from Lily and sent a chill through Joe. It depicted the classic symbol of death—a tall, gaunt figure, his face hidden within the folds of a cowl. He held a scythe. A white rose in full blossom graced the corner. The macabre card was surprisingly beautiful.

The old woman patted Joe's hand. "Death is not the horrible card you think," she said. "Isn't death merely the stepping through from one life to the next? Dis could be a foretellin' of the end of pain and a reminder of your mortality. I think a great and good change is comin' to you. With courage, evil may be overcome."

Joe blew out a breath and glanced back at Lily. She smiled thinly.

"Now, Miss Lily. I would read your cards." Madame Leveque slid the deck across the table toward her.

Joe slid from the chair and held it out for Lily. Lily sat and carefully shuffled the deck, before handing it back to the old woman. Joe placed his hands on Lily's shoulders and he felt some of her tension ease.

Again, Madame drew three cards. As soon as the first was turned, all three people leaning over the table laughed.

"The Queen of Wands! Appropriate, *non*? A woman of passion and energy. You are fond of nature—*wild things*, yet you are practical."

The second card brought the tension back. A man dangled by his foot from a rope that hung in the air.

"The Hanged Man. Dis indicates you'll experience suspense and change. There may be sacrifice for great gain, or a search for inner truth. A change in point of view may be needed."

"But what does that mean?" Lily asked.

Madame settled back in her chair and folded her hands on her stomach. "Your choices have brought you to dis point. Now it is up to you to gain wisdom from your search for truth."

Lily shook her head, but Joe squeezed her shoulders. He wanted to see the next card.

Madame's hands remained on her belly and she smiled at Lily. "Turn the next one, my dear."

Lily reached a tentative hand to the card, and Joe had to smile. For all her professions of belief in empirical proof, she was enthralled. She flipped the card.

A beautiful woman blended two bowls of water into a single stream.

"It is called 'The Star' and represents the blending of the past and present. An awareness and acceptance of two worlds." Madame glanced pointedly between Lily and Joe.

Feeling a little mesmerized, Joe murmured, "Thanks, Madame."

She nodded her acceptance, and then swept her hand toward the sofa. "Please, take a seat and we'll talk. "

Joe held his hope in check and sat down. Dragging a hand through his hair, he tried to figure out a place to begin.

"Joe wants to be human again."

Joe smiled ruefully. Lily's eagerness eclipsed his.

Madame's dark gaze seemed to look straight through him. "What about your new existence can't you accept?"

"I'm a damn parasite!" Frustration made his reply angrier than he'd intended. "I feed off humans."

"Do you take more than they can give?"

His hands dug into his thighs. "Sometimes, I want to. It's hard to fight the hunger."

"God gives us all tests."

"I don't think God has anything to do with my current state." *Darcy and her bloodsucking boyfriend do!*

Madame nodded. "I think you will find your mortality."

He stared, hope rising. He leaned forward. "How? What do I have to do?"

"You must face your past. Go home."

Not what he wanted to hear. He shook his head and looked at Lily. Her bleak expression reflected his heart's dismay. "I don't understand."

"I can't tell you anythin' more."

His head dipped. He'd come all this way only to hear that he had to go home. Something he already knew.

"Madame," Lily's voice broke through his disappointment, reminding him of the other danger lurking. "There's one other problem I need your advice concerning."

The old woman reached across the table and took Lily's hand. She turned the palm upward. "You haven't figure it out yet, have you child?"

"What?"

"Tell me first. What disturbs you?"

"There are so many things. I have intense…cravings. And then there's this …thing following me."

Madame tilted her head toward Joe. "Does this man satisfy your…cravings?"

Lily nodded her head, blushing.

"Then isn't your problem solved?"

"What I feel isn't normal." Lily gripped the edge of the table. "I want too much. Besides, he's leaving." She shrugged her shoulders and bit her lip. "And then there's the other…thing."

"The wolves? Do wolves follow you now?"

Lily exchanged a shocked glance with Joe before dragging her gaze back to the woman. "Yes. Or at least one does."

Madame turned to Joe. "The only way to keep them from her is to take her with you."

Joe nodded. "Why do they follow her?"

"For the same reason you do." Her little smile told him he wouldn't like what she said next. "To mate."

His body tightened. "Is it because of her increased sex drive?" he asked. "Do they smell her constant need?"

Lily's eyes darkened and Joe recognized the signs of her growing arousal. Just the mention of sex and she was primed. And like Pavlov's dog, her arousal kicked his into high gear.

"It is dat. And something more," the old woman said, her expression growing amused. She hadn't missed the exchange between Joe and Lily.

Frustrated with her cryptic comments, Joe blurted, "Why do they follow *her*?"

"Because she leaves her scent all over the city. She's in heat."

Chapter Eight

ℰℴ

Lily slid the strap of her handbag over her shoulder and shivered despite the balmy night air. Still reeling from shock, she wrapped her arms around her middle and stumbled toward Bourbon Street. "I'm one of them?"

"You heard what she said." His words were clipped, his face hard as stone. "Not yet." His hand pressed the small of her back, hurrying her along. "Although, I'm wondering why you'd fight the change! The wolves don't mean you any harm. They just want to fuck you. Something you want."

Anger burned away the chill. "So I should just give into my nature? I should let any Duke or Fido take me because my body is ready to breed? That's so hypocritical coming from you! Why do you fight what you are?"

"I wasn't born to be a vampire. You were born to be a werewolf."

"Well, I don't accept that."

"Now you know how I feel. Neither do I."

He sounded so angry she felt like crying. Didn't he care strange werewolves wanted to mate with her? "I don't want them. Besides, I won't just get pregnant—I'll whelp! I could have a whole litter of puppies." That thought led to another more horrifying. "Oh God, does that mean I'll grow a row of breasts?"

They reached the corner and turned right onto the busy thoroughfare, blending with the strolling crowd.

"You think that's a problem?" Joe asked, his voice purring close to her ear.

Cream trickled down to soak another panty liner. That's all it took. One sexy rumble from this man and she was ready to shuck her pants in the nearest alley and have a go. She was insatiable. No. She was in heat!

"Shouldn't you be eager to get home and start taking notes?" he asked. "You've obviously been studying the wrong breed."

She dug in her heels. "Stop it!" She rounded on him, her hands clenched. "There's no need to be snide."

The hard set of Joe's jaw indicated he wasn't ready to let go of his anger.

Lily wondered if he even knew why he was angry. "You can't just give me over to them."

Joe stepped close, crowding her against a wall. "Course not," he said. His head lowered until his face was inches from hers. His eyes glittered dangerously. "I thought you'd bake them up a bunch of doggie treats and invite them over."

Ignoring the amused stares from passersby, she grabbed a fistful of his shirt and pulled him closer. "I don't want them. I want you."

He planted his hands against the wall on either side of her shoulders, trapping her inside his embrace. "Well, that's too bad. I told you, I'm not staying."

Lily licked her lips, enjoying a little thrill of power when his smoldering gaze followed the motion. "You could take me with you."

A muscle in his jaw rippled. "Not possible."

Her hands swept up to caress the hills of his chest. "You didn't seem so averse to that thought when Madame Leveque first mentioned it."

"That was before I knew my interest was chemically induced. You're not any more human than I am."

Lily flinched as though he'd slapped her. "What? You think this thing we have going is all about werewolf pheromones?"

"Isn't it?" The muscle along his jaw rippled again and his nostrils flared. He ground his crotch against her belly. "Baby, it makes me as crazy as it does you. You wouldn't care if I dry-humped you right here, would you?" He slid his knee between her legs and raised it to grind against her pussy. "Would I have followed you to your apartment if I hadn't already been snared by your scent?"

"Silly me," Lily said around a gasp, her body already climbing the peak. "I actually thought my irresistible personality might have had something to do with it." The tips of her breasts swelled and she rubbed herself shamelessly against his chest while she rode his thigh.

His mouth slammed down on hers, his tongue stabbing between her lips.

Lily kissed him back with all the love she had. He thought this was just chemistry—an artificially induced arousal. She knew better. She'd fought her urges for months until this man presented himself on her balcony.

Joe groaned into her mouth and lifted his knee higher.

It was just enough to send her over the edge. Her whole body stiffened. Wide-eyed with shock, her body convulsed—her thighs clamping around his leg as waves of shuddering contractions gripped her empty vagina.

Slowly, the tight coil of desire in her belly unraveled. Spent, her body and mouth slackened. If not for Joe's knee still rammed between her legs, she would have melted to the ground.

Joe gave her a final sliding kiss and lowered his knee. His gaze smoldered darkly. "See what I mean? You'd let me take you anywhere."

Suddenly tired and near tears, Lily let go of his shirt and leaned back against the wall. "Why don't you just go now? You're wasting nighttime."

He stepped back a pace so their bodies no longer touched. "I'll see you home, first."

"You don't need to do that. I'm not in any danger, remember? They just want to fuck me. Something I want, right?"

"I'll see you home."

Lily felt like screaming. Any moment now she was going to break into a million pieces. "Joe, they won't harm me, but they'll kill you."

"They'll try."

"Only because you stand between them and me. I don't want you hurt because of me. You should just go."

"For all we know, there's only the one wolf. Even odds. What are the chances of a pack existing here in New Orleans?" His face tilted and suspicion twisted his mouth. "Or would you like that? A half dozen wolves nosing around your pussy?"

Lily stared, her heart breaking. He hadn't a clue how she felt—and he wouldn't care if he did. She turned on her heels and walked away from him.

"You're going the wrong way," he called after her.

She ignored him and walked faster.

"Dammit! Lily stop!"

She was running now, blinded by the tears streaming down her face.

Heavy hands landed on her shoulders, bringing her to a screeching halt. Lily didn't bother to turn. Instead, she drew ragged breaths and fought against more tears that burned the back of her throat.

"Baby, I'm sorry," Joe said. "I was out of line." His body pressed against her back.

Lily blinked rapidly. This was too humiliating. She'd thrown herself at him and been turned down cold. His pity was the last thing she wanted now.

"You sure don't run like a wolf," he said, next to her ear.

"I'm not," she said, hating that her voice sounded clogged with tears. "Not yet."

"That's right." His hands slid down her arms and encircled her middle.

Lily accepted his embrace, letting her head fall back against his chest. "But I'm a breeder. That's what she called it, right? I'm just a bite away from being canine. Sooner or later they'll find me—just like you did. By scenting me."

His hands closed around her shoulders and he shook her once. "You can fight it. You aren't turned yet."

"What am I supposed to do? Lock myself in my apartment every time I come into heat? Avoid anyone whose nose twitches when they draw near me?"

"Yes."

"What good will that do? I have to survive—I have to work. I'll meet some good-looking guy squeezing Charmin in the grocery store and my desire will overpower me. I'll let him take me home." She sniffed and rolled her head on his chest. "I won't be able to help it. One bite and it'll be finished."

Joe nuzzled her neck. "You're sure you don't want that? It might be easier to just go with the flow."

"You're not the one who's going four-legged." She scraped tears from her face. "I have no desire to run on all fours and smell other dog's butts. And think of the expense of all that waxing!"

Joe's shoulders shook. He turned her around, but she stubbornly kept her gaze on his oversized feet. He put a finger under her chin and brought her face up. By his crooked grin, she could tell he was exasperated.

Lily shrugged. "Think about it. No Remington razor will do the trick."

Joe drew his T-shirt over his head and used it to mop her face, ignoring the whistles from several grinning women as they walked by.

Lily scowled at every one of them.

"Let's get back to the car. We've got plans to make."

"Plans?"

"Like flight plans. And you need to pack."

Lily brought her gaze slowly up, hoping her heart wasn't shining in her eyes. She was so pathetic. "Don't say that unless you really want me with you."

Joe's eyes burned her like a four-alarm blaze. "Don't want you?" He pulled her hand down and forced her palm to follow the curve of his erection. His face was still hard. Still angry. But the remorse in his expression said the anger was for himself.

"Let's get back to my place quick," she said, her heart thrumming.

He grabbed her hand and pulled her back down Bourbon Street.

"Wait, put your shirt back on!"

He laughed and pulled her faster behind him.

She'd parked on another side street, but as soon as she turned the corner she knew something was wrong. She didn't need to have all her werewolf powers to know eyes followed her progress. "Joe?"

He slowed his pace and his head lifted. He sniffed at the air. "Yes. I know. They're here."

"What do we do now?" Her hand clutched at his like a lifeline.

"Make your choice, Lily."

What choice? A blood-drinking vampire or a pack of horny dogs? "I'm afraid."

"You can be what you were born to be, or you can come with me. But choose now."

"Damn, they followed my scent, didn't they? I should have bought that strawberry douche."

"What's it going to be?" he repeated.

"I think—" A low growl sounded from the far side of the street. "Run!"

Joe didn't need to hear her say it twice, he ducked down and his shoulder hit her belly. She draped over him like a rucksack, and he took off in the direction they'd just come.

Lily was glad for his strength and his speed. His feet ate up the pavement. She'd never have kept up. She leaned up and caught sight of a man straightening from his hiding place beside her car. The man from the diaper aisle! He leapt to the sidewalk and ran after them, tearing away his T-shirt and ripping open his pants.

What the hell was he doing?

He stopped for a second and pushed his jeans down his legs, and then he was running after them, again. Lily had a glimpse of his powerful, nude body as his legs stretched to increase their pace. Then he was changing, morphing, his face growing longer, fur sprouting all over his body. He lunged and he was running on all fours, his transformation complete. A werewolf!

She would have told Joe, but she hadn't the wind to scream with her body bobbing on his shoulder. Faster! Run faster, she wanted to say. The wolf was closing in on them.

Then there was a second wolf, loping into view from another side street—and another. They drew closer—so close she could see their eyes glowing like flat, gold disks in the light from the street lamps, their tongues lolling from the sides of their mouths.

At that moment, she was sure she didn't want to be a werewolf. A lolling tongue was not something she ever wanted to aspire to. *Faster, Joe!*

Joe turned onto Bourbon Street, but didn't slow his pace. She heard screams and lifted her head again to see the wolves loping around the corner. Exposure to the crowds didn't seem to be a deterrent. Her pheromones must indeed be a powerful thing.

Lily heard the squeal of brakes and a loud horn.

"Mister! This way! Get in the car!"

Lily found herself tossed onto the vinyl back seat of a taxi. Joe jumped on top of her. Heedless of the fact they were only half inside the car, the driver hit the gas.

Joe hauled her the rest of the way inside and slammed the door. Lily pushed Joe to the floor of the cab and scrambled on the seat to look out the rear window. The taxi was pulling away from the wolves. One by one, they stopped, their heads low to the ground, chests billowing, as they watched the taxi leave them in the dust.

Lily turned to Joe and for the first time realized the screams she'd heard could just as well have been for him. His wore his monster face.

He'd collapsed against the back of the seat, dragging lungfuls of air into his chest.

"Joe!" she hissed.

His eyes shone like the wolves in the dim light when he turned toward her.

"Your face!" She tilted her head toward the driver.

Joe took several deep breaths and his face reformed into the handsome one she preferred.

"Holy shit! Did you see that?" the taxi driver said, excitement in his voice. "What did you two do to piss those dogs off? Steal their bone?"

* * * * *

They booked a redeye flight from New Orleans to Orlando. From there they would rent a car. They'd be in Vero Beach by early morning.

The tickets would just about clean out Joe's account. He slid the card across the counter.

Lily put her hand over it and presented the ticket agent her American Express card. Joe's face burned.

"Don't be mad," Lily said. She chewed her bottom lip. "This is my fight. You wouldn't be going back there now if I weren't in danger. Let me do this."

Joe let go of his pride. He'd been on unpaid leave of absence since January. He didn't even know if he still had a job.

His stuff was in storage. The suitcase he'd retrieved from his hotel room with all his clothing was still behind Lily's couch. What the hell did he have to be proud about?

As they headed to the gate, her small hand slipped inside his, and he gave it a squeeze, reassuring her he wasn't angry.

Even while he dreaded returning to the place where life as he'd known it had ended, he was glad he wasn't going there alone.

* * * * *

"Can I get something for you sir?" the pretty flight attendant asked.

"A blanket?" Joe asked, smiling at the woman. "My girlfriend's cold."

"I'm not cold," Lily said flatly.

Joe dropped his gaze to the flight attendant's chest and raised an eyebrow. "She's cold."

The woman gave him a grin and opened an overhead bin. The blanket was thin, but would be enough of a screen for what he intended. He raised the armrest that separated their seats and spread the blanket over them both.

"Oh," Lily grumbled. "You're just too macho to admit you're the one who's cold."

"Vamps don't hold the heat very well," he replied, with glib amusement.

"I wonder if that's how you got your cold-blooded reputation."

Under the blanket, he slid his hand over her thigh.

Lily's eyes widened. "You're not thinking—"

"Open your pants," he whispered.

"You're not going to—"

The rasp of his zipper alarmed her and she stared at his movements beneath the blanket.

"There's no one around us—the plane's nearly empty." He reached for her hand and brought it to his aching cock. "Let's play."

Lily gave her fellow passengers, most of who were already settling down to sleep, a guilty glance, and then Joe heard the slow slide of her zipper. When she looked back, she leaned back against her seat, her eyes begging him to take her.

Joe reached for her tummy, pulled her blouse out of the way, and tunneled his hand into her underwear. Sliding past her belly, he raked his fingers through the soft curls covering her sex. Lily's eyes scrunched closed and her face turned bright pink. If anyone looked their way they'd know exactly what he was doing.

That was just fine with him. It had been too many hours since he's last been inside her. He didn't care who watched. His fingers parted her folds and speared inside her juicy cunt.

Lily's hand gripped his cock like a gearshift.

"Lily," he whispered.

Her eyes fluttered open. "Yes?" she asked, her voice high and thin.

"Move your hand."

She took her hand away from his cock.

"No. Jerk me off."

"Oh!" Her hand encircled him, but she moved with excruciating slowness up and down his shaft.

"You're killing me, baby. Faster."

"They'll see us," she hissed.

"If you don't do it faster, I'll turn you over the seat and fuck you now."

Shock widened her eyes, but her cunt gushed around his fingers.

Sitting side by side, their hands in each other's pants, Joe couldn't care less who saw the frantic rustling beneath the blanket.

"It's not enough," Lily panted.

"Speak for yourself," he mumbled, enjoying the friction from the coarse blanket and her hand pumping on his sex.

"There has to be a better way."

He gave her a sideways glance. "Meet me in the restroom?"

"Are you crazy? We can't both go in there. Someone will see us."

"Who'll notice? Everyone else is sleeping."

"There's no room—"

"I promise I'll make it fit," he purred.

Lily pulled her hand away. He swirled his finger inside her sex once and drew a wet trail up her belly, before he took his hand away. They both struggled with clothing and zippers, grinning at each other like children filching cookies from the cookie jar.

He leaned across her and gave her a smacking kiss. "Take the stall on the left, but don't lock the door. I'll be right behind you."

Lily hurried down the aisle, sure that anyone looking at her flushed face and mussed appearance would guess what she'd been doing—but she didn't care. Her pussy ached to glove Joe's cock again. With a quick glance to assure herself no one followed her progress, she entered the small restroom and quickly stepped out of her shoes, pushed her slacks and panties down her legs, then looked around for somewhere to hang them. The small overhead cabinet would have to do.

Just as she draped her clothing over the corner of the cabinet, the door swung open and Joe stepped inside, crowding her back against the toilet. "Glad to see you didn't waste any time." His hands were already unbuttoning his jeans. He slid them just past his hips. His cock bounded out of confinement, poking her in the belly.

She couldn't resist its invitation and sat on the cold metal toilet to take his thick cock inside her mouth.

"Christ! You catch on fast." His fingers tugged bobby pins from her bun and speared through her hair, encouraging her to take him deeper into her mouth.

Lily rocked back and forth, sliding her lips over his cock, sucking hard, and reveling in his gasps and the jerk of his hips as he glided in and out of her mouth. She cupped his balls and tugged gently.

"Baby, stop!" He pulled her hair.

With a last swirl of her tongue along his shaft and around his plump head, Lily lifted her face. "Fuck me?"

"Climb up on the toilet."

His hands steadied her as she climbed up and turned to face him. He opened his arms and she clasped his shoulders. Wrapping her legs one at a time around his narrow waist, she lowered her body onto his cock.

She was so ready and wet her vagina rippled as she slid all the way down his shaft.

He held her in his arms for a long moment. Then bracing his feet as wide as he could in the narrow stall, he rocked his hips. The gentle motion wasn't enough.

"Harder!" she begged.

His hands gripped her ass to lift her, and then he shoved her down on his cock at the same time as he rocked forward.

"That's it! Faster!"

His breath gusted out on a laugh. "Shhh. Bellow like that again and you'll wake the whole plane."

Lily didn't care. "Don't stop!"

"I couldn't if my life depended on it," he gritted out, sealing his mouth over hers to muffle her moans.

Up and down, he slammed into her. His cock thickening as his body changed. He flung back his head and Lily watched, helpless with arousal, as he transformed into her sexy, ravaging monster, his movements growing sharper, harder, faster.

"Yes! Please, more!"

Then her body exploded, warm honey gushing from her cunt, making the slap of their flesh sound wet and sticky. Lily bit his shoulder to keep from screaming out loud as her body stiffened and shuddered.

With a last deep thrust, Joe's cock released a stream of hot cum that bathed her womb in warmth like super-heated lava.

Slowly, he morphed and braced his hand against the wall. She felt his legs tremble, but refused to let him go. She kissed the deep grooves she'd left on his shoulder, then his chin, and finally his mouth.

When she pulled away, she looked into his reddened face, still tight with strain. "Do you think anyone heard us?"

Chapter Nine

🕉

Snuggled under the blanket once more, Lily fought the urge to sleep. Her body was as relaxed as a soggy noodle, but she hated wasting a moment of her time with Joe.

She turned her head, which rested on his shoulder, to look into his face. "Now that I've had a chance to catch my breath, do you mind telling me why we're going to Florida? I know Madame told you to go home, but how do you expect to find our answers there?"

Joe glanced away. "There's one person left who might know something. Although I hate like hell asking him for a damn thing."

"Why?"

He looked back, his anger barely banked behind his rigid face. "He made me what I am."

"Your sire?"

"Yeah." He must have seen the interested light in her eyes. "Don't go there. We're not talking about that—or him."

"All right. I'll change the subject. So what do you do? Besides…vampire things?"

"I'm a cop. Or was."

She nodded, not the least surprised.

"What? Not going to list the clues that gave me away?"

She frowned. "I don't think I like it when you tease me."

"Why?" His finger smoothed the lines furrowing her forehead.

"Because I wonder how you read me so well. Do I have a teleprompter on my forehead that repeats my every thought?"

He groaned. "I know you're dying to tell me. Go ahead."

She chewed on her lip. He was going to laugh at her. She just knew it. "Well, you have short hair and a well-conditioned body."

"I could have been military."

"True, but you knew how to break into my apartment."

"You didn't think that was just part of Intro to Vampire? Or I could have been military with a criminal past."

"Well, then there's the way you walk."

He raised one dark eyebrow. "The way I walk?"

"Come on. Tell me you've never been pulled over for a speeding ticket and seen that little strut cops do when something makes their day."

"I've never seen it."

"And you don't believe it just because you've never seen it?" This time she raised an eyebrow. "And I'm supposed to believe I snore just because you said so? Sometimes you've just got to trust." She grinned. She had him.

His eyes narrowed. "Okay. So I strut."

Satisfied for now, Lily yawned and snuggled closer. "Wake me when we get there." She fell asleep with the sound of Joe's soft laughter and his hand rubbing her breast.

* * * * *

Joe *strutted* into the Special Unit's station house, dreading the coming confrontation.

It was early morning, just before sunrise. The time the guys usually returned from patrol and gave their outbriefs to the Captain.

With Lily following behind him, he walked past the long row of empty desks, past the dispatcher's booth, straight to the conference room. He didn't bother knocking on the closed door.

A dozen faces, most belonging to teammates he'd known better than his own family, turned toward him. His old buddy Max Weir muttered, "Just another fucking vampire."

Joe's back stiffened.

Captain Springer looked over his shoulder, his eyes widening, a smile wreathing his broad face. Then it slipped and he darted a glance down the table.

Joe followed that glance to find Darcy in her usual place, Quentin at her side.

Darcy's face blanched white and she gripped the edge of the table. Quentin's arm encircled her shoulder and he leaned toward her to whisper something in her ear. Then he straightened and glared at Joe.

"I think, we'll talk in a little while," the Captain said, sending a meaningful look around the table.

The room cleared quickly, except for Darcy, Quentin, and two people Joe didn't recognize—one a dark-haired male and the other a busty blonde. Some deeply buried instinct told them these two were kin—vampires.

His teammates nodded their greetings as they passed, their faces betraying wariness. Max jostled him, giving him a deliberate shove as he left the room. Joe didn't care. His eyes were on his sire.

Suddenly, Quentin's nostrils flared and his eyes narrowed. He lunged to his feet. "Why the hell did you bring *that* here?" he bellowed, staring past Joe's shoulder.

Lily gasped and slipped her hand inside his. Quentin was staring at her like she was some kind of monster.

Joe stiffened and gave Lily's hand a reassuring squeeze. "She's the reason I'm here."

"Well, this is a pretty pickle. Do you even know what you have, cub?" The glib murmur pulled Joe's attention to the brown-haired man sitting on the opposite side of the table. The pointed glance he shared with Quentin marked him as the blond vamp's friend.

Joe lifted his chin with defiance. "A breeder, or so I'm told."

"She doesn't belong here," Quentin said, looking mad enough to tear his head off. "We don't mix."

Darcy, still seated, reached for Quentin's arm. "Why don't we sit down and talk? And what exactly is a breeder?"

"The enemy."

Lily clutched Joe's hand, trying to still her trembling. The way the tall, blond man stared had her cowering behind Joe. She should just leave. She tugged her hand, but Joe wouldn't let go. She tugged again, but he simply drew her to his side and put his arm around her shoulders, anchoring her there.

She glared daggers at him, but he never noticed. His gaze remained on the blond one. Then Lily saw the woman seated beside the menacing man. She was slender, with wide-set brown eyes and shoulder-length brown hair. Her face was devoid of makeup, but she was lovely. Her skin glowed with health—at least it would have if she didn't look like she was about to pass out.

In an instant, Lily guessed this was the woman who'd scorned Joe and stopped feeling sorry for her. The woman's gaze met hers for a moment and she gave Lily a tight-lipped smile.

"I think I better go, Joe," Lily said softly.

The man with the chestnut hair gave her a pitying look. "You don't even know, do you?"

"That you're vampires? I guessed that. I also know werewolves are on my ass," she said, lifting her chin.

"You're too valuable for them to let you go. You can give them the next generation of—"

"Vermin!" the blond man spat.

"—cubs. My name's Dylan O'Hara by the way," the chestnut-haired man said with a crooked smile. "That's my wife, Emmy."

He nodded toward a plump, blonde woman Lily hadn't seen because she was tucked in the corner next to a box of chocolate-covered donuts. She waved one and giggled, "Sorry, sympathy cravings." Her eyes widened and her glance darted to the dark-haired woman.

Lily was starting to feel dizzy. There was so much anger and intrigue going on inside the room, all she wanted to do was leave. "Really Joe. I want to go," she repeated.

A glance at his face and she knew he hadn't even heard her. He stared at Emmy for a long moment, and then his gaze flew to the brown-haired woman.

"That's Darcy Henry," Emmy said, drawing Lily's attention away. "Quentin won't ever get around to the rest of the introductions. He and Joe have a history."

Lily felt sick at knowing the source of the competition was wrapped in one willowy-slim woman.

"So do Darcy and I," Joe ground out, dropping Lily's hand. His jaw set like granite, he circled the table stalking toward Darcy.

"They are *so* competitive," Emmy said.

Quentin stepped in front of her, but again, Darcy reached up to stroke his arm. "It's okay, Quent." Darcy rose and Lily suddenly understood the tension. Darcy's belly was round. Obviously, she wasn't a vampire.

She was pregnant.

Joe stood in front of her, his hands clenched at his sides. "Mine?"

Quentin's arm slipped around the woman's shoulders, clearly stamping his possession.

"Your child, yes," Darcy whispered.

Lily reached for the edge of the table, something to hold onto because her legs suddenly felt like rubber.

"I wouldn't have left you if I'd known," Joe said angrily, his words stabbing at Lily's heart. He still loved her.

"I know," Darcy said, reaching up to place her hand on his cheek. "But it was for the best, don't you see?"

Joe shook his head. "Not really. You're pregnant. I'm responsible. Christ, I was stupid."

"Water under the bridge—and I am happy, Joe."

"With *him*? Is he treating you well?"

"We're married." Her smile reassured Lily that at least she wasn't in love with Joe. "I love him."

Joe closed his eyes and let out a deep breath. "What about the baby?"

"He's yours and ours. I'd like you to be part of his life."

"I will be."

Darcy nodded, and then she looked at Quentin. "Right?"

The blonde vampire glared at Joe, but he nodded, too. "I don't have to like it."

"I'm glad you don't," Joe murmured.

Lily almost rolled her eyes at the posturing from the two males. You'd think it was high noon at the OK Corral.

"I've just got one question for you, *Garcia*."

Joe's eyes narrowed and Lily hoped they weren't about to draw.

"Have you fucked her?" Quentin asked, nodding at Lily.

Lily felt the wind squeeze out of her lungs as she gasped.

Darcy looked just as shocked. "Quentin!"

"It's important," Quentin said, his jaw tight.

"What my eloquent friend is trying to ask is whether you've been in her bed?" Dylan repeated, his gaze also turning to Lily.

Feeling naked beneath their stares and knowing her face was as red as a tomato, Lily blurted, "My name's Lily!"

"It's none of your business," Joe said, rage making his voice gravelly.

"I'm afraid it is," Quentin said softly.

"Why?" Lily whispered.

"She's a breeder," Quentin said, his hard gaze unwavering.

"So?" Joe's stance widened, and he looked about ready to swing. "She hasn't been with any werewolves."

"But she's been with you, hasn't she?"

Joe nodded once, curtly.

"Well, shit!" Quentin took a deep breath and shared a look with Dylan.

"Quentin!" Darcy pulled on his arm. "Why is that important?"

"Werewolves will kill her and her get," he said, looking suddenly tired.

Lily felt like ice water ran through her veins. Quentin's anger was one thing—his defeated expression made her tremble.

"Then we'll protect her," Emmy said cheerily.

"It's not that simple, love," Dylan said, his voice devoid of emotion. "Vampires will want her dead, too."

"But why?" Her wide blue eyes stared back with innocence. "I'm a vampire, and I don't want her dead. Besides, he's not a werewolf. She can't bear the next generation of puppies if she's been with him."

"Because she's likely carrying an abomination in her belly, even now."

This from Dylan, the kind one, made Lily swallow nervously. *A baby? An abomination?* That wasn't possible. She'd never read of a hybrid child in all her research.

"But she can't be pregnant," Joe said, his face darkening. He turned back to stare at her, too. "Vampires can't impregnate humans." His glance dropped to her belly.

"But she's not *entirely* human, is she?"

Lily heard Quentin's smug comment as if from a distance. The room had started spinning. *I can't be pregnant!*

* * * * *

"Now see what you've done!" Emmy glared up at the three men who hovered around the sofa in the lounge. "And babies are never abominations!"

"What is it with you?" Quentin shoved Joe. "Are you single-handedly trying to populate the world?"

"Leave off, Quent!" Dylan said. "We've got bigger problems than your jealousy."

"So, tell me how this is possible?" Joe asked, raking a hand through his hair, trying to gather his wits. The last few minutes had scrambled what was left of his brains. Finding out he was a father—and might be again soon—had him feeling like a low-down, dirty bastard. Then watching Lily drop like a brick to the floor had scared years off his life—if he'd had one.

"We're not spermless," Dylan replied, "it's a temperature thing that keeps us from impregnating humans, or even our own kind. This woman" he said, nodding toward Lily, "emits a chemical that excites werewolves and vampires. Our temperatures rise—just enough."

"Oh yeah," Joe shook his head. She'd certainly made him hot the moment she'd parted her sweet thighs to pleasure herself. The one woman on the planet he should never have taken…

"I've only experienced it once or twice myself, but then I'd had proper mentoring," Dylan said, glaring at Quentin. "I knew we didn't mix."

"But why is it such a terrible thing if she's pregnant?" Darcy asked, wringing out a wet cloth above the station's coffee pot. She laid it on Lily's forehead.

"We survive because we keep a balance in nature," Dylan said, "vampire to human, werewolf to human. Even among us. The consequences of this union, vampire and werewolf, will upset that balance."

"Would you speak English for fucksake!" Emmy grumbled. "Get to the point. Has anyone else noticed how pompous he's gotten since we married?"

Dylan reached down and pulled her hair. "The point, my dear, is that any child of such a union may have extraordinary powers. Werewolves and vampires will want it destroyed before it can realize its full potential."

"But she's not a werewolf, yet," Joe protested.

"She carries their DNA. She can pass it to her child."

Feeling sick to his stomach, Joe said, "Maybe she's not pregnant. Hell, she's still in heat."

"She's capable of conceiving throughout her heat—it doesn't end until she stops ovulating. That doesn't happen in a day. It begins when she conceives her first cub, but can last a week."

"What are you saying? She might be having a litter?"

"Just how many times did you fuck her?" Quentin bellowed.

"Oh God! I *am* going to have a dozen tits!"

Lily sat up, her head still spinning. Quentin reached to steady her.

"Get away from her," Joe said, shoving the other vampire away. He knelt beside Lily. "Are you feeling better?"

"I want to leave," she said quietly.

"All right, we'll leave."

"No. By myself." She looked into his face and saw something that looked like pain. But that couldn't be. She was just someone he'd been attracted to because of the chemical she emitted.

"You should let her leave, Joe." Quentin said. "She's a danger to everyone around her."

"She's not going anywhere by herself," Joe said, with the menacing look that always managed to turn her knees to jelly.

"They'll have to move into The Compound with us," Darcy said.

"The hell they will!" Quentin bit out.

"What compound?" Joe asked.

"Nicky's old place," Darcy explained. "The SU confiscated it along with the rest of his property. They deeded it to us to set up The Council."

"Council?"

"You've a lot to catch up on," Dylan said.

"Look, I'm not going to any compound. I'm going home." Lily struggled to stand, but her legs didn't seem to have any strength and she crumpled back onto the sofa.

"Stay put," Joe said, placing his hand on her thigh to keep her there. "Why don't you want me to come with you?"

"Because I'm just a problem," she said, through a veil of tears. "You don't really want me."

He raised both eyebrows. "Don't want you?"

"If she moves in, she'll have to stay put until she has the baby," Dylan said, as though Lily hadn't spoken a word. "Otherwise she'll leave scent everywhere she goes. We can't have her drawing every wolf and vamp in the region."

"What about after the baby's born?" Quentin asked.

"We'll see," Dylan replied. "The baby may not show any signs of its nature until it reaches adolescence."

"But *she'll* have to be turned," Quentin said, staring at Lily.

"No!" Joe said, rounding on the two men.

The three males faced off, hands clenched.

Lily put a hand to her forehead and stripped away the cloth. Her head hurt just trying to keep up with the volleys the men shot at each other, she wasn't sticking around to see them beat each other bloody.

Emmy sat down beside her and patted her knee. "You just have to let them get it all out. It's a man thing. They can't just agree; it's always a contest."

"If you don't turn her," Dylan said, "she'll continue to come into season."

"But how will she raise a child—or children," Joe said, "when she'll be damned to the night for half her life?"

"Auntie Darcy can babysit," Darcy said, waving her hand to get their attention.

"Absolutely not!" Quentin said. "If the child were discovered there could be a bloodbath. I won't risk your safety, Darcy."

"Will he be furry?" Lily asked.

This drew the first smiles from Dylan and Quentin. Lily began to understand their attraction. Or maybe it was just her pheromones going into overdrive.

"No," Dylan said. "He'll appear human. Of course, there's every chance he may be human."

"She may be a girl," Joe said.

"Not likely. Why do you think Lily here's so valuable?" Dylan said, his gaze sweeping over her.

Lily blushed as all three males threw her interested stares.

"They mostly whelp males."

"I may not even be pregnant," she said doubtfully.

"And you make it a habit to swoon?" Dylan raised an eyebrow.

"Never!"

Three male heads nodded sagely.

Lily huffed. "I'm not staying. Joe isn't going to want me once my heat ends—it's just the pheromones. Hell, I might not want him."

"Oh, you'll want me," he said, stalking toward her. "I'll make sure of that."

Lily held her breath as he squatted next to her. He lifted her hand and pressed a kiss to her palm. "You're staying. Period. End of story." The firm set of his mouth told her he'd sit on her if she tried to leave.

She just wished he wanted her to stay because he loved her—not because she might be carrying his child. "I never cry," she said, with a sniff.

Dylan and Quentin grinned.

"They're counting off clues," Joe said.

"Clues?" she asked stupidly.

"Fainting, crying—"

"She's preggers all right," Quentin said.

"You don't like me," Lily wailed, hating she sounded like a child.

Quentin rolled his eyes. "I have to like you. Darcy won't let me sleep with her, if I don't."

"Got that right," Darcy growled

"How will we protect her during the day?" Joe asked, glancing back at the two men.

"Dylan's loaded," Emmy said, her eyes dancing with amusement. "He can hire security to guard The Compound."

Dylan nodded. "Most of Nicky's surveillance equipment is still in place. Won't take much to get it up to snuff."

"What do you say, Lily?" Joe asked. "Will you go peacefully, or do I have to cuff you and drag you there?"

"You mean I have choices?" Lily felt like an idiot. All he had to do was give her that intensely sexy stare and she melted like goo.

The corners of his lips turned up, forming a smug smile.

She narrowed her eyes. "That's not fair. You're using my own nature against me."

"If it's the only way I can get you to be reasonable—"

"All right," she scowled. "I'll stay until the baby's born. I know I'll need protection until then. After…we'll see."

Joe nodded. "Good enough." He leaned forward and kissed her, sliding his tongue into her mouth.

Lily melted against him, her arms circling his neck.

"And we thought it got loud when the Albermarles moved in," Emmy murmured. "Sweetie, these two are gonna rattle the roof."

Chapter Ten

&

"So do you know what you're having?" Lily asked Darcy.

The women had gathered in the kitchen at The Compound for an early morning snack before they all headed to bed.

She was getting used to a vampires' hours. Looking down at the remnants of her rare steak, she realized more than just her sleep patterns were adjusting. The final transformation once the baby was born would be a cinch.

"I'm having a boy," Darcy said, around a mouthful of Cookies 'n Cream. The woman had already put away a pint and was starting on her second. How she maintained her slim figure was a marvel to Lily.

Lily had made a study of her two companions over the past couple of days. She now understood Joe's attraction to the reed-thin, muscular woman. Emmy on the other hand was lush and everything feminine, with her golden hair and plump curves. Between the two of them, Lily felt like a plain, brown wren.

"Joe will be thrilled," Emmy said. She'd claimed she wasn't hungry at all, but had picked at both their dishes. She glanced up at Lily's face. "Oops. Sorry."

Lily gave her a small, tight smile. "It's okay. I'll have to get used to all this togetherness. At least until my baby comes."

"Why are you so set on leaving?" Darcy asked, concern shadowing her eyes.

Lily shrugged. "I couldn't bear for Joe to stay with me because of the baby, when he's in love with you."

Darcy shook her head. "He's not in love with me. We're just friends. He wanted me because Quentin wanted me. If anything, Joe has a thing for Quentin."

"Not a man on man thing, mind you," Emmy piped in. "Like I said, everything's a competition. Who's the meanest, toughest—"

"The best lover." Darcy shivered. "That was pretty irresistible, when they were trying to one up each other."

"I bet it was," Emmy said dryly. She waggled her eyebrows with wicked amusement. "So how was it? With both of them?"

"You had Joe and Quentin in bed with you—at the same time?" Lily asked, feeling a little queasy.

Darcy winced. "It's not like it sounds. I mean, it was the ultimate thrill, but Joe needed me. It was just after Quentin turned him. He needed blood—and sex."

"And you just had to be the one to give it to him?" Emmy asked. "Sure."

"Yeah," Darcy said, a lovely pink tingeing her cheeks. "Something like that."

"So who's the biggest?" Emmy asked slyly.

"Is size really a characteristic of vampire males?" Lily asked. "I mean, I'd guessed that, but sometimes I think Joe's just teasing me."

Emmy's eyes gleamed with amusement. "Yup. At least, I've seen Dylan and Quentin's man-things. They're both pretty impressive."

Emmy and Lily turned to Darcy, who blushed brighter.

"I didn't exactly see his…thing, after he was turned. He was behind me."

"I knew it!" Emmy crowed. "You had a man-wich!"

"Emmy, Christ!" Darcy's lips twisted into a wicked grin. "Actually, yeah. So you see, I can't attest to the fact that one or the other is larger, but Joe was certainly…"

"Substantial?" Lily couldn't resist asking.

Darcy nodded and the three shared embarrassed glances before bursting into laughter.

"Let's go back to what you said before," Darcy said. "Lily, you just have to stay. It would tear Joe apart not to see his child grow up."

"And there's so much work for us to do here," Emmy said, spearing the last chunk of Lily's steak. "What with The Council starting up and the work with the Special Unit."

"Joe tells me you're a professor, an expert in vampire traditions." Darcy's expression reflected true interest.

Lily snorted. "I don't think my research has taught me all that much. Look how I was blindsided with this werewolf thing."

"But you could continue your research here," Darcy insisted. "You'll have plenty of subjects to study."

"Joe's not very supportive of some aspects of my research," Lily grumbled. "He'd have a cow if I pulled out a ruler." Lily brightened. "But I haven't seen everything yet, have I? I mean, I've never seen a vampire fly."

"Fly?" Emmy asked around a mouthful of steak.

At the two women's amused expressions, Lily's shoulders slumped. "Tell me he wasn't teasing me about that."

"Don't you see?" Emmy said. "You just can't trust what they tell you. These guys are jokers. You have to stick around to see for yourself what they can do."

"They really can't fly?"

"Nope. But they are wickedly agile and fast. Maybe you could set up some kind of physical trials to make some comparisons—human to vampire."

"They're fast tongued, you mean. It looks like I'll need to pull together a whole new survey."

Darcy's expression grew solemn. "Why don't you think Joe loves you?"

Lily sighed. "Because he's never said it. And because all he ever said was that he wasn't staying."

"I think you're wrong," Emmy said. "You should have seen his face when you fainted."

"Maybe," Darcy said, tapping the side of her cheek with a finger, "you have to make him say it."

"How would I make him say anything?"

"Darc is right. They may be big, bad vampires, but they're vulnerable too. Our guys are especially so. They're macho men. They think they have to keep those emotions deep inside — hidden. They don't like being weak."

Darcy nodded sagely. "Yeah, they think love makes them weak. Until you do something to really shake them up."

"Like what?"

"Well, there's this little thing I tried on Quentin. He'll do anything I say if I use it on him."

"Anything?" Emmy leaned closer.

"What do you do?" Lily asked.

"They are macho men, and very nervous about anything that they can't control."

"Are we talking about a sexual act?" Lily's body alerted. Good Lord, just the thought of sex had her wet!

"Come on, Darc! Out with it." Emmy squirmed with excitement.

"Well," Darcy glanced nervously over her shoulder then leaned across the table. "I put my finger inside him. He says he hates it, but when I do it he shivers all over."

Emmy screeched with laughter. "You finger-fuck him — in the ass? Oooh, Dylan would never let me — "

"Exactly."

Emmy and Darcy turned to Lily. She realized her mouth was still hanging open and shut it. "No way he'll let me do that." She bit her lower lip. "So how did you work your way around to doing that?"

* * * * *

Dylan and Joe turned from the monitor to stare at Quentin whose face had blushed a fiery red.

"Ballocks!"

Joe enjoyed the other vamp's discomfort immensely.

"So that's what all the bellowing is about." Dylan grinned with delight. "Quentin, I've known you for a hundred years, I don't think I've ever seen you turn quite that shade of red."

Quentin's eyes narrowed dangerously. "You are never to mention it again."

"What do you think, Joe? Will Lily get up the nerve to give you a poke? Will you let her?"

"Fuck no!" He shuddered at the thought.

"Dylan, are you going to tell the women about the surveillance cameras in the kitchen?" Quentin asked, a very unsubtle change of topic.

"Nope. How will we ever know what they're plotting?"

"Have to keep a few steps ahead of those three," Joe agreed.

"Looks like you still have some work ahead of you to convince your little lovebird to hang around," Quentin said.

"Yeah, it does." Joe took a deep breath. "And now's as good a time as any."

"Let's get the women to bed before they hatch any more plots," Dylan murmured.

* * * * *

The door to the kitchen slammed open and Joe stalked inside. By the look on his face, he had a bone to chew. Lily stood and circled to the far side of the table.

"Hi Joe," Emmy chimed. "He looks mad—or horny as hell, doesn't he, Darcy?"

"I'd say he looks mostly pissed," she said grinning. Her smile slipped when the other two vamps entered the room. "He's not the only one."

"Why don't you join us?" Emmy asked innocently. "We were just talking about...things."

Lily didn't like the way Joe's eyes narrowed, nor did she like the grim smile curving his lips. She feinted right, intending to make a getaway through the kitchen door, but Joe was on her in a second. With an effortless heave, he lifted her over his shoulder.

"Joe, put me down!"

He headed for the door.

"Remember the finger thing!" Emmy called after her.

Joe swatted her bottom. "Forget the finger thing."

"Emmy I think they knoooow!"

* * * * *

Once again, Lily felt the raspy stroke of her vampire's tongue against her most intimate flesh.

She held her breath, trying to decide whether she should let him know she was awake. But his tongue took the choice from her, stabbing deep within her pussy to circle her inner walls, a delicious scraping against tissue already super-heated and swollen from hours of lovemaking.

She moaned and pressed her mound closer to his wicked mouth. She opened her eyes and stared down her body, shocked to discover her thighs draped over his shoulders, his arms wrapped around them. His hands burrowed between her legs to hold her lips apart. He lowered his head and his mouth ate at her delicate folds.

He'd tilted the lampshade to direct light in a long halo across their bed. Lamplight bathed their bodies. The sight of his dark hair and latte-colored face between her white thighs triggered a primal response. His male animal appealed to the wanton core at her soul.

The intimacy of his act, with her legs spread wide and his mouth sucking where few men had ever wandered, shook her. A wave of tender longing caused her a moment's panic. *Keep it light!*

"Do you always raid the leftovers in the middle of the night?" she asked.

Joe caressed her outer lips and looked up into her eyes. The hard edge to his features frightened her, reminding her she was tweaking a tiger's tail.

"Not much for sweet-talk, are you?"

"Do you really want to talk?" he asked, and drove two fingers inside her vagina.

Lily bit her lip to keep from crying out. His fingers had unerringly found her G-spot. She couldn't move more than an inch or two up or down, yet the urge to pump her hips was so strong her belly trembled and her thighs quivered within his arms. "Later," she moaned. "We'll talk later."

She sank her fingers into the short, dark curls on his head, tugging him down to encourage him to stroke her with his tongue—which he did.

"Joe..." Her head thrashed on her pillow as a wave of heat swept over her breasts, tightening her nipples into exquisitely tuned points. She lifted a hand to caress one turgid tip and squeezed her breast, shooting more heat to her melting core. "Come inside me!"

Joe didn't let up, didn't give any indication he even heard her plea. He sucked the hood of flesh that covered her swelling clitoris and let it pop noisily out of his mouth, then he sucked it again, and again at the same time shoving his fingers deep.

Lily's belly spasmed and her shoulders lifted off the mattress. Her fingers tugged her nipples, pinching, twirling them between her thumb and forefinger. Her other hand scraped his scalp, digging in to push him closer.

But he resisted and smoothed his whisker-rough cheek against her open cunt. The friction, so acute it was painful, caused a shudder to wrack her body and her vagina convulsed, opening and closing, clutching his fingers, squeezing her passion-milk from her inner walls.

His tongue lapped at her cream, a low moan rising from his chest to vibrate against her. Still, he didn't stop.

Lily mewled, her throat tightening around an incoherent litany of moans and pleas. "Please, please, pleeease!"

He pressed back the hood guarding her clitoris and closed his lips around the glossy, engorged button, his tongue rubbing in delicious circles, wringing a second wave of dark ecstasy from her loins.

As the last deep shudders shook her body, her hands fell to the bed and she stared at the ceiling.

Now his strokes soothed, and her mind wandered to the coming months when she would leave him.

She'd found her proof of vampires' existence in his living, breathing form. A lifelong quest satisfied. Her victory however, was hollow. Despite the fact she'd known him less than a week, she knew her heart would be irrevocably torn when she left.

She loved him without knowing a damn thing about how he really felt. She did know the dimensions, textures, and colors of his body. And she knew that something in his relentless pursuit of her surrender, the harshly, etched pain that clung to his broad shoulders and handsome face, and his barely leashed power called to something equally primitive and pain-filled in her soul.

Joe's face lifted from between her legs and he shifted first one thigh, then the other, from his shoulders. A predatory gleam glinted in his eyes and Lily's breath hitched. He wasn't finished with her yet.

He rose on his hands and knees and "walked" up her body until his knees prodded the back of her bent thighs and his face was directly above hers.

Her gaze swept down his taut belly to his heavily engorged sex and she reached for him, curving her palm around him, drawing a hiss of breath from between his teeth.

Reaching lower, she cupped his balls, rolling them in her palm, and watched with growing satisfaction the expressions that crossed his face — dark need, taut restraint.

"Now, can we get back to what we were discussing previously?"

Joe lifted an eyebrow. "Oh, were we talking?"

"I was thinking about my last choice."

He quirked an eyebrow. "You want me to use my cuffs? The Captain gave them back to me when I resumed my job."

"No, I still want to finish exploring the last of my *previous* choices." Lily smiled at his hungry, alert expression. "Are you ready to be at my mercy?"

Joe's heavy-lidded glance burned her. "I can't wait to see those pink lips stretched around my cock."

Lily's pussy tightened and her cheeks and breasts flushed with heat. "Do I get to finish you this time?"

"Baby, I'm not making promises I can't keep."

She tilted her chin. "Then I'm not going down on you."

"Do you play poker?"

She looked him straight in the eye and lied. "Never."

"Damn!" He climbed off her, a frown creasing his forehead. Slowly, he stretched out on the mattress, his body rigid, his hands clenched at his sides.

Lily grinned. He looked as though he awaited his execution. "Put your hands behind your head."

He glared at her, but he clasped his hands, and slipped them beneath his head.

"Now, you can't interfere, understand? If you do, I'll stop. And I won't let you have me."

"Do you really think you can tell me no?"

She shook her head and gave him her meanest look. "I know you can make me want you, but I think you'd rather I didn't hold a grudge."

He took a deep breath that stretched his skin over his rib cage. "I won't interfere. And I won't take over…" He shot her a furious glance. "…unless you beg me."

Lily bit her lip. The way he said that had her worried. What did he know that she didn't? Of course, she'd never had a man's body totally at her mercy. "Well, fine. That will never happen."

He raised a single eyebrow and his expression turned smug.

Her blood boiled and her gaze narrowed. He'd thrown down the gauntlet. Opening her legs wide, Lily straddled his waist, knowing her moist center slid across his skin. His eyes glittered dangerously, but Lily felt powerful. In control. It was about time she greeted the monster on her terms.

She raised her hands to her breasts and cupped them. "I need a little encouragement. Give it to me." She leaned down and pressed one nipple to his lower lip, tracing the curve with her tip.

His lips remained a firm line.

She leaned back and narrowed her eyes. "So that's how it's gonna be, huh? We'll see about that."

She scooted a little lower on his belly and felt his sex nudge her buttocks. "Oooh! Look who wants to play."

Rubbing her breasts in the whorls of hair on his chest, she continued to work her way down his torso, licking his nipples, then biting them, all the while rubbing her body on his hard cock.

She lifted her hips and let his engorged shaft fall between them. A slide of her moist cleft down his length drew a hiss from between his tightly clenched lips.

Lower she went, until her knees settled between his legs. She raised herself on her arms and looked up into his face.

"What was it you said you wanted? To see my pink lips around your cock?"

She circled her mouth with her tongue, and then grinned when he groaned and closed his eyes. "Poor baby. Don't be such a coward."

Joe's eyes slammed open, but then they narrowed with sexy menace.

Lily's heart tripped as she stuck out her tongue and lapped a drop of dew from the head of his cock. She spread it around her lips, painting it on like lipstick. "Mmmm."

"Lily?" His tone held a warning.

She opened her jaws wide and sank over his cock, loving the way his thick shaft filled her mouth, loving the taste of his satiny skin as it glided over her tongue. The plump head butted the back of her throat and she relaxed to take him deeper.

"Baby!" His fingers that were supposed to be clasped behind his head combed through her hair, caressing her scalp as she raised and lowered her head, suctioning hard on every rise, relaxing on every downward glide.

Slowly at first, she worked over his throbbing flesh, noting how his thighs quivered and his breath became labored with his growing arousal.

She scraped his shaft with her teeth and Joe groaned, his hands fisting in her hair now. Her hands wrapped around the base of his cock and worked the moisture from her mouth up and down his shaft. She squeezed her fists, twisting in opposing directions.

Then the telltale pulse of his hips, shallow, circling, encouraged her to move faster, until she bobbed noisily on his cock, faster.

His body strained, his thighs, balls and belly turning hard as stone, shuddering with delight.

Lily held on, working his flesh, all the while her own pussy grew drenched until her arousal dripped down her thighs and her vagina spasmed audibly, releasing moist sighs.

Suddenly, she halted and withdrew her mouth, shaking with her own need. When she raised her gaze to his, she found him waiting.

"Please," she begged. "I need your cock. Inside me."

In a blur of motion, she found herself on her knees, her buttocks high in the air, his large, hard hands holding her still as he rammed his cock inside.

"Yes! Yes! Oh please, more!" she begged in endless supplication as Joe slammed his hips against her buttocks, driving his cock deep, again and again, his thrusts driving the air from her lungs. She grunted loudly, clutching the bedding in her fists, her eyes closed tight to shut out sight while she concentrated on the feel of his body, filling hers, pounding at her cunt.

Then it was happening, that miracle of escalating power that transformed his body and elevated his loving to the next plane. His cock expanded, his thrusts, supercharged with his vampire strength, rocked her body.

Her thighs clenched as her orgasm built, layer by layer, until she lost herself, lost her mind in an explosion of fiery colors.

Lily collapsed to the bed, panting, crying. How could she give this up?

Joe's arms closed around her and he pressed kisses on her shoulders and neck. He kept the connection, his waning erection still planted deep inside her body.

"Why are you crying?" His gravelly, deep voice surrounded her.

Lily shook her head. She wasn't going to say it. He didn't want the words.

He sighed and withdrew from her body and turned her in his arms.

Lily kept her gaze averted. She didn't want him to see her tears, or see the love in her eyes.

A finger lifted her chin. Joe's expression was…satisfied. "Why are you crying?" he repeated.

Her face crumpled. "You don't love me."

"Why do you think that?"

"Because this is just lust." She sniffed. "Artificial lust. You're just reacting to my heat."

"You humans have no nose."

"What?"

"Your heat is past, love."

"You're wrong. We did it four times tonight. That's not normal."

"It must be for us." He pressed his loins against hers. His erection was already recovering.

"I don't think I can keep doing this," she whispered.

"Course you can. Want me to prove it?"

She shoved at his chest, but he didn't budge. "You're such a man! You don't get it."

"What don't I get? That you're in love with me?" His eyes studied her face.

"It's not fair for me to feel so much."

"You think I don't?"

She shook her head slowly. "No. You can't. You're just trying to do the noble thing. You want to take care of me because I may be carrying your child."

"You are carrying my child. And you're right. I want to take care of you."

Lily's heart squeezed. "But it's not enough. For me. I know I need help because I don't know a lot of things about what I am and what my child or children will become. But *I* need more."

Joe rubbed his thumb on her lower lip. "Do you know I died in this house?"

Lily blinked, shocked. "How could you bear to come back?"

"Because you need to be here. And somehow, the end of my human life isn't as important now. I've found my humanity." His hand slid down her belly. "My children are my humanity. Maybe yours will be something a little more than human, but I'm still man enough to feel pride and love for what we made."

Lily took a chance. With her heart in her eyes, she said, "I love you Joe. I love you human, I love you monster. You thrill me."

Joe closed his eyes. When he opened them, he brought her hand to his lips and kissed her. "There's only one way I can say this." He pressed her to her back and entered her with a single, strong thrust. "I love you, Lily. You make me strong. You make me crazy—and I don't think eternity will be long enough for all the loving I want to give you."

Tears streamed from her eyes as he gently rode her. Their mouths mated as their bodies blended, pouring together.

When at last they lay spent in each other's arms, Lily turned to Joe and smiled slyly. "You said the words and I didn't even have to use the finger thing."

His eyes narrowed. "Don't you even consider it."

She wrinkled her nose. "Why do you guys get so uptight about an itsy-bitsy little finger? You've shoved a much larger—"

"Lily!"

"I'm just saying—"

"Don't you ever."

She sighed and snuggled into his arms. "Will our loving always be this…" She shrugged. Words couldn't express how happy she was.

"Hot?" He kissed her forehead. "Sexy?" He nuzzled her face until she lifted it to receive his next kiss on her lips.

"Wonderful." She closed her eyes, reveling in the slide of his mouth along her chin.

"I don't see why not, and it's not like we won't have years to practice." He drew her earlobe into his mouth and bit.

She shivered. "Decades."

He lifted his head and stared into her eyes. "Centuries?"

"Boggles the mind, huh? Just think of all the time I'll have to complete a thorough study of vampire behaviors."

Joe winced. "About some of your conclusions…"

"Don't!" She placed a finger over his lips. "I want to discover everything for myself."

"But…"

"I know you want to help, but I'll need to conduct my own interviews—get a sampling of the population."

"So long as your *sampling* doesn't require a ruler."

She grinned and tweaked his nipple. "Maybe Emmy could help me with my research."

Joe shuddered and rolled his hips, nudging her sex with his. "God helps us. I'll have to have a little talk with Dylan."

"Don't worry. That's still a long way off." She grimaced. "I have to deliver this litter first."

"They'll likely keep you too busy for mischief for many years to come."

"Don't look so hopeful." She raised her legs, encircling his waist and pulling his hips into hers. "It's all your fault anyway."

"Mmmm. What's my fault?" By his smoky, half-lidded stare she could tell the topic was losing his interest.

"If you'd cooperated in the first place, I wouldn't have to look to other vamps for outside verification."

"I'll cooperate!" He screwed his cock in ever smaller concentric circles deeper inside her.

"Nope. Too late. My objectivity is compromised."

"Baby, more than your objectivity's been compromised."

"Too true. But I just can't trust you'll give me the straight skinny."

His sexy movements halted. "Are you saying I'm a liar?"

She raised an eyebrow. "I don't ever think I'll forgive you for letting me think you could fly!"

"Who says I don't?" He pulled out and slammed back inside her. "Don't we?" he growled.

Lily's mouth opened on a gasp. "Emmy told me the truth."

"Maybe Dylan's doing it wrong." His buttocks flexing beneath her heels, Joe's powerful thrusts drove Lily higher with each stroke. "Fly with me, baby."

Lily soared.

RELENTLESS

∽

Chapter One

ନ୍ତ

With only slivers of moonlight to guide his way, Max Weir crept through the saw palmetto and pine thicket toward a house curtained by vegetative neglect. He'd forgone the use of the night-vision goggles that most of the human members of his team wore. On the prowl for a monster, he preferred his own senses, his own two eyes.

The Special Unit's stealthy assault was aided by a wind that howled through the trees, bending the tops so pine needles pelted the team. A constant low roar, like the sound of the ocean, filled his headset. God or Karma was with the SU tonight. The wind blew away from the house and its occupants, disseminating the scents of gun oil and the uninvited humans — they'd never know what hit them.

A cancer grew inside the small, cinderblock house at the center of the property. Max had been in this line of work long enough to know what took place in the nondescript house, but he'd never understand the attraction that brought humans willingly to the door of a vampire's den.

Anger knotted the muscles of his chest. Not until the disappearance of a college student was linked to one of the parties hosted here did the SU kick into gear. This killing field should have been ringed with fire and its occupants consigned to hell when the den was first discovered and documented.

But that wasn't how they operated now. It wasn't simply enough to find a vamp and stake his heart to dirt. Now the vermin had to be proven guilty of crimes by the Masters' Council before the team got the green light to strike.

"So Dylan, how'd you talk Emmy into sittin' this one out?"

Max ignored the chatter in his headset. Not long ago, he would have joined the banter, which eased the guys' tension as they waited for the order to move on their target.

"We could sure use her tonight. Emmy's got a ruthless side to her," Phil Carstairs, one of the good guys—a human—continued.

"Toward a doughnut, maybe." Darcy Albermarle snickered from her position in the command van. Darcy, once upon a time a friend, consorted with the enemy now—fucked one of the bastards on a nightly basis.

"Em would take offense to that comment," Dylan O'Hara replied. "Her tastes have become a little more refined over the past months."

Max's shoulders bunched with revulsion at the sound of the Irish vampire's dry amusement. The vamp and his growing coven didn't belong in the SU—they belonged at the end of a stake. *His*, preferably.

"Yeah, she's moved on from doughnuts to the Danish!" Phil said. "Although, I gotta admit, your wife has no conscience. She'd try to talk the bastards to death."

Soft laughter followed. Emmy O'Hara's penchant for running off at the mouth when she grew excited was a well-known fact.

Max's lips twisted in disgust. They acted like the female vamp was part of "the family" now. Was he the only one of the original unit who understood how wrong it was to befriend the demons? And worse, let vamps lead a hunt for other vamps? As far as he was concerned, the only good vampire was a dead one.

"Get set," Darcy said, her voice suddenly sharp. "Traffic barriers are in place. Mobile phone jam is on. No one's driving in or calling for backup."

Max's hand tightened on his crossbow, which was already cocked with a steel-tipped arrow. The first of many, he hoped. He itched for a battle, something he could pour his adrenaline into.

"Captain says, move in," Darcy said. "Good hunting, guys."

"You heard it, men. Team One, circle around the back," Dylan said.

From the edge of the seedy lawn, the first team raced across the clearing to nestle close to the house before circling to the back entrance.

After a few tense moments, Max heard a crackle in his headset, then, "Team One's in position," Phil said.

"Team Two," Dylan said, "wait for my command."

As if the house sucked in all sound within its vicinity, an ominous silence settled around the clearing. There was no music, no shouts of laughter from within, even though a couple dozen people and vamps had to be inside going by the number of cars lining the driveway and street. This was supposed to be a party — an orgy of sex and blood sharing.

From the corner of his eye, Max watched Dylan streak across the lawn and flatten his back against the wall beside the door. Unencumbered by a flak jacket or heavy armaments, the vamp held only a stake in his hand.

Max tensed, waiting for the signal to rush the door.

Dylan straightened, his head lifting to scent. "Something's wrong." His whisper broke the silence. "Do you get that smell, Quent?"

"Coming." The second vamp, Quentin Albermarle rushed across the lawn in a blur of black, his blond hair shining silver in the moonlight. Flanking the door, he too paused and lifted his head. "That's not something you find every day," he said, his British voice even, yet hard-edged.

"Team, have your pistols ready," Dylan said. "Safeties off. We've a different sort of monster inside." Without further explanation, he whipped around, lifted a booted foot, and kicked the door open.

Max cursed. "Team One, the front door's been breached. Go, go, go!" With his crossbow raised, Max charged toward the house, his heart pumping so fast blood roared in his ears.

"Maybe, we should wait for Dylan's signal," Joe Garcia said, easily keeping stride with them.

Max wished he could ignore the vamp beside him. A twinge akin to pain reminded him Joe had been his friend. "Why? So he can help them escape out the back?" he asked, without trying to mask the acid in his tone.

Joe didn't respond. Since his "death", he'd remained aloof. Probably knew Max could hardly stand the sight of him. Still, old habits seemed to die hard—even when one was undead. Joe looked and acted as he always had. He still wore the SU's black uniform and used his issued weapons. The only difference was he'd left off the flak jacket.

Were all vamps arrogant assholes? A jacket could have protected him from an arrow or a stake. His cockiness would get him killed.

Not that Max gave a damn.

He reached the door, propped the stock of his weapon on his shoulder, and then stepped through the door. Sighting down the beam of his crossbow, he found the living room empty, save for clothing lying in piles among small hills of brownish-black soot. Vamp remains.

"Shit!" Joe said. "Did they leave us anything to do?"

Max caught himself before he smiled. Joe had always been eager for action.

"There's no way those hotshots took care of this alone. What do you think happened here?"

Max barely heard him. Odors assailed his nose. Singed flesh—the vamps, he guessed. And something else, wet and musty. He tensed. *It can't be.*

A prickling unease raised the hairs on the back of his neck. He followed another smell—which grew more overpowering the closer he came to the source—followed the sound of muffled voices, Dylan's and Quentin's, he recognized as he drew closer. He stole down a hallway toward a brightly lit space that opened wide into a game room.

Once again shouldering his weapon, he stepped through the entrance. He found what his nose already told him was there. Human carnage in vivid splatters that dotted the ceilings and drowned the shag carpet. Opened carcasses with bowels unstrung like wads of yarn across the floor.

"Holy Mary, mother of God," Joe whispered beside him. "No fucking way a vamp did this."

Max's body tightened in rejection of the horror he witnessed. For all his years on the force, he'd never seen carnage on this scale. Shit like this had never happened before the SU went soft on vamps. A monstrous evil had found Vero Beach's leniency too inviting and was making itself at home. Once you negotiated with one evil…

Like hell he'd let it continue! His finger closed around the trigger of his bow. Dylan's back was exposed as he knelt over one body. Damn, but he was tempted!

"Don't do it, Max," Joe said, his voice low, but firm. "My wife would never forgive me if I let you dust one of her new friends."

Max trembled with outrage, but he slowly lifted his finger off the trigger and lowered his bow. Now wasn't the time.

At Quentin's nod, Dylan looked over his shoulder. His glance fell to Max's crossbow and he lifted one eyebrow in challenge.

"Good choice," Joe said and slapped his shoulder as he passed him to squat next to his new buddies.

Max stared at the three of them, thick as thieves. Max could remember a time when Joe swore he'd rather die than turn— even asked Max to set him in the sunshine to fry if it ever happened.

"So what the hell did this?" Joe asked.

Dylan cast Quentin a wary glance, before replying softly, "Werewolves."

"Did I hear you right?"

Max jerked at the sound of Phil's voice as he stepped through the door. He'd been so engrossed in the scene before him he hadn't heard Phil's approach.

Phil's eyes widened. "Shit!" His face tightened as he took note of the bodies strewn around the floor. "The rest of the house is secure. Only dust bunnies left."

"When did werewolves move into the neighborhood?" Joe asked, his hands fisted at his sides.

Phil, his gaze still glued to the floor, asked, "Am I the only one who didn't know werewolves existed?"

Max shook himself. He had a job to do. "I'll start the teams on a sweep of the area. See what we find." As he turned to leave, he cast a scathing look at Dylan and Quentin.

Joe, he ignored.

Dylan sighed and stood up as Max left the room.

"He's not going to change—voluntarily, that is," Quentin murmured.

"I know," Dylan said. "I've already made the call to Navarro."

Quentin nodded. "We can't let anyone stand in the way of our setting up a southern council." He waved his hand at the room. "This only makes it all the more vital we handle him quickly."

Dylan glanced at Joe to see his reaction.

The younger vamp was still torn by old loyalties—trying to ride the fence between his new "life" and his old friends. Joe took a deep breath, his face a grim mask. "Well, shit. How are we going to keep a lid on this mess?"

* * * * *

Max pushed through the door of the bar determined that tonight he'd either get shit-faced or fucked. Which, didn't matter. So long as he could blow off the steam that had been gathering a head since the botched mission hours before. The bar was a regular haunt—only a block from his house. If need be, he could crawl home. The smoky air, the loud grinding music, and the smell of stale beer appealed when he had an axe to grind.

The SU had swept the area for signs of the wolves that killed the vampires before turning on the humans in a mutilating frenzy. Their bloody paw prints led beyond the house to a gravel road where they'd disappeared. The pack had made their getaway in cars. This hadn't been a roaming band's target of opportunity, but a takedown.

The grim faces of the vampires telegraphed their worry. He hoped they were shaking in their boots. Not that the thought of a rogue wolf pack wasn't just as unsettling to Max.

But seeing the cocksure Quentin lose his perpetual smirk was gratifying. Dylan had been grim-faced and pale. Perhaps the bastard saw his own fate in the house.

However, Joe's silence had been the most telling. He hadn't looked the least bit surprised.

Max made his way through the tables ringing a small dance floor. The place was nearly empty, save for the men hovering near the bar for the night's last drinks. The tension in his shoulders knotted tighter. All it would take would be one smart-ass comment. He hungered for an excuse to drive his fist through something.

The crowd parted, and a flash of a slim white ankle snagged his attention. Every trace of anger, bitter regret, and frustration coalesced into a single, burning need.

The men blocking his view shifted, and the ankle drew his glance upward to a bare knee. The woman's legs parted, and one slid atop the other. Her foot sawed up and down, and a slender, functionless sandal dangled from the tips of her painted toes. God, he wanted to help her lose the shoes altogether.

He advanced toward the men standing between him and his goal. Their faces registered annoyance for only a moment before they stepped aside. The hard hunger that rode his belly must have turned his face into an implacable mask.

As he drew near, her shape was revealed one tantalizing curve at a time. Sweetly turned hips were clothed in a stretchy black skirt that ended at the top of her thighs—not a hint of underwear marred the smooth fit. Conveniently tied behind her neck, a miniscule top bared the gleaming, supple skin of her back and midriff—again, no sign of a bra. Her nipples puckered invitingly against the black fabric that barely contained the apple-like curves of her small breasts.

Finally, his gaze rose to her face. She could have been a whole lot less than appetizing, and he'd still have wanted her on the merits of that ride-able frame. But her face only made him more determined to have her.

Large, doe-like eyes, framed by thick lashes, blinked as she caught his stare. Her upper lip was a fraction fuller than the lower and inspired delicious, succulent fantasies. Her face was round, her jaw small, and a thumbprint dimple carved her chin into two delicious halves. His tongue itched to slide along that little notch.

As he reached the bar, he drew a deep breath, eager to catch the scent of her perfume. He wasn't disappointed. The woman smelled like sex. Hot, nasty, spicy sex.

His body hardened along with his intentions. With only a fleeting thought for how aggressive he might appear, he loomed over her, his gaze sweeping downward. When he glanced back up to her eyes, he schooled his expression into something shy of predatory. He didn't want to frighten her away before he'd even learned her name.

Instead of looking intimidated or frightened by his intensity, as so many women would have, she raised a single dark eyebrow. She didn't say a word, just returned his stare. Somehow, her bold action felt out of sync with the wariness lurking in her eyes.

Then he noticed the movement of her throat as she swallowed. Did he make her nervous?

Her expression betrayed no such fear. Part amusement and part calculation, it changed as her gaze dropped from his face to sweep down his chest and lower. Interest with only a hint of alarm flared her nostrils and tightened her jaw, causing her to open her mouth to take a deeper breath.

She had good reason to be wary. If she told him to back off, he'd be hard pressed to obey. Every male chromosome in his body screamed at his groin to take her.

His gaze never leaving hers, he took a deep, calming breath and forced himself to follow the ritual. "Can I buy you a drink?"

"I'm not thirsty." Her voice pleased him. Feminine, but not too dainty, with a hint of aged whiskey.

Undeterred, he nodded to the bartender hovering behind her. "Two draft beers."

Her brown eyes narrowed, but she remained silent.

He raised an eyebrow. "Maybe I'm just thirsty."

"Or impossibly arrogant," she muttered, just loud enough for him to hear.

He bit back a grin. "I haven't seen you here before," he said, and then cursed himself for using such a tired line.

"I'm new to the area," she said, sounding bored. Her foot sawed faster.

Great! They sounded like trained parrots. How could he think of conversation when all he wanted was to slide his hands around her naked back? "What's your name?"

"Pia."

Pia. Cute name, a little sassy like she was. Or rather, like he thought she might be if he could just figure out how to get her talking.

At least she hadn't tried to bolt. He leaned past her to reach for one of the beers the bartender laid behind her on the bar. He held it out.

Her hands remained in her lap, her expression defiant.

Well, hell! His luck wasn't running any better. He lifted the glass and gulped the foam.

She watched him, her eyes following the movement of his throat. Her tongue licked her full lower lip.

Before he gave it a thought, he handed her the same beer again.

Rather than pouring it on his shoes, her hands slid around the glass. Her gaze remained on the beer.

Satisfaction throbbed in his belly. She'd probably like an introduction before he asked her to go home with him. "Name's Max."

Her lips pressed together and then curved into a smile that stretched the full lower lip. The lady had a rather large mouth. It was perfect. "As in Maximus?"

The smile warmed him while giving him confidence he hadn't totally blown it. He shifted his feet and stepped closer, bringing her crossed legs between his. "Do you doubt it?" he asked, his voice low.

Her head tilted back, and a frown drew together her finely arched brows. "Do you think I'm impressed with your caveman tactics?"

His glance slid down to her breasts. Her headlights were erect little points that stabbed toward him. "Damn right," he said, hoping he hadn't read her body language wrong.

With a toss of her hair, she uncrossed her legs, her knee caressing the inside of his thigh. "Sorry about that," she murmured, although she didn't look sorry at all. She'd just checked him out.

His heart kicked into a slow, thrumming throb. The lady knew where this was leading. She'd accepted his beer.

The part of him that had tensed in pursuit relaxed. She could be his if he didn't overplay his cards. And he had a decision to make. Savor a slower rise to climax or take her hard and fast? "Dance with me."

She shook her head, which swept the ends of her curly brown hair across the tops of her bare shoulders. "I don't dance."

He reached for the beer she held in her lap and set it on the bar. His fingers closed around her slender wrist, and he tugged her up from the stool.

"What do you think you're doing?" She tottered on her heels for a moment, and her nipples brushed his chest. Her gaze, wide-eyed, set his heart thumping in a slower, heavier beat. He swept his arm around her waist and pulled her along to the dance floor. He needed her in his arms *now*.

They were the only couple on the small square of parquet-printed linoleum. Max didn't give her a chance to protest, he simply pressed his body to hers—chest to hip, and slid his leg between her thighs. The heavy, grinding rhythm of the rock music suited his mood just fine. He shifted on his feet from side to side, not so much a dance as foreplay. His body introducing itself to hers.

She stiffened inside the circle of his arms. "Do you ever pay attention to what a woman tells you?" she asked, her words clipped.

Encouraged she hadn't hauled off and slapped him yet, he leaned down to whisper in her ear, "Sweetheart, I was listening, but not to what your lips were saying."

Her head jerked back, and her gaze bored into his. "Perhaps you should."

The look halted him in his tracks. He'd pushed her too hard. "All right." Sighing his regret, he stepped away. "I'm sorry. I misread the situation."

But she didn't walk away as he expected. Instead, her head tilted to the side, and she studied his face for a long moment, her teeth worrying her lower lip.

He wiped his expression free of hunger, hoping for another chance.

Finally, she looked around the bar and shrugged. "Well, seeing as I'm here…"

He didn't wait for her to change her mind. He pulled her into his arms.

She nestled her face in the crook of his neck and groaned. "This is happening too fast."

Relaxing to savor the sensations, he chuckled and pulled her closer. "I know what you mean," he murmured. A dark, musky floral scent rose from her hair and skin, wrapped him in heat.

Her arms snuck up around his neck, and her small, firm breasts pressed against his chest.

Once again pretending to dance, he shifted her slightly to glide her nipples across his chest. They'd been erect before their bodies met—they were hardened little bullets now.

"Do you think you'll overcome every one of my objections as easily?" she asked, her breath gusting gently in his ear.

"I promise you won't have *one* when the time comes." He lifted his leg and rubbed his thigh against her crotch.

Her head fell back, and her chocolate eyes glinted with amusement. "Sure of yourself, aren't you?"

He was getting there. He leaned down to whisper in her ear. "I smell your arousal."

Her breath gasped, but she didn't pull away. A tremor shook her body. "Do you think you're just going to get a quick-"

Placing a finger over her lips to shut her up, he said, "Whoa, sweetheart." He nuzzled her cheek. "Nothing about this'll be quick. This is just the appetizer." He bent his neck and kissed her sleek shoulder.

Her head fell back exposing her creamy throat, inviting him to slide his lips along her throat—which he did.

"You sound like you're going to eat me," she said, half-laughing, half-moaning.

Max stiffened and spoke between tightened lips, "I will, if you ask me sweetly."

Again, she gasped, following with a burst of soft, strained laughter.

Not the outright "yes" he hoped for, but promising just the same. He wished he had a glib tongue so he could put her at ease, but his body was too insistent, too ready to pounce for him to think straight.

Every sense tuned to her. Her body draped languidly across his chest. Her legs slid along either side of his thigh, and he wondered if she wanted another rough caress. He decided to test her by rubbing his thigh against her femininity.

She moaned—a sexy sound that made his dick throb.

His hands glided over her back, then smoothed to her sides. With his thumbs, he caressed the edges of her breasts. She didn't stiffen in his arms. "Look at me," he said.

Her head tilted back. Her eyes were wide open.

He swept his thumbs beneath the fabric of her top and went straight for the ripe little berries at the center of her breasts.

Her gaze darted beyond his shoulder to the bar.

"They can't see a thing. It's too dark." He swooped down to capture her lips.

Sounding like a kitten, she whimpered, pressing hard against his thumbs. Her hands clutched his shoulders.

He raked her tongue with his, and then swept around her mouth to touch her teeth, the roof of her mouth, before he pulled away to drag air into his lungs. "Baby, I want a bed beneath your back for what I'm gonna do to you." No way could he be subtle or patient with this one. *She has to want this as much as I do…*

Again, her throat moved. "And if I can't wait?"

He stilled for a moment, and then muttered, "Christ!" His need crowded insistently against the placket of his jeans. With a quick glance around the bar for the nearest exit, he pulled her down a hallway and into the restroom.

Once inside, he locked the door. Then he turned and stalked her, backing her into the old-fashioned wooden stall. "You have to spell it out for me. Do you want me to stop?"

Her eyes rounded. "I don't know. I don't know *you*."

His jaw clamped tight. "I won't hurt you. Or at least I'll try not to."

Her tongue wet her lips. "Good enough," she whispered.

Max palmed her breast with one hand; his other hand glided up her bare thigh and pushed up her short skirt. He went straight to the scrap of nylon covering her sex. He tipped the lid of the toilet closed with the toe of his boot and sat.

The woman, Pia, wasted no time climbing onto his lap, her thighs straddling him. Her breasts were level with his mouth, and she pushed the hem of her cropped top up, exposing them.

Max took the hint and groaned, rooting with his lips until he held a burgeoning nipple between them.

She grasped the back of his head, pushing her breast deeper into his mouth. Her sex ground against the hard ridge of his cock, riding him, wriggling her hips so eagerly he thought he might spill his seed in his pants like a teenager.

He dragged his mouth from her breast. "Wait." He pushed her off his lap and stood, then placed his hands on the sides of her waist and lifted her high. "Hold onto the top of the stall, sweetheart."

Quickly catching his drift, she spread her arms wide across the top of the wooden stall and gripped the edge. He hefted her higher and stepped backward. She "lay", suspended from the top of the stall, her legs parted and draped over his shoulders. His face was poised at the opening of her legs.

He glanced up at her flushed face. "I did say I'd eat you, if you asked sweetly."

Chapter Two

๛

Pia D'Amato wondered how things had gotten this out of control so quickly.

She'd planned to play hard to get ever since she'd glimpsed him striding toward her. His large, heavily muscled body had radiated hunger, and he'd moved with a rangy, masculine grace that raised her nipples in an instant to full alert. When his gaze had found hers, she'd felt the searing heat of his brand.

Never one to question the vagaries of fate, she accepted that tonight was meant to be.

His golden eyes had honed sharp as an eagle's on a bunny rabbit. Assholes she could deal with, and she'd prepared her standard rebuff. However, the hint of wary desperation—and his expectation she'd resist—made her hesitate. She'd sensed he needed to win their battle of wills, but that he also needed her to give him hurdles to overcome. Why pleasing him became important mystified her.

Not that she intended to refuse him, *ultimately*.

Then she'd found herself uncharacteristically tongue-tied, overwhelmed by his relentless pursuit. At first, all she could do was blink dumbly and try her best not to drool. What woman could resist the mesmerizing intensity of his full-frontal assault?

His gaze had stripped her while she sat on her barstool. The look he'd given her once he'd finished said he'd staked his claim. If any other man had so blatantly given her the once-over, she'd have delivered a setdown he'd not soon forget.

But Max was a man like no other. He embodied a mix of strength, stubborn determination, and an underlying vulnerability she was sure he kept buried from the world. He attracted her—*madly*.

When his jeans-clad thigh had scraped the tender flesh between her legs, she'd laughed at herself, at her eagerness to rub on him like a cat in heat. And she'd thought to manipulate *him*!

All she wanted was him—inside her. *Now.*

His head turned and his hot mouth kissed each thigh, the scrape of his evening shadow glancing against the lips of her pussy. Covered by the sheerest silk thong she owned, she felt moisture dampen them in an instant. As uncomfortable as she found her perch, there was something pretty damn exciting about having all this mega-male's attention concentrated on the core of her femininity.

His gaze smoldered, and his nose twitched as he inhaled deeply. But he didn't give her the kiss she wanted. He really was going to wait for her to ask him sweetly before he plundered her body.

The man was blatantly male; he called to her body on its most primitive and elemental level. Built large and rugged, his shoulders were so broad they easily spanned her spread thighs. His biceps were so thickly muscled they strained the arms of his dark T-shirt.

His face was too hard and masculine to be handsome. A square jaw, heavy brow, and a broad nose that was slightly askew on his face, were a match for his rough and ready attitude. He was too much man to manipulate. Too much man to refuse.

His hot breath gusted against the wetness gathering at her entrance, and her belly tightened around a coil of desire so strong she trembled.

But her pride demanded she couldn't beg for release. Bad enough he'd managed to ride roughshod over her willpower. She still wasn't certain how he'd managed to get her into this predicament—holding on to the top of a bathroom stall with her legs draped over his shoulders—waiting for him to fulfill the promise in his golden gaze.

And why her? She took a deep breath and glanced down her body. Why had he chosen her? Had she somehow given herself away? Or was she just an easy conquest to him?

While the thought rankled, she had to admit, the evidence was pretty damn convincing. She was after all splayed wide for his taking, her small breasts squeezed beneath the hem of her halter. Her nipples constricted so tight and so long they begged for attention.

Like she would have to beg, if she was ever going to feel the warmth of his mouth on her dripping sex.

And how long had it taken him to convince her? Fifteen minutes? Maybe!

He tongued the crease between her thigh and her pussy, wetting her skin. The air conditioning blew cool air on her open thighs. The contrast of the cool air on her crotch, and his warm hands, each cupping a bare buttock, drove her over the edge. To hell with who had control. And to hell with the last remnants of her dignity. She needed his mouth on her most intimate flesh.

"Please," she said, surprised by the husky timbre of her voice.

He kissed her thigh. "I like the way you say that, but I want the words, baby," he said, and lapped at the fabric covering her sex again.

Her womb tightened. He wanted the coarse, nasty words — the ones that made her flinch. Saying them would strip away any pretense she might want to keep for her pride's sake that this was anything but what it was — a physical mating, a carnal fuck.

Pursing his lips, he blew a stream of warm air over her open, weeping flesh that she felt through the fabric.

Her breath caught on a sob she didn't know was coming. "Eat me, Max."

His lips lifted, baring his straight, white teeth. Not a smile — more an animalistic grimace of triumph. His hands slid from her ass and around the tops of her thighs. They met at her mons.

Oh God.

He bent his head and licked the seam of her pussy through her underwear. He rubbed his tongue over her, pressing into the silk, poking inside her opening to swirl his tongue in the shallow sheath he'd made.

She moaned and felt her womb clench. All too soon, it wasn't enough. Why hadn't she taken off the goddamn panties?

One clever hand tugged rhythmically at the strap that rode between her buttocks, drawing the elastic tightly against her anus. The other traced her slit through the crotch of her panties.

"More, please," she begged, looking away from the hard-faced man who was quickly ratcheting up the heat of his caresses.

"Tell me, you want me to fuck you with my fingers," he said, his voice rough as gravel.

Oh, yes. She pumped her hips, eager for him to hurry.

"No, baby." He nipped an outer lip through her panties. "Tell me."

She gritted her teeth. "Please, fuck me with your fingers," she said, her voice rising. "Please fuck me, Max."

With his nose, he nuzzled aside the crotch of her panties, and his tongue touched her directly for the first time, delving between her labia to flutter the tip against the notch at the top of her slit.

Pia nearly screamed, biting her lips to hold it inside.

His gaze slammed into hers as he curved his fingers to plunge inside her.

She wished he wouldn't watch her so intently. She didn't want to reveal how vulnerable she felt this near to release. Or how close she was to tears at the powerful rush of desire that swept through her.

"Come for me, baby," he growled, while pressing his fingers deeper. Then his lips closed over her clitoris, and he sucked—*hard*.

Pia flung back her head and howled, her body shuddering as the coil unwound, pulse by pulse.

When finally her climax waned, she clung limply to the wood, gasping for breath, her body sagging.

He kissed the nest of hair that covered her mons before sliding her soaked panties back into place. "Come home with me." Not a request. But not *exactly* a command. His expression betrayed his naked need.

Naked as hers still was.

Her throat closed. This powerful, but needy, man was her quarry, and she'd betray him tonight.

* * * * *

Max's foot was heavy on the gas pedal as he sped toward his house. His body was so hard he hurt. His engorged cock felt strangled inside his jeans.

He couldn't get the picture of her unraveling out of his head. Her body had been his for the taking. Open, trembling, then convulsing around his fingers. The sound of her loud wail had filled him with triumph and still rang in his ears. The taste of her arousal remained in his mouth, and he savored it. Her spicy flavor drove an urgency so strong and insistent inside him, he fought the need to pull his truck to the side of the road. But there wasn't room in the cab to fuck her hard and long, the way he had to—or die.

She'd been silent ever since they'd left the bar and that worried him. He'd waited impatiently for her to retrieve her purse from beneath the front seat of her car, and then hurried her to his truck. If she changed her mind, he feared he wouldn't have enough control to stop.

Perhaps he shouldn't have waited. But as hard and horny as he was, he knew a quick fuck against the bathroom stall wouldn't have been enough to slake his need.

Something about this woman told him getting her out of his system would not be quick. He wanted — *no, needed* — to hammer at her pussy for a good long while. He just hoped that when he had her underneath him, he didn't scare the shit out of her.

Pulling into the driveway, he hit the garage door opener. The seconds it took for the door to rise and close them inside were interminable. He was out of the truck and pulling open her door before she'd finished fumbling to release her seatbelt.

He held out his hand.

Her face was pale, her mouth a tight line.

He didn't give her time to refuse. He clasped her hand and pulled her from the seat and into his arms. His kiss wasn't gentle or tempting — his mouth ate hers, and he swept his tongue, still flavored with her release, into her mouth.

Pia groaned, her hands clutching his shoulders, while her body pressed so hard against his, he thought she might try to crawl inside his skin.

His hands reached for her soft bottom and he squeezed, bringing her hips flush with his arousal. He slipped his hands beneath her skirt to grip her warm, naked flesh and ground his cock between her thighs while he massaged her ass.

The small whimpering sounds she made in the back of her throat drove him crazy — if he waited any longer to take her he might not keep control.

The flimsy fabric of her panties gave beneath his tug, and he growled with satisfaction when he heard them tear. He dropped them to the ground and then encouraged her to raise her legs, one at a time, to hug his waist. Max pumped his cock against her exposed flesh, drinking her sighs. As moisture seeped from her to soak the front of his trousers, he trembled with the need to be inside her.

He dragged away his mouth, his gaze boring into hers, and walked through the door into his kitchen and down the hallway to his bedroom, not bothering with lights.

When he reached the bed, he climbed onto it, never letting her go, until she was beneath him, his arms cradling her. "Tell me now, if you want me to stop," he said, straining to get the words past his lips. All he wanted was to tear their clothes from their bodies and get her naked skin next to his—his cock crammed inside her cunt as far as he could reach. "Spell it out for me, baby. I can't make a mistake. Don't want to hurt you."

"I don't want you to stop," she said, her voice tight.

He rose on his arms. Light from a streetlamp outside filtered through the blinds, painting her face and body with pale gray stripes. Her eyes were huge in her face, her mouth already swollen from his earlier kisses. His belly and thighs tensed. "Be sure," he said, fighting his body for control. "I'm so far gone, I can't be gentle."

Her lips opened around a gasp. "I don't want gentle. I want you inside me now."

Straightening, he pulled his T-shirt over his head. Then his hands went straight for his jeans and he opened them, closing his eyes with relief when his cock fell free from its denim tourniquet.

Her breath caught. When he opened his eyes, he found her glassy stare glued to his dick. Her teeth bit her lower lip, and she moaned.

He closed his fist around his cock. "Baby, I'm gonna fuck you like an animal," he said, his voice growling his promise.

Then he reached for her hips, shoving her skirt up to her waist to expose the nest of black hair that beckoned him like a siren. It glistened with her arousal. The spicy scent of her made his dick pulse.

With shaking hands, he stripped the skirt and her halter-top from her body.

Pia eagerly parted her legs and reached out with her arms. Her pale skin was luminous in the lamplight. Her nipples were dark, dimpled circles that made his mouth water. Every pale hill and shadowed valley of her body was on display—his for the taking. She appeared tiny beneath his large hands, everything about her as feminine, fragrant, and soft as a man could want. She made him ravenous as an animal to possess her.

Unable to wait a moment longer, Max fell between her thighs, his cock prodding her warm, wet slit. When he was sure of his aim, he tilted his hips and rammed inside her, crowding past the tight, soft tissues of her vagina. Without giving her time to adjust to his size, he claimed her with a single thrust.

Her muffled scream halted him.

His chest heaved and his body trembled, but he held himself still above her. "Christ, I'm sorry. Baby, I can't stop now," he said, desperation making his voice thick.

Pia's breath panted. "Fuck me, Max. Fuck me hard," she whispered.

With another growl, he came down on top of her, pushing and grinding into her wet cunt until she sheathed his length. He couldn't stop to savor the feel of her body closing around him when his own clamored for him to move. His buttocks tensed, pulling away, and then he flexed forward, cramming his cock back inside. He pumped into her, the rhythm hard and jerky. The force of his strokes drove her body up the bed.

Her voice rose on a moan, and she reached above her head to brace her arms against the headboard. Her legs settled around his hips, and her face grew taut. "Fuck me, fuck me," she chanted.

Max grunted as he pounded at her cunt, hammering hard, twisting to drive to one side then the other, needing to stroke the sweet spot inside her, needing to hear her say the words.

"Fuck me, fuck me!" Her body grew rigid. "Harder!" Then he felt the clasp and roll of her inner muscles, drawing him deeper, summoning her climax.

He gritted his teeth, the muscles in his back and ass expanding with the strain, clenching as he set his jaw and plunged. His head felt ready to explode, his cock and balls hardening like steel.

Still, he jackhammered his hips until her groans turned to guttural gasps for air.

Her legs and belly trembled, and her cries grew higher and incoherent. Her back arched off the bed, and then she screamed, long and loud.

Max's body burned like a match to dry kindling. He paused and pulled her legs from around his waist. Then he pushed them high, using his shoulders to force them upward so he could reach deeper inside.

She moaned, and her head thrashed on the mattress, her hands fisting around the bedding.

He had to get deeper—so deep he'd feel her heartbeat against his dick. He pressed her thighs into her chest and coaxed her to clasp her ankles around his neck.

"Too much," she gasped, squeezing her eyes shut. "It's too much!"

He turned his head, kissed her ankle, and drove his cock upward.

Her breath hissed inward.

"Baby, relax," he said, realizing how absurd that had to sound when his body was clenched, readying itself for the final assault. Braced on his arms, her ankles snug around his neck, he rocked against her cunt, trying to keep it slow and steady, not wanting to hurt her.

Pia's gaze clung to his face, her eyes dark, her mouth rounded with her gasps.

The tension built in his belly and his strokes quickened, aided by a hot wash of creamy arousal from inside Pia's body. He stroked and pounded, varying the length of his thrusts, reveling in the wet slaps of his belly and balls against her flesh. The bed shook and shimmied with the strength of his powerful fucking. Faster, harder, until the bed banged loudly against the wall.

"Now! I'm coming again, now!" she keened. "Yes!"

Max flung back his head, his eyes scrunched tight, and he howled as his body exploded, pumping scalding liquid from his cock in a stream of fire to bathe her womb.

Finally, his hips slowed their pounding motion to long gliding, inner caresses. He opened his eyes and stared down at the stranger beneath him and bent his head to kiss her. Thanking her with his body and mouth for the gift of sweet release.

* * * * *

More comfortable now that her body wasn't folded like a pretzel, Pia yawned. What a night. *What a man!*

Her limbs remained as limp as overcooked linguine, and she ached deliciously. She lay on the bed still stunned by the strength of her climax. If anyone had asked her—before Max— whether she preferred a gentle lover or an animal, she'd have chosen gentle. Not that he'd given her more than a few little bruises where his hands had gripped her ass—oh, and a pussy that felt pretty raw and hot.

Her hands smoothed over his back in lazy circles. His breathing had returned to normal, and the sweat on his chest and shoulders was dry, or drying on her. It was nice just lying beneath his weight, blanketed by two hundred plus pounds of prime, Grade-A human male.

"Are you okay?" he asked, his voice rumbling against her breast.

"Sure." Her jaw nearly cracked with the next deep yawn.

"Do you need to rest?"

Pia's hands circled faster. "No, why?" she asked, her heart already skipping in front of his answer.

"You'd tell me if you were too sore, right?"

Pia was thankful for the darkness. No way did she want this man to see how flustered his intimate questioning was making her. "Sure."

"Good. I want you on your belly."

Did he expect her to snap to his order just like that? "In case you didn't notice, you're anchoring me to this bed."

He kissed her nipple and hauled himself up to kneel beside her.

Pia rolled immediately to her belly. Who was she fooling? She couldn't muster an ounce of irritation. She had to know what wickedness he had in store for her next. Round one had been mind-blowing.

Besides, there was still time to complete her mission.

Max's hands palmed her buttocks as he crawled over her to straddle her thighs.

Pia groaned and pressed her bottom upward.

He kissed her shoulder, nuzzled through her hair to nip her neck, all the while his hands massaged her ass, squeezing, separating her cheeks, reigniting the fire that had only banked its embers.

Then he stretched out on top of her, his weight pressing her into the mattress again while his cock nestled between her buttocks. The scrape of the denim still clothing his legs only added to the wild excitement clamoring throughout her body.

Pia sighed and wriggled, wishing she could open her legs to take his hard cock into her body. Which place he chose to tunnel inside didn't particularly matter. She wanted to be filled with his masculinity.

He lifted a knee and nudged it between her legs.

Relieved they were both hurtling forward at the same speed, Pia moved one leg to the side, then the other, as he climbed between. He stretched over her again. But this time the hard ridge of his cock pressed directly against the super-sensitive flesh between her legs, while his weight squashed her to the mattress, leaving her breathless. Her body responded with liquid encouragement, seeping out to lubricate his cock as the rolling motion of his hips stoked the flames higher.

"I wanted to take it slow this time," he said, an edge of desperate laughter in his voice.

"Slow—fast, I don't care," she said, gasping for air. "Just come inside me, please."

"I wouldn't be much of a gentleman, if I didn't get you ready first. Your cunt is red-hot. I'll hurt you."

Oh, he'd used the C-word! Her body clenched. On any other man's lips, she'd have taken offense, but he said it so easily, so naturally. The gravel in his rough voice made the word erotically charged.

"So get to work," she whispered, "on my...cunt...please," she whispered.

He growled next to her ear, and his teeth grazed her neck. Apparently, he liked her saying the word, too. Then he lifted off her body, and she heard the sound of rustling bedding.

"Lift your hips, baby."

She groaned and lifted her bottom.

"Higher." He shoved two pillows beneath her, raising her bottom. "Do you mind if I turn on a light?"

Pia's breath hitched. The man wasn't going to leave her any shred of privacy. With her face pressed to the mattress, he'd have a view of...everything. Places *she'd* never seen. "Do it."

He didn't choose the lamp on the bedside table. No, he went for the one on his bureau, even angled it to remove any chance of shadows marring his view.

Pia groaned and pressed her hot cheeks to the bed.

Max laughed as he returned, the mattress dipping to one side with his weight. His hands caressed her ass. "Don't worry about it. You're beautiful." His fingers combed the down between her legs. "Open your legs wider, sweetheart."

Once again, Pia obeyed. One part of her was eager for his exploration, the other cringed inside at the intimacy he forced on her. A coupling in the dark was one thing—even hanging from a stall with her legs spread wide had been different. She'd been able to see him. Now, she was vulnerable, under his control. Waiting for the next wicked thing he would do.

He cupped her sex with his palm. "You're red here, and hot. Would you like me to cool you down?"

"I thought me being hot was the whole point," she said, her words muffled in the bedding.

"Aroused—not irritated. There's a difference. You're red—raw-looking, actually," he said, his voice not sounding the least bit regretful.

"Are you going to give a tour?" she asked, with a bite in her voice.

"Would you like that?" Again, the sexy hint of a growl made her fingers curve tightly around the sheets. He squeezed her ass.

"I would never have guessed you were a man of so many words."

"I was focused before." His fingers traced a lazy trail between her buttocks. "I don't talk much when I have a target."

"You have two targets now." She couldn't believe she'd just said that! "Shouldn't you be doubly quiet?"

"But I'm enjoying making you squirm." He nipped her ass.

She yelped and lifted her rear higher. "A sadist, then?"

"Do you like pain?" He circled her anus.

"Augh!" She bunched the bedding around her face and tried to control the trembling excitement building in her belly. "Sometimes," she whispered.

"I've left bruises on your ass. I'm sorry about that." His mouth gently placed wet kisses on each one.

"I didn't mind."

"I may leave a few more before I'm done."

"Oh, please…"

Chapter Three

"Seduce him or turn him."

Pia shuddered at the memory of Navarro's tight-lipped order. His scary, intense stare had made every hair on Pia's body rise.

Some of the female vamps, and a few of the males, thought he was pretty hot with his dark, shoulder-length hair, olive complexion, and a slender face that looked like a picture she'd once seen in a textbook of an ancient Byzantine king.

The others were convinced he had to know a lot about pleasing a woman, as old as he was. That he had to know dark, ancient techniques when only a look could make their flesh burn for him. But she'd never actually heard of him taking a lover.

The only thing he inspired in Pia was a major case of the willies.

For one thing, the man never smiled. His mouth was beautiful, perfectly symmetrical, curved at the corners like he'd been a man who smiled a lot—while he'd lived. Sitting in his study in his large, leather armchair, the center of his mouth had formed a straight line. Betraying no hint of emotion, he'd talked about the human who served as the only impediment to the Masters' plan to extend their reach into southern Florida.

And his dark eyes never seemed to blink. She'd stared transfixed the few times she'd been in his presence, waiting for him to lower his lids or do something that would make him seem the least bit—well, human…like.

"So, if he's such a problem, why don't Dylan or Quentin handle him?" she'd asked, after gathering her courage.

"They are our diplomats. They must remain blameless. Besides, their wives care about this human."

"Do they know you're sending someone?"

"Yes, that's why I offered you the option of seducing him." He waved a negligent hand. "Otherwise, I'd have said, turn him or kill him."

"Oh." She looked down at her hands and realized she was clutching them together so tightly her knuckles were white. She unclasped them and wiped off the sweat from her palms onto her slacks.

Raising her gaze, she found him watching her curiously, like a bug beneath a microscope, his palms pressed together and fingers steepled under his chin.

She took a deep breath. "Do they know I'm the one you want to send?"

"They are not to be apprised of my plan," he said, his words clipped. "They don't even know things are already underway. It's best this way."

"Quentin might not be too happy to see me," she said, working her way up to broaching the subject that really bothered her about this assignment.

"Quentin has softened since his marriage. I doubt he still holds a grudge."

If she didn't know better, she'd have sworn there was a smile in his voice. "Well, if you're certain I'm right for this job…"

"You'll be perfect," he'd said, his gaze boring holes into her. "Try seduction…first."

With her ass in the air and Max's lips trailing kisses across her bottom, Pia wondered who was doing the seducing here.

When his tongue laved the hot skin of her swollen labia, she forgot about Navarro, forgot about her assignment. Her whole world narrowed to the glide of Max's talented tongue.

He licked and fluttered, teasing her with shallow inward strokes that had her lifting her bottom to follow the motion. "I need more. This is torture," she said, her voice sounding thin to her own ears.

His response was to blow a stream of cooling air over her, and then he pressed apart her lips to direct another cool stream at her opening.

Her thighs and buttocks trembled with her excitement. "Max! I thought this was going to be fast."

"It will be," he murmured. "Are you complaining?" His lips closed over her hooded clitoris, sucked and released.

She released a shaky breath. "'Course not," she grumbled. "You'd just go slower."

"Smart girl. Are you ready for a new adventure?" The pointed tip of his tongue dipped into her anus.

She yelped in surprise. "What are you doing?"

"You don't like that?" His tongue fluttered like the wing of a butterfly.

"That's not the point." She groaned. Was he trying to thoroughly embarrass her?

"That was *the point*—shall I prove it to you again?"

"Why don't you go back to being tall, dark, and mute?"

"So you're saying you're ready?"

Was this a trick question? "Uh…yes…"

"Finally." His hands left her rump, and he shifted on the mattress. Then she heard his feet hitting the floor.

"Where are you going?" she asked, rising up to glance over her shoulder.

His back was to her as he bent to remove his boots. "I'm taking off the rest of my clothes."

She blushed and looked away. She'd forgotten he still wore boots and blue jeans. While she'd been naked as a newborn for the last hour, he'd been half-clothed. She buried her face again to the sound of his soft laughter.

Then the mattress dipped and she braced herself, her body already shivering in anticipation of his touch.

His hands settled on her buttocks, and he silently encouraged her to come to her knees, raising her bottom into the air.

Pia buried her hot face into the bedding, a little embarrassed he could see everything—including proof of her overwhelming arousal trickling down her thighs.

Then his tongue lapped the cream seeping from her pussy. His moan vibrated against her sensitive flesh, and her trembling grew stronger. His fingers spread her folds, sliding inside once, before something broad and heavy pressed into her entrance.

And that was only the beginning of the wonderful sensations that left her breathless with need.

Below, his blunt, calloused fingers circled her clitoris as his cock eased deeper into her vagina. Above, fingers teased the second little orifice, circling then dipping inside.

Pia's body quaked on the edge of release. "Oh Max," she moaned, as she rubbed her aching nipples on the nubby fabric of his comforter. "Deeper, please. Please, Max. Deeper!"

"Give me the words, baby," he said, his voice raspy as his shallow thrusts built a fire inside her.

She had to tell him? Did he want whole paragraphs? "Damn you! This sex talk is new for me."

"Shall I stop?" He rotated his hips, circling his cock inside her.

"What do you want me to say?" she asked, the words coming out in a rush.

"Tell me what would please you—what you want to feel."

"That's easy. I want your cock deeper inside me."

"Is that all?"

"No." her breath caught on a sob. "Your fingers. Fuck my ass with your fingers. Please. If you don't mind."

"Mind? Ask me anything."

"I just did! Fuck me with your fingers!"

"Oh baby, keep talking to me." His strokes grew longer, reaching deeper. His fingers tunneled in and out, keeping rhythm with his hips. "Christ, you feel so good. Hot, tight. Your cunt's soaking wet."

"It's for you," she moaned.

His thrusts were harder now.

"Please, just like that! Fuck me hard, Max."

"Can you take more?" he asked, his voice harsh, strained. "I want my balls snuggled up to your clit."

"Give me all of you, Max. Please, pound my pussy!"

His chuckle sounded strained. "Pound my pussy?"

"So, I told you I'm new to this. Just do it, buster!"

He growled and his teeth closed on her shoulder, not piercing her skin, but hard enough to bruise. His taut belly slapped her bottom with the force of his movements. Harder, sharper, faster.

Pia went wild, jerking her hips back to slam against his belly, taking him as deep as her vagina would allow. "Oh, that hurts so good. Damn, you're big. I love your big cock."

"Wiggle on it. Just a little."

Pia lost control, egged on with his encouragement, slamming backward, her hips jerking.

"Oh baby, I can't wait." His hand settled between her shoulder blades, and he pressed her chest down to the mattress. "I'm gonna come." Another finger joined the two pumping in her ass. Then he hammered faster.

"Can't talk. Can't breathe. Faster! Oooh!" Pia felt her orgasm rush over her like a firestorm, sucking the wind from her lungs, flashes of color bursting behind her tightly shut eyelids.

"Yes, yes!" she chanted, until she could only moan as he delivered the final, powerful thrusts.

He folded over her back, both of them raised in the middle by the hummock of pillows. He kissed her shoulder and murmured, "Pound my pussy?"

She dug her elbow backward into his ribs. "See if I ever talk dirty again."

His arms closed around her, and he hugged her tightly. "Baby, I don't mean to tease you."

"Don't you?"

"Well, yeah, but not in a mean way. It was pretty funny." He shifted over, dragging her off the pillows, but keeping the connection with her body. He settled on his side, her body spooned with his.

With his arm as her pillow, Pia felt her eyelids dip. She'd been truly fucked and fondled to the edge of her endurance. And vamps had a lot of that—endurance. She smiled softly at the thought that Max might be her match. And he was a human!

Just a quick nap, she thought, *and then I'll take care of business.* Her mouth opened wide around a yawn. The last thing she remembered was the feel of his hands cupping her breasts, and she slept.

* * * * *

Max woke to find that Pia hadn't moved an inch. She still lay inside the circle of his arms, her rump snuggled against his groin. His cock appreciated the soft pillowy mounds as it rubbed against her. He squeezed her breast, but she didn't stir. While disappointed she didn't wake, a primal satisfaction made him smile—he'd exhausted her.

His hands glided over the shallow indentation of her waist and lowered to the womanly swell of her hips. She was a tiny thing, really. He wondered how she'd taken him. Not that he'd given her much choice. He'd ravaged her body, inside and out.

Pia would have pleased him if she'd simply given him release—but she'd done so much more. The tension that had knotted his body was gone, melting beneath the rays of her warm, womanly smile, her lusty appetite, and the funny things she said. In the light of day, would she change toward him? He hoped not. He wanted her again.

Glancing over his shoulder, he gauged the hour by the gray, morning light sifting between the blinds. Dawn was breaking.

Deciding to close them and let her sleep a while longer, he rolled out of the bed and padded to the window.

An indrawn hiss sounded behind him. He swung around to see something like steam rising from a stripe of skin on Pia's shoulder where the sunlight touched her. She whimpered and reached a hand to cover her shoulder.

He flipped the blinds closed and stood stock-still. The stripe sizzled, red and blistered.

Fucking hell! A vamp was in his bed. *Sweet Pia was a goddamn vamp bitch!*

A chill wrapped around his heart and he slowly walked around the bed, staring.

Deceptively innocent, her face was as soft and beautiful as an angel's. A dark angel.

Her eyes were closed, her breath so slow and shallow he could barely tell she breathed. She'd cried out in her sleep.

When had she planned to take him? If he hadn't loved her to sleep, would she have nuzzled her sweet mouth against his neck and bitten when he'd been so close to orgasm he didn't care? Or would she have drained him dry while her mouth closed over his cock? Now she'd never get the chance.

Although his stomach churned at the thought, he knew what he had to do. Pia's fate had been decided the instant she'd died the first time. All he could do now was send her soul to hell along with the rest of the demons who'd made her and her kind.

Damn her for getting under his skin!

Bending, he dragged his duffel from beneath the bed and slid open the zipper. He dug inside until his hand closed around warm, smooth wood. He pulled the stake from the bag and straightened.

His chest rose and fell swiftly as he fought anger and disappointment. This was his calling, what he lived to do. That the most appealing woman he'd met in a long time was one of them ate a hole in his gut.

He reached out and gently rolled her on her back.

She didn't wake—not a flutter of an eyelash or a sleepy murmur.

He climbed onto the bed and straddled her body, moving stealthily so as not to jar her awake. He'd observed enough vamps at rest to know they slept like the dead. Pia was no exception.

And he'd make no exception for her. Careful not to note the sweet curves of her breasts, or the dimple he'd promised himself to explore, he closed his mind to her spicy scent and the feel of her butter-soft skin between his thighs. Better to get this over with quickly. He traced an X above her heart with the tip of the stake, drawing two thin lines of blood to mark the spot.

Then holding the stake with both hands, he raised it high above his head. He drew in a deep breath. A shudder racked his naked body. Every muscle in his arms, back and shoulders shook as he fought himself. This was the right thing to do. Every demon deserved her death.

But the bloody X looked obscene against her milk-white skin. His belly clenched at the thought of looking into her startled eyes the moment she disintegrated into dust.

Slowly, he lowered the stake and tossed it on the mattress beside her. He'd let her find it when she awoke. If she were smart, she'd make damn sure they never crossed paths again.

* * * * *

A sharp rap on his kitchen door was all the warning Max got before his brother Alec swept into the room. Like a free-ranging dog, he scouted the kitchen, opening the pantry door and tipping the lid to the bread bin, before finally choosing a beer from the fridge. He popped the top, and then straddled one of the chairs next to the table backwards.

"Make yourself at home," Max said, more distracted than irritated. The problem lying in his bed down the hallway still claimed his attention.

"You're in a sour mood today."

Alec's cheerful tone set Max's teeth on edge. As usual not one hair on his blond head was out of place. His khaki slacks were pressed with a knife-edge crease, and the cuffs of his cotton shirt were buttoned.

Max scratched his whiskered cheek and glanced down at his rumpled T-shirt and sweat pants. His brother always made him want to take a bath.

"Kill any vamps lately?"

Max started guiltily. "Not a one," he murmured and took a sip of his lukewarm coffee. "Why do you ask?"

Alec took a long draw of his brew and set the can on the table. "It explains your grumpiness."

"So, is this a social call?" Max's question sounded like a snarl to his own ears.

Alec's brows rose. "What? I can't just drop in and say hi to my big brother?"

"Do you need money?" Much as he loved his brother, he wanted him gone before he nosed around the rest of the house.

Alec's amusement crinkled the corners of his eyes. "I'm twenty-five, not fifteen."

Max stared pointedly at the beer. "But you still can't afford your own groceries?"

"It's just a beer. Man, you woke up on the wrong side of the bed." Alec's green eyes narrowed. "Quentin still giving you shit?"

Max shrugged. "We made a raid last night — it was a bust."

"Not the first time. You're edgy as a bear with a thorn in its paw." At Max's glare of warning to drop the subject, Alec grinned.

"Someone beat us to the party."

"Who?" Alec asked, his brows rising. "Rogue vamp hunters?"

Max shook his head. "Werewolves."

"Well, fancy that." He took another draw of his beer. "Shit's coming out of the woodwork around here. Have you had a chance to get inside The Compound?"

Max's hand tightened around his coffee cup. "No. Security's pretty tight. No civilians have been invited in."

"If the breeder's pregnant, it'd explain why it's sewed up tighter than a virgin's panties."

"Could be they're just a wary bunch of vamps," Max replied evenly.

"You were right the first time, brother. Why do you think we have a new dog pack in the neighborhood? Think it's a coincidence?" Alec's expression grew hard. "The woman, Lily, have you seen her since she arrived?"

"Nope."

"But you've seen the other women?"

Max nodded, knowing where this train of logic was running. "It does look damn suspicious. If she's carrying a vamp kit —"

"If she's breeding for a vamp, you have to take out her and the monsters she's carrying."

Max felt acid burn in his gut and he put down his coffee cup. "She's human."

"She's fucking a vamp."

Max felt his cheeks burn with guilt.

"You're the only one who can get close enough." Alec's gaze pinned him to his chair. "Joe's your buddy."

"My friend died," Max said, between gritted teeth. "Besides, he'd be suspicious if I suddenly wanted to hang out again. He knows what I think of his kind."

Alec lifted an eyebrow. "So have a change of heart."

Max shifted his head from side to side to loosen the tension knotting his shoulders. "I'll try to get close enough to see whether she's actually pregnant."

"Good enough." He canted his head, leveling a questioning gaze. "What is it with you today? Are you going soft on the demons?"

Max forced his features to remain relaxed. "No."

"Remember what they did to our mother," Alec said softly.

"How the hell can I forget? They left me with you to raise on my own." He gave his brother a small, tight smile.

"Yeah!" Alec raised his beer and swallowed the rest in one long gulp. "Hold onto that thought. By the way, can I borrow your motorcycle?"

So that was it. Max heaved a sigh. "I thought you were just here to see your big brother."

"That too. Got a date tonight—can't take her out in my Civic. She'll think I'm a real geek."

"If you take the chopper, you'd better lay off the beer."

"Really?" Alec stood, eager to be away now that he'd gotten what he'd come for. "You'll let me have her?"

"Sure." At least it would get him away from Pia. "But if you leave a single scratch on her—"

"I know, I know." Alec grinned and swiped the keys from a dish on the counter. "You know what your problem is…"

Max raised an eyebrow.

"You need to get laid, brother."

Max threw a glare at Alec as he walked out the door laughing, then he glanced at his watch. Only an hour before sunset. Time to get dressed for work—and time to get lost before Pia awoke.

But first he couldn't resist one last look.

He walked slowly to the bedroom and pushed open the door. Pia lay on her back just as he'd left her, naked and sleeping peacefully.

The dim light did nothing to hide the sweet curves of her body. Her hair was a dark cloud—he'd remember the sight of it fanned out on his pillow for a long time. He lifted a strand and rubbed it between his fingers—*fine as spider's silk*.

Her small body was just as deceptively beautiful. His gaze lowered to the silken thatch between her legs, and he shifted his feet apart. He could still remember the feel of her inner muscles clutching his body in rhythmic waves. Could hear her throaty cries as she'd come, luring him over the edge.

He reached and cupped a breast—the one marked with dried blood. His thumb caressed her nipple, and it budded instantly. He drew away from the temptation of that rosy crest, and cursed silently as his body reacted to the sight.

Damn her! Did she know what he was? Was she playing some sort of game to draw him out?

First, a murderous pack of werewolves. Then a sweet, fanged temptation.

Max didn't believe in coincidences.

Chapter Four

ɞ

Stretching, Pia woke slowly, moaning as her sleep-fogged mind noted each delicious ache. With her eyes still closed, she slid her hand along the mattress, only to find the source of her languorous state gone. Sighing, she rolled and pressed her face into Max's pillow.

For a long moment, she let her mind wander back through the evening's love play. Max's stern mouth softened by long, carnal kisses. Strong hands kneading her breasts and buttocks. Blunt, clever fingers that brought her to the edge. And a cock that filled her to the brim.

But the words! Sexy, nasty words that made her flinch while at the same time incited her to orgasm. She wanted his whispers again.

Where the devil was he?

Her eyes opened, blinking at the fading gray light filtering behind the blinds. She listened, stretching her senses to determine whether he stirred anywhere in the house. Instead, she found she was completely alone. Only lingering traces of his tangy blood and spicy cologne remained, and no footsteps could be heard anywhere in the house.

Her disappointment was keen. She'd hoped to feel the slide of his strong hands and snuggle next to his chest, and perhaps, enjoy a slow ride into erotic wonderland. Then an appalling thought occurred.

She'd slept!

Pia jackknifed to a sitting position. She'd slept in Max Weir's bed! Had he guessed she was a vamp? Or did he just think she was a very heavy sleeper? Her gut told her he had to know. She couldn't imagine a man with his libido letting any woman in his bed sleep throughout the day. And if he'd tried to wake her for a little morning action...

Her heart galloped, and she raised a shaking hand and stared—nope, she wasn't disintegrating, and by the ache in her shoulder and other parts best not considered at the moment—she wasn't a ghost.

As deep as his prejudice was reported to run, she didn't know why he'd left her alive. But here she was in his bed—not even a splinter of wood poking from her chest. She glanced down and gasped. A burnished brown X was painted on her breast.

She scratched at the flecks of dried blood. It didn't take a brain surgeon to understand his warning. He may have let her live for now, but he'd been mighty tempted to end her life.

When she scooted to the edge of the bed, something smooth and hard rolled toward her hip. Her hand closed around it, and she raised it in front of her face. He'd been more than tempted! She screeched and tossed the stake across the room. Then she leapt off the bed, searching the floor for her clothing.

They were folded in a neat pile on top of his bureau, her shoes beside them. Like he wanted her to dress in a hurry and haul her ass out of his house.

Her shoulders drooped. What had she expected? One night of incredible sex and he'd leave her a love letter?

Best not to tempt fate twice. She dressed in a frenzy and hurried out the door. She'd gotten the message loud and clear—the next time he'd play for keeps.

* * * * *

Pia fretted with the fringe on the hem of her sleeve. She'd found a dangling thread and yanked it. "Shit!" Now, the gold fringe was only half as long as the one on her other sleeve. And she'd wanted to make a good impression.

The Compound, as its new owners had dubbed it, was a work in progress. From the details she'd gleaned since a security guard let her through the gates minutes earlier, the estate would be a cozy beige and gold haven with none of the opulence that usually marked a Master's residence. Overstuffed leather chairs and sofas faced inward, inviting one to linger for a chat. But Pia's nerves hadn't settled after her mad dash from Max's house, so she paced, trying to think of what she'd say about her latest failure.

Had she made a mistake coming directly to The Compound? What if she ran into Quentin? Did he still hold a grudge? She'd only been a lowly operative in the Masters' Northwest Council when she'd last seen him. Maybe he wouldn't remember her.

Perhaps she was just being paranoid, feeling off-kilter since her debacle with Max. If she ever saw him again and his expression held one ounce of the disgust she now felt for her deception, she'd crumble.

No, she'd best slink back to Seattle, her tail between her legs, and forget about the brawny human whose strength and dark sensuality had so captivated her. She couldn't bear to face him again.

Not that she hadn't dreamed in a corner of her bruised heart of seeing him one last time. At least to apologize. During the short taxi ride here, she'd entertained any number of scenarios, all of which ended horribly. Her staring down the shaft of an arrow buried deep in her chest... Her hand reaching out to him as she disintegrated into a grimy dust heap...

Okay, so she was getting melodramatic. She'd fucked up. Time to face the truth. She simply wasn't cut out for this cloak and dagger stuff. This latest episode in a long string of disasters should have told her that.

Worse, her first solo assignment outside Seattle and she'd botched the mission in less than twenty-four hours.

"Do you think she'll have a sleeve left if we leave her to stew much longer?"

Pia started at the feminine voice coming from the doorway of the den where she'd been cooling her heels for the past half hour.

A woman with golden hair that hung past her generous bosom grinned and sauntered into the room.

The man following her inside was Dylan O'Hara. And wherever Dylan was, Quentin was sure to follow. "Well, well," Dylan said, following the woman inside. "Won't Quentin be surprised?"

Rats! He'd recognized her. She needed to get out quick.

Emmy swung back to Dylan, her eyes narrowing. "You know her?"

Dylan flinched, appearing ill at ease beneath the woman's displeasure.

Pia had never seen the vamp anything but cool. Interesting.

"Well, I know her, but I don't *know* her, love," he said, his hand curving around the woman's fleshy hip.

"Good, then I don't have to tear out her hair." She turned back to Pia and gave her a blinding smile. "I'm Emmy O'Hara. Seems you two are already acquainted." She stared at Pia expectantly.

Pia straightened and offered her hand. The last thing she should expect was a polite introduction from Dylan. "I'm Pia D'Amato. From Seattle."

"How was the weather when you left?"

Pia shrugged. "Wet."

Emmy wrinkled her nose. "I don't miss that one bit. So, you're one of us? I can't tell just by looking. Dylan can, but he's older than Methuselah."

Dylan's eyes narrowed, but a hint of a smile curved the corners of his lips. "You're Navarro's solution to our little problem?"

"Some solution…" Pia muttered, then blushed when she realized she'd said it out loud. "He sent me."

"She's here to help with the werewolves?" Emmy asked, her eyes widening. "That was really quick."

"No love," he said. "Another little problem. One not worth mentioning."

Pia took the hint. The subject of Max's "conversion" was not for Emmy's ears.

"I can't wait until Quentin arrives," Dylan said.

Pia's face flamed brighter. "Actually, I just stopped in to tell you I'm heading back home tonight."

"So soon?" Emmy looked genuinely dismayed. "But you just got here! I know Lily would love to meet you. She hasn't had any female vamps other than myself to interview."

"Lily?"

"Yeah, Joe's wife. She's been with us for several months now. She's working on a book. *The Definitive Guide to Vampirism.*"

Dylan cleared his throat. "She'll likely be too ill to see our friend, seeing as Pia's leaving so soon."

Emmy bit her lip. "Oh right. I forgot."

"Anyway," Pia said, hoping to take control of the situation, give her debrief, and hit the road before Quentin burst through the door. "I'm packed and on my way to the airport."

"Like I said before, leaving so soon?" Dylan asked. "Did you already take care of that little bit of business for us?"

Pia stared at her ragged fringe. "Um…actually, no."

"But you've met him?"

Pia nodded, but still couldn't meet his gaze.

"Met who?" A dark-haired man strode into the room. By his Latin features, Pia assumed he was the newest vamp, Joe Garcia.

"Max," Dylan said.

"Is *she* the solution?" Joe's dubious glance swept her from head to foot.

"We have a problem other than the werewolves that requires a solution?" Emmy asked.

"Navarro's diabolical," Joe said, a smile stretching his sexy mouth.

If Pia hadn't already met Max, she might have melted into a puddle, this man was so handsome.

"I think I need a drink," Dylan said. "You're still in a hydrated state, Pia—so I assume your meeting wasn't a total disaster."

Joe glanced at his watch. "You work fast. It's only an hour past dusk."

Pia looked from one curious male face to the other. How could she admit she'd been a dismal failure? "Well, I-I met him last night."

Joe's eyebrows rose. "Oh, I see." His gaze turned speculative. "I take it, he didn't know you were a vampire."

Pia wished they'd change the subject. "Not at first," she said, her teeth grinding with annoyance.

"But he does now, and you're still standing." Joe glanced at Dylan. "I'm impressed."

Dylan shrugged. "Seems our girl here has found a chink in the tough guy's armor. Tell me why you're so eager to leave? Looks like your work's just begun."

Pia blew out an agitated breath. "He made it quite clear he didn't want to see me again."

"You!"

Pia jumped at the familiar voice and her stomach sank.

Quentin Albermarle—the bane of her professional existence—filled the door, a look black as thunder on his face. "What the devil are you doing here?" The large, blond vampire advanced menacingly.

Pia refused to back up a step. "Hello, Quentin. Don't worry about me. I-I was just leaving."

"Do I detect a bit of animosity?" Emmy asked, her eyes too wide and guileless to be believed.

"She's a menace!" Quentin said, pointing a damning finger in Pia's direction. "A walking disaster!"

Annoyed he could still hold a grudge when she'd obviously done him no lasting harm, Pia straightened to her full height. "How was I supposed to know you weren't killing that woman? She sounded hysterical."

"I was tickling her—she was laughing *hysterically*!" he said, his face turning purple. "Besides, if you thought I was killing her, why didn't you aim higher?"

Pia glanced at the others to see whether a rescue was imminent, but Dylan merely coughed, and Joe's lips twitched.

She scowled at them both. "Who said I missed?" No way would she tell these arrogant assholes she'd been aiming for his heart. She couldn't help it her palms had been moist, and the crossbow slipped.

"You *meant* to shoot me in the ass?" A tic pulsed next to his eye.

Pia decided discretion might be the better course. After all, she didn't ever have to see this odious vamp again. She crossed her arms over her chest and glared. "I apologized. It was a natural mistake."

"Natural?" He leaned down, so close his nose nearly touched hers. Then his face grew still. "Bugger me. Tell me Navarro didn't send this chit here."

"'Fraid so," Joe said, his tone mild.

"What the hell was he thinking?"

"She spent the night with Max."

Quentin drew back and stared. "Fuck me. And she's still standing?"

"Boggles the mind, doesn't it?" Dylan said dryly.

Quentin looked her up and down, and then walked around her. When he'd finished his circuit, he frowned. "I need a drink."

"Drinks all around, it is!" Emmy said gaily.

"Make a note, Dylan," Quentin said, his voice still hard. "She's never to hold a weapon within a hundred yards of me."

"Looks like you're staying," Emmy whispered in her ear as she handed her a tumbler of amber liquid.

Pia didn't even sniff to see what she'd been given. She tossed it back and then coughed. The whiskey warmed her all the way to her belly. "Who says I'm staying? He knows what I am. If he sees me again, I'm potting soil."

Emmy pressed her down into a chair. Then her gaze turned mean as she surveyed the men. "So is someone going to tell me what this is all about? What problem is Pia supposed to solve with Max?"

"Now, love," Dylan said, reaching for her.

Emmy held a hand out to block the move. "Don't you dare 'Now, love' me and pat me on the head. I'm not a puppy."

"No, love," Dylan purred. "You're my pussy kitty."

"You are not going to distract me." Emmy's nostrils flared. "What are you guys up to?"

"Ballocks!" Quentin said. "That wife of yours never keeps a secret. Darcy will have my ass."

Dylan sighed and reached for Emmy's hand. "Haven't you noticed Max's intense dislike for us?"

"Max just needs time to get to know us," Emmy said. "Darcy says he's a great guy when he's not being an asshole. Look at Joe," she said with a nod toward the Cuban. "He hated our guts."

Joe raised an eyebrow. "Who says I still don't?"

"Lily says so," Emmy said with a nod. "Did you tell her a lie?"

Joe muttered under his breath and slumped into a chair.

Emmy turned to Pia. "What exactly were you supposed to do with Max?"

"Not what she did, obviously," Quentin muttered.

Pia squirmed in her chair. She knew Emmy wouldn't be pleased to hear the details of her mission, or that Navarro's first inclination was to kill Max outright.

"I take it you slept with him?" Joe asked, his expression closed.

"Yeah, that was kind of the problem."

"Why?" Emmy asked. "What were you supposed to do?"

Pia glanced around the room.

Dylan sighed and shrugged.

Pia took a deep breath. She may as well get this over with. "Um…I was supposed to seduce him or turn him."

"Turn him?" Joe's brows drew together in a frightening scowl. "Over my dead body."

"Too late," Quentin murmured.

Dylan frowned at both the male vamps. "Well, you almost got the first part right, Pia. So what happened?"

"I fell asleep."

Joe snorted.

"And when did you wake up?" Dylan asked.

"A couple of hours ago."

Dylan stood still for a long moment, and then a grin teased the corners of his mouth. He turned to Joe. "He's going to be surly as a grizzly bear."

Joe's expression didn't betray his thoughts. "Yup."

"I want you to stick close," Dylan said. "See if he says anything about our girl here."

Pia bristled at the "our girl". "And what am I supposed to do in the meantime?"

"Stay here," Quentin said. "Out of trouble."

Pia had the urge to click her heels and salute, but Quentin's fierce expression didn't reassure her she was out of the woods yet.

"Let's head to the station," Dylan said.

"Try not to make it too obvious we're sussing him out," Quentin said, looking at Joe. "Do you suppose he'll put two and two together and figure out we're responsible for her being here?"

Joe rose from his chair. "Max is so ready to think the worst, he'll probably jump straight to believing it was a setup."

"Then we have to make sure he never makes a firm connection," Dylan said. "Keep him doubting."

"Pia," Joe said, turning back to address her. "I want your promise you won't attempt to turn him."

Pia lifted her chin. "I can't do that."

His face turned menacing. "Then I'll have to tell him why you're here."

"Let's see if she can win him over first," Dylan said. "She may not have to resort to draining him."

"You're not to move a muscle until we return," Quentin said. "Got that?"

Pia didn't try to hide a scowl. Her hot stare should have blistered their backsides as they swept out of the room.

"Whew!" Emmy said, fanning herself. "Was the testosterone stinking up the place or what?"

Pia felt her lips twitching at the outrageous remark. "They are a bit overwhelming."

"Did you really shoot Quentin in the ass?" she asked, her face alight with laughter. "God, what I wouldn't have given to see the look on his face."

"It was a Kodak moment, all right."

The two women burst into laughter. Pia felt the tension drain away. For the moment anyway, she was safe—and it looked like she might be given a second chance to redeem herself. She'd worry about how to keep her body solid around Max later.

"Did I miss a joke?" a feminine voice said from behind Pia.

Pia whirled.

"Not a joke. But you'll be sorry you missed it," Emmy said. "Meet Pia. Pia, this is Quentin's wife, Darcy."

Pia nodded to the woman, then her gaze trailed downward. Darcy was reed-thin except for her very round belly. Quentin's wife was pregnant. Pia gasped. "Are you a breeder?"

"Not the kind you think," Emmy said quickly. "The baby's not Quent's—but that's a long story."

Pia looked from one woman to the next. They couldn't be more different. One blonde and voluptuous, with a face that sparkled bright as Christmas lights. The other brunette, slender, and serene. But there was no mistaking the bond between them as they traded meaningful glances. Pia felt a twinge of envy for their friendship.

"Pia is here to take care of Max, Darcy."

Pia nearly groaned aloud.

"What's to take care of?" Darcy said, stiffening.

"That's a very good question." Emmy turned back to Pia, her eyes narrowing. "You're gonna have to spill, girlfriend."

"Shit."

* * * * *

"So what was-sh Max like?" Emmy asked, her reddened eyes alight with curiosity.

Pia wished her glass wasn't empty, she could use another shot before she answered that one. She glanced over her shoulder to where the bottle sat on the kitchen counter—too far to walk. She sighed. "Intense."

"I bet." Emmy burped and then giggled. "He looks like the kind who would walk through walls to get at a woman."

Pia's cheeks filled with heat. "He is relentless." She pursed her lips to keep from giggling, guessing it was probably time to stop drinking. She never giggled.

Darcy's mouth turned up at the corners. "Well, well. I always knew he had it in him."

Emmy leaned over the kitchen table and spread a generous daub of liverwurst on a cracker and popped it into her mouth. "Mmmm. Love organ meat. So's Max...hung?" she asked, her hand covering her mouth.

Darcy tilted her head back and groaned. "She's obsessed."

"I'm not the only one," Emmy snapped. "Lily carries a measuring tape."

Pia intercepted Darcy's swift headshake and a glare in Emmy's direction, and alarm bells rang. That was the second time she'd heard that name. Wasn't it? She shook her head—*big mistake*, the room swirled. "Lily? There's another woman in The Compound?"

"Oops," Emmy said, eyes rounded with guilt.

"Joe's wife," Darcy said. "She's ill."

"Oh." The secretive glance the two women shared only heightened Pia's curiosity. She tried to sit straighter in her chair. "Is she a vamp or human?"

"Human, like me," Darcy said, quickly. "So is Max...hung?"

Her attempt to change the subject was too obvious to be casual, but Pia let it drop—Max's penis was a much more interesting subject. "He's impressive...especially for a human."

"I knew it!" Emmy said, slapping her palm against the table so loudly Darcy jumped.

Pia, on the other hand, guessed her nerves were too well insulated. Not so much as a flinch. She lifted her glass to her mouth, then cursed when she remembered it was empty.

"The guys are always saying they're just un-ush-unusually large for vampires." Emmy smiled. "The braggarts. So tell me, have you ever had a vamp who couldn't wield his cock like a weapon?"

Darcy spluttered with shocked laughter. "Em!"

Pia grinned. Whatever the two were trying to hide, it wasn't any of her affair. Nope! She was strictly short-term. "Vamp cocks are the biggest. Although..." she leaned over the table to whisper, "I've heard werewolves are just as impressive."

"Werewolves!" Darcy shuddered. "Monsters, every one. You should have seen what they did to those people."

Having heard the story of the botched raid earlier, Pia could sympathize. "Not that I have any personal experience, but I have heard things."

Darcy's gaze sharpened. "Is it true they're hard to kill?"

"You have to destroy their hearts or their brains," Pia said.

"Why do they hate us so much?" Emmy asked, looking like she was about to cry.

"Well, like I said, I can only tell you what I've been told—strictly third-hand info. But werewolves are like vampires—they can be made or born." Pia shrugged. "But the ones that are made, usually from a bite, are very unstable and vicious."

She paused as Darcy poured another finger of whiskey into her glass. Her throat was really dry. She took a drink and looked up to find both women staring expectantly. "Well, those who are born don't like the made ones very much—they tend to bring attention to the whole population. That's partly why there are so few."

"Purges, hunts?" Darcy said.

Pia nodded.

"But that doesn't 'splain why werewolves hate vampires," Emmy said.

Pia frowned, trying to remember the rumors told by other vamps on the fringes of those who would know—the ancient ones. "Their population is very small. They don't usually risk turning humans to werewolves because those creatures tend to be unstable. They need breeders."

Emmy's flushed face blanched pale. Darcy shot her a strained look.

Pia noted the byplay, but her brain was a little too muzzy to understand. "And not many breeders exist," she continued. "So werewolves take it personally when a vamp mates with one." Pia shrugged. "Wouldn't you take it personally if a vamp robbed you of a chance at continuing your species?"

"Bugger," Emmy muttered, shoving her glass away.

"Funny how our two senior citizens never mentioned that story," Darcy murmured.

"It's not common knowledge among vamps — there are very few opportunities for the two species to tread on each other's toes. Breeders are that rare."

Darcy's eyebrows lifted. "Well, I'm glad we had this little talk."

"Me too," Emmy said glumly.

"You don't think your werewolves are sniffing around a breeder, do you?"

"'Course not. What would be the chances?" Emmy said briskly. "Is there any more of that liverwurst?"

Pia looked from one woman to the other. Both their expressions were pinched with worry. Something was definitely up. "So when are you due, Darcy?"

The dark-haired woman's face relaxed fractionally. "At the end of the month," she said, smoothing her hand over the mound of her belly.

"I think that's the only thing I miss about being human," Pia said, sighing.

"Have you been one for very long?" Darcy asked.

Pia grinned. "Well, I'm not as ancient as your old man, Emmy, but I've been around the block a time or two. I was turned back in the twenties."

"You were a flapper girl?" Emmy said, her face lighting with enthusiasm again.

"A gangster's moll, actually. Can't you picture it?"

Emmy tilted her head to the side, smiling. "Carmine red lipstick, one of those chiffon and silk chemises—yeah, I can picture it."

"So what happened?" Darcy asked.

Pia blew out a breath. "The usual. Wrong place, wrong time. I went to a dance hall where the bootleg whiskey was pouring a little too freely." She raised her glass. "I've always loved the taste of whiskey. But I swear, that night I only had two drinks and there I was dancing on a table. I'm sure someone put something in my drink."

Emmy wrinkled her nose. "So, some studly vamp fell for you in a hard way and had to 'trink your blahd'?"

"No. I distracted the partygoers, and G-men raided the party. My table got flipped and next think I knew, I was waking up with a cracked skull and a vamp who looked like Mortimer Snerd sucking me dry."

"Who's Mortimer Snerd?"

Pia laughed. "You're such a baby."

"Well, I liked the sucking you dry part," Darcy said, waggling her eyebrows.

"Darcy! You have such a dirty mind," Emmy cried.

"I can't help it," Darcy said, blushing. "All I think about these days is sex. Quentin won't do the mambo with me until I pop."

"You make it sound like you aren't doing anything!" Emmy rolled her eyes. "What's all that commotion I hear from your wing of the house?"

Darcy swatted Emmy's arm, while Pia chuckled.

"So, was anyone going to tell me there was a new vamp in town?" a new voice chimed from the doorway.

Pia peered around her shoulder, swaying in her chair. "You Lily?"

The newcomer strode inside, dressed in an oversized T-shirt and stretchy pants. Her brown hair glinted red in the light from the chandelier.

Pia's glance caught on the small mound of her stomach pressing against the cotton shirt. "Good God! Is it in the water?"

Chapter Five

໑

Max sat at the far end of the conference room table with his arms folded over his chest, waiting for the rest of the team to assemble. He felt like hell and knew he looked it, too. He hadn't bothered with a shave, and his uniform had that "lived in" smell.

When he'd left the house he hadn't brought a clean uniform with him. He'd just wanted to put as many miles between him and that woman as he could. So he'd changed into the uniform he'd discovered at the bottom of his locker and hit the firing range. Two demolished targets later, he still hadn't worked the rage out of his system.

He'd let her go. His mission in life was to keep people safe—and he'd let a bloodsucker walk. His gut told him she wasn't a stone-cold killer.

For one thing, she'd missed several opportunities to take him out when he was his most vulnerable—sleeping a deep, dreamless sleep beside her, or lost in the wonder of the most powerful orgasms he'd ever experienced.

He snorted, disgusted with himself. He should have known then she wasn't human.

Further, she had puppy-dog eyes—wide, brown, liquid—the kind that tore at your heart. *Not* that she'd touched his. How could anyone who had her soul shining in her eyes hide homicidal tendencies?

The conference room door swung open, and he pushed the memories aside. He had work to do. Werewolves to track and kill. Vampires to expunge from the planet.

Joe walked in, dressed in SU black, a coffee cup in his hand. "Hey buddy."

Max bristled, grunting his displeasure at Joe's familiar greeting.

Despite the less-than-polite acknowledgement he'd received, the vamp sat beside him. His gaze swept over Max. "Looks like you had a rough day."

Max's arms tensed, bulging his biceps as he tried to contain the growl rumbling in his chest.

Joe's lips curved, and he tilted his chair, balancing it on two legs. "Captain Springer had the daytime team pull every report of animal attacks in recent weeks," he said casually. "Other than a few missing dogs attributed to gators, nothing came up. Think we have an isolated incident?"

Max grunted, wishing the others would hurry it up. Making small talk with the undead thing wearing his friend's face made his stomach churn.

"We're going to make the rounds of the 'blood banks' tonight. See whether anyone's heard anything. We'll also check out any new vampires in town."

Max stiffened.

Joe lifted an eyebrow and gave a slight smile—the mischievous sort Max had often seen before Joe turned. "You'll be with me."

"Wearing your flak jacket tonight, *Garcia*?" Max said, keeping his voice even.

"Will I be needing it—*Max*?"

"You never know, *old buddy*."

The door opened again, and the rest of the team filed in. Max forced himself to relax. He felt so wound up, he was a hair-trigger away from exploding. The Captain knew better than to partner him with Joe—he'd made his feelings clear on that issue.

However, the sly look in Joe's face when he'd mentioned scouting for new vamps in town had raised red flags. He knew about Pia. Max had known the bitch was too good to be true—

even before he'd discovered she was a bloodsucker. Just his damn luck the most appealing woman he'd met in years…

Maybe shadowing Joe for the night wasn't such a bad idea. He might get a chance to figure out what she was doing here and how The Council might be involved. Remembering his brother's suggestion to pal around with Joe, Max decided to play it cool and keep his ears and eyes open.

He glanced across the table and found Quentin's gaze trained on him. Something was definitely up. The bastard's face always sported a smirk. Now, his expression was a blank slate.

* * * * *

Max's head pounded in time with the heavy beat of the rock n' roll blaring inside the last stop of the night. Nine Inch Nails music couldn't have been more appropriate for his rotten mood.

"Look, I'm going to speak with the bartender," Joe shouted into his ear. "Why don't you have a look around the backrooms, see whether everyone's playing nice."

Max nodded, glad for the chance to shake Joe off his back for the first time since they'd left the station. Maybe he'd even find some vamp action he could sink his stake into.

The scene in the "blood banks" had undergone a dramatic change since The Council came into being. Before, vamps had always sought their victims in dark alleyways or the restrooms of the "blood banks" — seedy bars where the pickings were easy. Lured by the erotic and sometimes hypnotic nature of the vampires, humans followed them into darkness.

If they were vampires with souls or at least a healthy streak of self-preservation, they played by the rules and drank only enough to sate their appetites while leaving their human hosts slightly dizzy from blood loss. The gift the humans earned in return for serving as meals-on-legs was a powerful sexual release.

Since vamps were hard to spot unless they forgot to retract their teeth or wore their monster faces, Max had often crept into dank, dark hidey-holes to catch a vamp in action and dust him.

Now vamps had public places, poorly lit backrooms in bars, where humans and vamps could mix and be watched. This was considered an improvement. So long as the sexual conduct remained fairly PG, no one interfered with consensual blood sharing. Prostitutes and thrill-seekers were the only human fare—that was another rule: No innocents could be taken here.

When Max pushed through the door of the "feeding room", he hoped for one little scream so he could let loose.

The heavy thump of the drums was just as loud here as in the main hall, because the room was packed. The sound of the bass beat was muffled, but insistent, like a relentless, throbbing heart. A colorful light ball spun overhead, painting the patrons in strobing, rainbow colors while they undulated to the music and their sexual fervor.

Max edged around the room, checking the humans to make sure they were conscious and pink-cheeked. Unfortunately, everyone appeared to be playing nice.

Then he caught a glance of a familiar mane of glossy brown hair among the dancers. He shoved between gyrating bodies until he stood behind Pia and her human meal. The young man was groping her backside, grinding his hips into hers while her face snuggled into the crook of his neck.

Max's shoulders bunched tight as steel, and he saw red. His hand sought the stake deep inside his pocket, but he realized he didn't want to kill her.

No, he wanted to plant it deep inside the chest of the man who looked ready to shoot his load in his pants.

Max watched the pair, letting his anger grow with each passing second until the man's face tightened with his release. Pia held him while the young man spasmed, gasping as his orgasm rushed through him. Then she slowly pulled away, licking his neck to close the punctures.

At the sight of Pia raising her face to kiss the guy's cheek, Max had all he could take. He stepped forward and clamped his hand on her shoulder, squeezing hard.

Pia glanced back, but didn't look particularly surprised to see him. Blood stained her lips, and her vamp teeth peeked beneath her upper lip. She turned to her host and murmured something that made him smile. He let her go and headed for the bar. Then she shrugged her shoulder.

Max dropped his hand, but reached for her wrist and tugged her hard, pulling her into his arms. "Didn't you get my message, *sweetheart*?"

She pressed her hands against his chest and glared. "A girl has to eat. I worked up quite an appetite last night."

Slipping the stake from his pocket, he glided it along the bare skin of her midriff. "Don't think I won't carry through. I let you off light the last time."

She shivered, and her nipples flowered, scraping his chest. "I'm a girl who appreciates a good, hard poke." Holding his gaze, she licked the last traces of blood from her lips with a sensual sweep of her tongue. Her incisors remained protracted.

Max's body tightened, hard as the stake inside his fist. "You just happened to be here, right? My last stop of the night."

Her eyelids shuttered her expressive gaze. "And if I said, I've been following you?"

"No way. You got here before I did."

Pia lifted her lips fractionally, baring the length of her fangs. "I work fast."

"You wanted me to see you feed on him?"

"I want you to know what I am. I don't want secrets."

"Why would it matter to me?"

Rising on her toes, she whispered next to his ear, "Because I don't want to worry that when I sleep in your arms, you'll destroy me."

With the stake still in one hand, Max gripped her upper arms to push her back. Looking down into her face, he said, "That's assuming we'll ever share a bed again."

"Won't you? Don't you want me?" Her hand crept down the front of his pants and cupped him. "Tell me this isn't all for me."

His erection burned at her touch. Much as he would have preferred to deny her, he did want her. But it was just a physical thing, he told himself—she was one hot little lay.

He grabbed her hand, intending to shove it away. But through his slacks, he could feel the heat from it, and her fingers curved around him, squeezing. Instead of doing what he should have, he held her hand against him, encouraging her to rub up and down his length. "I hate this," he bit out. "I hate you."

She tongued his nipple through his T-shirt. "But you love the sex, don't you? So do I." Her mouth pouted, and her gaze smoldered. She glided her hand beneath to cup his balls. "I want you to fuck my brains out, Max."

Max drew a deep breath, fighting his need for this woman, reminding himself—*she's the enemy, a demon in a pretty package.*

A demon who was driving him out of his mind with her sexy little nibbles. Her fangs scraped his skin through his shirt, while her hands played with his dick and ass.

He shuddered, knowing he was quickly losing this battle of wills. He snagged her wrists and forced her arms behind her, bending her back.

Excitement brought a rose flush to her skin. "Are you going to do it here, Max? Are you going to sink that stake deep inside me?"

Witch! Oh, he wanted to sink something into her—the same something they were really thinking about. He wanted to drill a hole through his uniform to get at her. He slid his fingers around her arm and pulled her to a dark, shadowed corner, pressing her back against the wall.

Her expression wasn't gloating—it was tight, flushed. She wanted this as badly as he did. He dug beneath the hem of her cropped top until his fingers spread out, cupping the mound of her breast—the one he'd painted with her blood.

Her nipple hardened, and Pia leaned into his hand, encouraging him to strengthen his grip.

He squeezed the little globe and plucked the velvety nipple with his fingers.

Pia opened her legs and slipped her hands inside the back pockets of his pants to pull his hips between hers.

Max couldn't help but rub his erection against her. With one hand, he sought the juncture of her thighs. This time no scrap of silk covered her sex—she was naked.

"See?" she whispered. "I've been waiting for you."

Her sex was hot—so wet, moisture trickled down his fingers as he delved between her lips. "For all I know, you've been fucking your way through dinner tonight."

She flinched, but quickly relaxed her expression and offered him a sly smile. "Jealous? I promise the only cum you'll find inside me will be yours."

He fingered her nether lips, sliding back and forth in her juices. "You want this? You want to do this here?"

Her hips danced on his fingers. "Yes," she moaned. "*Now.*"

He groaned and then remembered what was in his other hand. Although, his body was so hard he could break bricks, he went cold at his core. He trailed the tip of stake up the inside of her thigh.

Her eyes widened with alarm.

"Don't you trust me?"

She swallowed hard, her gaze locked with his. "If you tell me you won't kill me now, then yes."

He pressed the blunt end about an inch into her pussy. "Don't worry about splinters. I sanded it myself. It will slide in smooth as satin."

Her eyes widened, but her body shivered and gushed its approval. Her mouth trembled and Max noted a battle seemed to be fought behind her brown eyes—she didn't want to want this, and she was frightened.

Good. He lifted one eyebrow—a challenge. "Tell me what you want."

"Kiss me," she said, her eyes glistening with tears, "and then fuck me with that stake. Satisfy your need to drive it into me, Max."

Max leaned down and kissed her, sliding his mouth over hers, drinking her moans. His tongue licked her lips and slipped between, touching the tips of her fangs then sliding deeper to stroke her tongue.

Opening her legs wider, Pia lifted a leg to hook over his thigh. "Do it," she whispered.

With both hands between her legs now, he spread her lips wide and pushed the stake gently inside her, his thumb flicking her clitoris. Her moans deepened against his mouth, and he made his kiss rougher, harder, until he drew her tongue into his mouth and sucked.

He'd thought he had control—a dispassionate distance from which he could love her body and steal her pride. But his hands shook with his own raging desire.

Her body writhed against him as he pushed the wooden stake deeper and began stroking her vagina with short, pulsing glides. Pia's hands shook as she sought the belt at his waist and unbuckled it, found the snap at the top of his pants and lowered his zipper. Then her strong, hot hands were wrapped around his cock.

Max forgot where he was, forgot there were people all around them. The woman groaning against his lips and fisting his cock was his whole world. He growled and stroked his penis between her hands.

"Bastard! Tell me you're not fucking her with a goddamn stake!"

Max jerked at the deadly sound of Joe's voice. He lifted his mouth from Pia's and stared down at her. Slowly, he slid the stake from her. His body shook with unspent desire and rage at his partner's interruption. But in the back of his mind there was also a healthy dose of shame for himself.

He slipped the stake into his pocket, while Pia lowered her leg and straightened her skirt. He shoved his engorged cock back into his pants, and then he turned to face the vampire behind him.

Joe's face was a mottled red. "Pia, get behind me."

"So you know each other," Max said quietly, feeling his stomach clench that his suspicions about Pia might be true.

"Just met today, *partner*."

"I'm not in any danger, Joe," Pia said.

"You don't know Max, sweetheart. Get behind me."

Feeling like a bear protecting his mate, Max stepped between Joe and Pia, clenching his fists. "I gave her my word I wouldn't harm her here."

"No, you didn't," Pia said.

Max leveled a narrow glance at her.

Pia shrugged. "I asked, but you never promised."

Joe's shoulders bunched like he was ready to take a swing. "We're still on the fucking job."

Max shrugged. "So we were blending in."

"You went too far."

Knowing Joe was right didn't ease the ache in Max's groin. He turned to Pia. Unfortunately, looking into her face didn't help matters any either. Her lips were still dewy and reddened from his kisses, and her nipples poked at the fabric of her miniscule top. He forced his shoulders to relax. "I have to get back to the station."

"Can I ride along?" she asked, leaning into him, her eyes wide and pleading. Her nipples scraped his side, and it was all he could do keep from sliding his palm over them again.

"No!" He almost shouted the word. "It's probably best this way. This thing between us won't work."

"Because I'm a vampire?" she asked, her eyes glistening.

"That's just the beginning of our problems."

Her expression fell, but she nodded. "I understand." Turning to Joe, she said, "I'll just get a taxi."

"We can drop you off on our way." Joe gave Max a searing glance and then spun on his heels.

Pia followed him out of the bar with Max trailing them at a distance. Distance he needed to get himself back under control. Moonlight from a full moon in a cloudless sky drew his gaze, but he shrugged aside its allure. He'd had enough moonlit madness for one night.

At their sedan, Joe tossed Max the keys. "You drive. I want your hands occupied."

Max twisted his mouth into a hard smile. "What's your problem? Gone all righteous, have you?"

Joe opened the back door for Pia while Max climbed inside.

"Whoo!" she gasped as she settled on the seat. "The vinyl's a little cold."

Remembering she wore no underwear beneath her short skirt, Max closed his eyes for a moment and took a deep breath. Then he jammed the key into the ignition and cranked the engine into life. Before Joe could close his door, Max stomped on the gas and the car leaped forward.

"The sooner we get there the better," Joe mumbled, slamming the door closed.

Pia clutched the back of their bench seat and leaned forward. "Do we have to go straight back?"

"Yes!" Max and Joe shouted.

"Just asking."

Max's fingers gripped the steering wheel hard. "Where am I taking you?"

"To The Compound. My rental's there. I'm already packed."

Max grew still. "You're leaving Vero Beach?"

"The climate's a little too sticky for me," she said, her breath licking at his neck.

"Good." Joe's response was more of a grunt.

Max told himself this way was best. Let her go. Save him the bother of dusting her later. Because he knew if she stayed, he wouldn't be able to keep his hands off her. Eventually, she'd show her true colors, and he'd never allow a vamp to take a drop of his blood.

The radio squawked, and Phil Carstair's voice broke over the channel reserved for SU business. "I need back up. Wolves have been spotted at the Piki Tiki. Anyone in the vicinity?"

Max's body grew rigid while adrenaline shot into his veins. Not fucking again!

Joe grabbed the handset. "Max and I are on our way. How many do you ha—"

"We got to drop off Pia first," Max interrupted.

"Hell no!" she said. "I'm weapons-trained. You might need me."

"Weapons-trained?" Max asked. The flame fanned beneath the fire of his suspicions regarding her reasons for being here. Sweet Pia was weapons-trained—and she just happened to be in that bar last night...

"Pull the car over," Joe said. "We'll let her out at that gas station." He pointed ahead at a well-lit parking lot and raised the handset to his mouth again. "Wait for backup. I repeat, wait for backup."

"Roger that," Phil said. "What's your ETA?"

"You're not leaving me behind," Pia said. "You need all the help you can get."

"You're damn well going to do as you're told," Max said, his voice hard and loud. No way was she going to get into the middle of this operation. The only danger she'd face would be him, after the pack was taken care of.

"Max is right," Joe said. "You're staying out of danger."

Max slowed down to pull into the parking lot.

"I'll just tell the man pumping gas to follow you," Pia said. "I can be *very* persuasive."

Max cursed under his breath. He knew damn well just how persuasive she could be. Her sweet body was another weapon in her arsenal. All she had to do was lift her skirt an inch…

He shot a glance at Joe, but his partner's mouth was tight-lipped.

"You better hurry," Pia said. "Your friend sounded a little worried."

The little witch! Joe and Max shared a glance. They didn't have time to ditch Pia.

Joe cursed and raised the mike again. "We'll be there in five."

"We've already cleared out any civilians along the boardwalk," Phil said. "See ya, buddies."

Max peeled out of the parking lot and gunned the engine again. "Just how much experience do you have with a gun?"

"Plenty. And I almost always hit my target."

"*Almost* always?" He glanced in the rearview mirror.

Her eyes sparkled with excitement. "I *usually* hit where I aim."

"Sweet Jesus!" Joe groaned. "Quentin's gonna have my ass if I give her a weapon."

"Should we let her go in without one?"

"I don't suppose you just want to watch?" Joe asked. "From a safe distance?"

A scowl darkened her expression. "You're not leaving me behind. I'm not helpless. I've been in Special Ops for twelve years now."

"And just how many of your fellow officers have you shot?" Joe asked.

Max blinked and looked at her in his rearview mirror.

Pia's mouth twisted in disgust. "Just one...well, two...if you count the time I tripped on a fallen tree limb. But that wasn't my fault."

"What are you?" Max asked. "The Barney Fife of vamp cops?"

"I excel at 'undercover' work," she said snidely. "You should know."

"Sweetheart, I've half a mind to lock you in the trunk while we answer the call."

"Do you really think that will hold me?" she said, her voice dripping sweet sarcasm.

"Fuck!" Max turned into the parking lot that flanked the boardwalk along the beach. He killed the engine, hit the trunk latch, and bounded out of the car.

With light shining from the streetlights above and the pale lamp from the trunk lid, Max and Joe strapped on their web belts and slid percussive grenades into metal loops. Almost in unison they drew their Glocks and depressed the buttons on the sides of their weapons to eject the clips with the standard issue bullets. From an ammo box, they drew clips with the special new issue—silver-filled bullets.

"What about me?" Pia asked as she peered into the trunk from behind Max's shoulder.

He stepped on the bumper of the car and reached beneath the hem of his trousers. He pulled out a gun and laid it in her palm.

"Don't I get ammo, too?"

"It's already loaded with what you need."

He watched as she drew back the barrel and pressed the button to drive it forward again. Satisfied she knew which end of the gun she held, he reached for the flak jackets. He offered one to her.

"Uh-huh," she said, shaking her head. "I might need to move fast."

Max continued to hold it out. "You'll wear it, or I'll hog-tie you and strap you to the steering wheel."

Pia's eyes narrowed, and her lower lip jutted out.

Max lifted one brow.

"Oh, all right." She swiped the flak jacket from his hands and shrugged into it.

Max assisted, closing the Velcro tabs.

She scowled ferociously. "If one of those puppy dogs bites my ass because I couldn't get away fast enough, you'll be hearing about it."

Max leaned down and put his forehead against hers. "Baby, no one's biting your ass but me."

Chapter Six

"Promises, promises."

Max found himself grinning as he heard Pia mutter beneath her breath. He made quick work of his own jacket. When he finished closing the fastenings, he glanced up to see Joe staring, a one-sided smile quirking his mouth.

Max wiped the smile from his lips. "Not one fucking word from you, *partner*." The last piece of equipment he donned was the headset. He slid it over his head, lowered the thin microphone wand to his lips and flipped the switch. "Phil, we're in the parking lot. Where are you now?"

"In back of the bar. We're going in through the kitchen."

"We'll take the front door. I'll give the signal when we're ready." Max spared a glance over his shoulder to make sure Joe and Pia were wired in. Then he climbed the steps to the boardwalk and loped toward the bar.

"I'm taking the rear," Joe said. "I'm not getting in front of Pia while she's waving that gun around."

"Scared, Joe?" Pia asked, her breath even despite the pace.

"Spitless, sweetheart. Quentin told me the whole story."

"Huh! Betcha he didn't tell you everything. Quentin's a pussy."

"I heard that!" Quentin's voice broke over the channel. "Tell me that walking disaster doesn't have a gun."

"Quentin!" Pia said, her voice filled with aggravation. "That was four years ago. I'm quite the markswoman now."

"So long as it's someone else's ass you mark, my dear."

Max was glad when the Piki Tiki's bamboo awning came into view. The vamp banter was making him ill. That hint of history between Pia and Quentin pricked his jealousy. He halted at the corner of the building and held up his hand. "This is the way it's going down. Joe and I'll go through the front door. Pia, you'll cover us from the window."

"I'm awfully glad I'll have the pots and pans to duck behind," Quentin said. "I'm coming through the kitchen with Phil."

"When I count three, Pia will start laying down cover fire." Max swung around to stare hard at Pia. "You are up for this, right? You weren't exaggerating your skills."

"She's the real deal, Max," Joe said. "She has the training. But she did shoot Quentin in the ass."

Max snorted. "Well, that's no sin in my eyes."

"Don't say I didn't warn you," Quentin said, his voice wry.

Pia rolled her eyes. "Showtime," she said softly, holding Max's gaze. Then she shook her head.

In three shakes, all traces of the soft, sexy kitten he'd held in his arms half an hour ago were gone. In her place stood a vamp with long curved incisors. As he watched, her forehead changed shape. The bones beneath her skin shifted outward, growing until she was unrecognizable—except for the chocolate shade of her eyes.

Her lips curved into a maniacal smile. "Some men only worry about what their girlfriends look like without their makeup." Her voice was deeper, with an odd, gruff inflection.

Max winced. "Why are you the only one donning a mask?"

"I'm only partway transformed. I need the extra muscle." She held up her arm. "Wanna feel?"

Max shook his head. "So long as you keep your monster reined in, I don't care. Come on, Joe." He strode to the side of the building, and peered through the window. The scene inside was chilling.

Three wolves in various stages of transformation had half a dozen vamps and a human bartender trapped in a corner. A dark-furred wolf, still walking on two legs, swiped his claws at a male vamp, shredding his clothing and drawing four bloody lines across his chest. The vamp screamed through a row of jagged teeth and charged, wrapping his arms around the wolf to lift him off his feet.

The pair crashed to the floor and rolled. But the wolf quickly gained the advantage and opened his jaws wide to close around the vamp's throat. With a shake of his powerful shoulders, the wolf separated the vamp's head from his body and the vamp exploded into a dark cloud of dust. His clothing floated to the floor.

"Bastards," Pia whispered beside him.

"They're just doing what's natural," Max said, giving her a steady stare. "Offing vamps."

Pia turned her head and lifted her upper lip, baring her fangs.

"Not your best look, baby."

"Good thing I'm not trying to impress you then, hmm?"

Max turned his attention back to the interior of the Piki Tiki bar. This place had quite a history—a long association with the vamp scene well before they came out of the closet.

He hoped the owner had good insurance. The bar was trashed. Tables were overturned, chairs lay in splinters, attesting to the battle that had raged inside. Broken glass sparkled like diamonds on the tiled floor.

A wolf with golden fur circled in front of the group huddled in the corner, snapping and snarling. Suddenly, he faced off with the vamps, lowering his head until it nearly touched the ground. A rumbling growl built in his chest. Each time one of the vamps looked ready to answer his challenge, he neatly corralled him back like a dog herding sheep.

The vamps returned the rumbling, snarl for snarl. However, they soon didn't attempt to step outside their corner.

It was a standoff, with the golden wolf in the superior position. His pack mates had only to wait for him to cull the vamps from the herd, one by one.

"I hadn't realized they were so goddamn big," Joe's whispers came through the headset. He still hovered behind Pia at the end of the building.

"How would anyone mistake them for dogs?" Pia said in her odd, gruff voice. "They're all monsters, but that gold one's the worst. He knows what he's doing."

Max agreed this wolf was a bigger danger than the others. His actions were calculated, intelligent. However much he might empathize with these wolves' lust for vamp blood, they weren't discriminating about what they chomped on. They'd kill humans just as quick. "We better move now," he whispered, and gave Pia a final look. "Make your shots count, baby. The head or the chest."

Pia nodded and crouched beside the corner of the window, her weapon held steady in both hands.

He ducked beneath the window so the occupants within the bar wouldn't see him as he sped toward the entrance. At the door, he counted, "On three. One, two, three." As gunfire erupted from the front and back of the bar, he shoved open the glass door, tossed a grenade, and rolled into the room. When he came to his feet, he aimed and fired at the golden wolf just as the grenade exploded, shattering more glass and distracting the wolves momentarily.

His first shot struck the wolf in the shoulder. The wolf staggered back and then shook himself. Rather than doing the expected and charging toward Max, he leapt into the air, bypassing Max. In a second bound, he broke through the large plate glass window, landing on the boardwalk outside.

Max had only a moment to spare a thought for Pia, before a dark-furred wolf crashed into him.

He rolled with the beast, struggling to bring up his gun.

The wolf clamped his teeth over the shoulder of Max's flak jacket in a bone-crunching grip and shook his powerful head.

Max flailed, helpless for a moment, and then clutched the fur at the wolf's neck. All his strength focused on raising his gun. He pressed the barrel beneath the wolf's jaw and pulled the trigger.

In a spray of blood and gray matter, the wolf crumpled on top of Max. He shoved it away and struggled to his feet.

Joe and Quentin battled the third wolf. By the looks of things, Max almost felt sorry for the beast. In the close confines of the bar, the vamps had forgone their weapons for hand-to-hand combat. They wore their vamp masks and traded blows and bites with the wolf. The muddy brown wolf was quickly losing the fight. Blood streamed from his mouth and nose, his chest heaved.

Max swung back to the window and realized Pia's weapon was silent. With a roar of anger, he ran to the door and jerked it open. The boardwalk was empty.

His heart thudded. The wolf had taken Pia—might already have destroyed her. But which way had he gone?

"Pia! Can you hear me?" he shouted into his mike. He stood still, trying to separate the shouts and sounds of fighting inside the bar. Then he heard it—feminine gasps. She was hurt and scared, but she was alive. "Baby, hold on. I'm coming."

The streetlamp barely illuminated the beach beyond the wooden planks. The shadows hid the wolf's tracks. He jumped over the railing onto the sand below.

They could be anywhere. He had to find her. But first, he needed to be able to follow the scent of the wounded male.

Max's hands stripped open the Velcro fastenings, and he dropped the jacket to the ground. He ripped at the rest of his clothing and equipment until he stood naked beneath the lamplight.

Please don't let me be too late.

Pulling strength from the glare of the full moon, Max let the transformation come over him in a rush powered by his anger. His teeth slid from the roof of his mouth. His face stretched, the bones cracking as they reached outward. Then he dropped to the sand as his body lengthened and fur sprouted from his skin. Within seconds he caught the musty scent of the male wolf — and the acrid smell of a woman's fear.

Max, the wolf, leapt from the boardwalk onto the beach and followed the trail of the other male's scent. Lost was Pia's name. Only a vision of a dark-haired woman with soft skin and round, wide eyes shimmered in his mind to match the scent. His strides stretched as he neared them, the woman and the golden wolf, and a deep-throated roar broke from him.

The golden wolf spun to face him. He held the woman by her torso, his large jaws clamped over the black covering encasing her upper body. The wolf was a powerful, potent adversary — and this close his scent was…familiar.

Weakened, the woman beat the golden wolf about the head with her fists, trying to dislodge his powerful jaws.

The dark wolf lifted his head and howled. His mate was in danger. Another had attacked what belonged to him alone. Fur lifted on his shoulders and back as he stalked toward the rogue wolf.

Pia gasped in agony. She figured the enormous wolf that held her had crushed every rib along her right side. Why he hadn't killed her outright? He could have so easily. Sure he'd go for Max inside the bar, she'd stared transfixed with horror when the wolf broke through the glass and landed beside her.

When he'd swung toward her, she hadn't time to raise her weapon before he was upon her. In the attack, she'd lost her weapon, and could only offer a feeble defense once he'd crushed her side with his enormous jaws, preventing her from taking a full breath. Then he'd lifted her and ran into the darkness while she flailed like a rag doll.

She'd thought he took a bullet in the shoulder, but the wound didn't seem to slow him. Obviously, someone had missed the two vital organs that could have brought him down. But why hadn't the silver bullet affected him? She wondered if perhaps it had passed through him, and therefore the poisonous affect of the silver hadn't had a chance to do its work on his body.

Now a second wolf, slightly larger than the monster that held her, stalked toward them. His coat glistened like polished coal in the moonlight and rippled with the flex of his powerful muscles. Believing the next few seconds would be her last, Pia's thoughts skipped to Max. She prayed hard that he was safe, and harder still that he'd find happiness.

The black wolf growled and snapped its teeth, and suddenly, she was released. She hit the ground and rolled to the side. Searing pain took what little air she could suck into her lungs. Slowly, she came to her knees.

The black wolf sidled toward her, answering the golden one's growls with a rumbling roar that emanated from deep inside his chest. The sound sent shivers up her spine. He stood between her and the golden wolf now.

Despite her pain, Pia tried to edge backward, but the black wolf turned and nudged her with a cold nose—an oddly tender action that confused her. Had he just told her to sit tight?

Dimly, Pia grew aware of shouts from the direction of the boardwalk. If she could have drawn a deep breath she would have screamed, but the effort of breathing was quickly diminishing her strength.

Then the black wolf raised his head and howled.

"Over here," Quentin shouted.

The golden one snarled and darted forward, snapping at the black's front hocks.

The black answered with a lunge and sank his teeth into the neck of his foe.

The two, well-matched in size and strength, rolled in the sand, their snarling growls growing deeper, their gnashing teeth inflicting more vicious wounds by the second.

Pia tried to retain her mask and vamp bulk, but she felt her strength seep from her body until her human form slipped to the sand, panting to ease the pain burning her lungs.

The pounding of booted feet hitting the sand drew nearer, and the golden wolf wriggled free of the black's hold before dashing away into the darkness.

Then the black wolf turned back to her, his fur glistening now from saliva and blood. He padded toward her, his head down, his chest heaving, until his face was inches from hers.

"Pia, hold very still. We're going to take him out." Quentin's harsh monster-voice echoed as if rising from a deep well.

She stared at the wolf, drawn by the unblinking gaze of his gold eyes. He was magnificent! Larger than any wolf she'd ever seen in a zoo. His head was broad, his neck thick, and his chest wide and deeply muscled. His black coat looked soft and lustrous. Slowly, she lifted her hand beneath his snout, half expecting he'd bite it off.

Instead, he gently nudged her palm with his nose and lowered himself to the sand.

"Don't hurt him," she whispered, raking her fingers through the matted fur around his face. He smelled like a dog— fresh, slightly musty, except for the tangy scent of the blood on his neck and shoulders. "He's a friend. He saved my life." She wasn't sure how she knew that, but the certainty grew stronger as she stroked his fur.

"We have to destroy him, Pia," Quentin said. "He's part of the pack that's been murdering humans and vamps."

"Not right," she gasped to get the words past her lips. "He...wasn't inside. Came later."

"Anyone seen Max?" Joe asked.

Pia peered up to see Joe and another officer, Phil she guessed, join Quentin. Their weapons were raised and pointed straight at the dark creature beside her. She struggled to her knees and crawled in front of the wolf.

"Dammit, Pia. Get out of the way." Quentin stepped forward, but the wolf's growl halted him.

Grasping his fur, Pia leaned into the wolf. "Go!" she whispered. "I'm safe." She wasn't sure he understood.

He whined and nuzzled his snout against her neck.

She turned slowly to the men. Their faces were hard, determined. They'd shoot him without a second thought— unless she pulled out a bigger weapon. "Shoot him, Quentin…and I'll tell Darcy…exactly where that bullet hit you…and who dug it out of your ass."

"Pia!" Quentin's voice rose in warning.

"I'm not kidding."

Quentin's mask melted. "For fuck sake. He's a goddamn werewolf—not a lapdog. He's dangerous."

"I can start with where the surgery was performed…"

Quentin blew out a breath. "Lower your weapons," he said, his voice sounding as disappointed as a child denied his dessert.

Pia shifted back to the wolf. "Go!"

But he lay there, and his tongue lapped at her fingers.

Tears filled her eyes. Her chest burned like fire and this stupid lupine was quickly losing his chance to lift his leg on another fire hydrant. "Go!" she shouted, shoving him as hard as she could manage.

Finally, the wolf rose to his feet. With a glare at the men standing beyond her, he turned and loped into the darkness.

Quentin stepped forward and knelt beside her in the sand. "Are you all right?" he asked, reaching to tuck her hair behind her ear.

Fighting to keep from crying like a baby now the danger was past, she asked, "Did you get the other two wolves?"

"Yeah," Joe said, as he joined them. He reached for the fastenings on her jacket and stripped them open. "What the hell happened with the light-colored one?"

"Blackie chased him off."

Joe's eyebrows lifted and he gently shoved the jacket off her shoulders. "Blackie? You want a pet that bad, why don't you move in with Max?"

"Max isn't housebroken." Pia winced as she pulled her arms from the jacket. "Where is he, anyway?"

"That's a good question," Joe murmured. "Quentin, you want to go back and see where he went—he might have followed another trail. If that yellow dog circles back…"

"Do I have to save his ass?" Quentin asked.

"You do unless you want me to tell your secrets, Quentin," Pia said, working her face into a scowl.

Cursing, Quentin swiped her flak jacket from the ground and headed back the way they'd come.

"You must be feeling better if you want to boss him around," Joe said.

"I am." Thank God for a vamp's rapid healing. She could actually draw a deep breath. "Just help me to my feet."

"You are one stubborn woman." Joe bent to place his shoulder beneath her arm and helped her rise to her feet.

Pia swayed and then pushed away from Joe. "We have to look for Max."

They walked back to the boardwalk. Joe assisted her as she climbed the steps. A crowd of black-clad SU officers hovered outside the Piki Tiki. The first of the body bags passed out the door.

Pia scanned the crowd, anxious to find Max to know he'd escaped injury. But she was disappointed when she didn't see him.

"He can take care of himself," Joe said, quietly.

"Is it so obvious I'm worried about him?"

"You're biting your lip."

"Who are you worried about?" Max asked, from directly behind her.

Pia screeched and whirled. She launched herself against his chest, throwing her arms around his neck to hug him hard. "Where the hell have you been?"

"Hunting." He hugged her back.

Pain shot through her side and she gasped.

Max dropped his arms and tried to step back.

Pia wouldn't let go of his neck and snuggled close to his chest again.

"Are you all right?" His arms closed gently around her this time.

"Mmmm. Fine now." She closed her eyes and rubbed her hands up and down his back. His bare back. Tilting her head, she gazed up at him. "What happened to your jacket and shirt?"

"I wrestled with a wolf—they stink."

Something in his eyes told her there was more to the explanation. But she'd kept secrets. In fact, she still had one, so she figured he was entitled to a few of his own. She snuggled close to his chest and inhaled. He did smell like a dog—just like Blackie had.

"Next time, let someone know where the hell you've gone," Quentin said.

Pia lifted her head to watch his approach. When she did, she noticed for the first time the angry red scratches on Max's torso and the deeper cuts on the side of his neck. "Why the hell did you remove your flak jacket?"

Max's smile was strained. "So I could move faster."

"You need to have those seen to."

"Later. We have some clean-up here, before I can leave."

"For fucksake, get out of here," Quentin said, waving him away. "Stow your gear in the SU van. Joe will make sure it gets turned in. Go to hospital."

Max stiffened.

Pia reached for his hand. "He's right—even if it's Quentin saying it—you need to go to the hospital." She tugged to pull him along.

Max walked stiff-legged behind her. When they reached the car, he pulled the keys from his pocket.

"You're not driving," Pia said, holding out her hand, palm-up.

Max planted his hands on his hips—and intimidating look from such a large man. "If your driving is as dismal as your shooting, I want to be behind the wheel."

She jutted her chin. She wasn't backing down from this one. "You're not driving. You could pass out on the way to the hospital."

"I'm not hurt that badly—and what about you? You need to have those ribs seen to."

"I'm a vampire. I heal fast." The way the blood zoomed through her veins now, she was well on her way to recovery. Arguing with Max ought to be prescribed for pain-relief.

"I'm only scratched."

"Those don't look like scratches to me," she said, pointing at his neck. "Give me the keys."

He sighed and looked toward the star-bright sky, stubborn tension bunching the muscles of his arms. "You're not going to leave me alone, are you?"

Pia grew still. "Is that what you want?" she said softly.

Max lowered his gaze. He stared at her for a long moment.

So long, Pia worried he would tell her something she didn't want to hear.

Instead, he laid the keys in her palm. "Take me home."

She closed her hand around the keys and dragged in a relieved breath. "To the hospital, you mean."

"I have supplies at home. You can take care of me there."

Taking him home meant he wanted to have sex. Her heart leapt at the prospect. "Is your tetanus up to date?"

"Last year. And werewolves don't carry rabies." He raised her chin with a finger, and his thumb caressed her lower lip. "Take me home, Pia."

Although framed as a demand, his voice held invitation. A warm, softly feminine feeling, a feeling she hadn't known for a very long time, settled inside her chest.

But the wounds on his neck were blood-encrusted. He might not think he needed a hospital, but she couldn't bear it if something bad were to happen. She pushed his head up to get a closer look at his neck. "Were you bitten?"

Max's expression shuttered. "I'm fine. Take me home, Pia."

She jerked open the car door. "Fine. Get in the car."

Max let himself into the car and leaned back against the seat.

She started the car, and then looked over at him. "You'd tell me if one of those bastards bit you, wouldn't you? I wouldn't want you going all furry on me."

Max leaned his head against the headrest and closed his eyes, shutting out Pia's face. Her worry warmed his heart.

If she only knew…

Chapter Seven

Pia pushed Max into a chair in the kitchen, and busied herself with the contents of his first aid kit. If she thought he might let her, she'd just lick the wounds until they closed. But she was pretty sure Max would be funny about vampire "gifts".

"You don't have to do this," Max said quietly. "I'll get a shower."

"Just stop, will you?" She grabbed cotton gauze and peroxide and hurried back. "Is this a macho thing? You have some ugly scratches."

His hand closed over hers. "I didn't bring you here to nurse me."

"You didn't bring me here—I did the driving." She uncapped the bottle. "These scratches could get infected."

Standing between his open legs, she poured some of the peroxide on the gauze and wiped at the bloody wounds on his chest. "I should really be pissed. You made me wear that heavy vest, but you couldn't keep yours on for five minutes."

"It got in the way," he murmured.

The blood dissolved, and she used a fresh piece of gauze to blot the rest of the dark brown smears from his chest and neck. When she was finished, she drew back her hand. The wounds were nearly healed. Only faint pink tracings remained on his skin.

Her mouth gaped and she looked up. *How was it possible?* Her gaze locked with his.

Max's mouth curved into a feral grin. "I told you I didn't need it."

She swallowed, suddenly uneasy. His stare was too intent—too predatory. "You heal fast."

"Fast as you," he whispered. He trailed his fingers from her shoulders to her wrists.

Shivering with equal parts of fear and desire, she stepped back. His hands closed on her hips. She jerked away—but he held her fast. The strength of his grip was surprising—*inhuman*.

She pushed back a niggling suspicion, one that would make her desire for this man a betrayal to her own kind. "Y-you must have some metabolism," she said, dropping the gauze to the floor.

"It's hereditary. All my line shares the same…metabolism." His eyes glinted as he pulled her closer. His legs were a vise, holding her immobile.

Pia's heart thundered. Her brain screamed caution, but her body melted against his.

His hands swept up her back to tangle in the hair at her nape. He jerked her head back and brought his lips to her neck.

If what her mind suspected were true, she shouldn't trust him not to harm her when she was so vulnerable to his bite—*but she did*.

"We share the same appetites." He bit her neck, hard enough to bruise, but not break her skin.

Pia's breath caught, and her body trembled. She was either in very deep shit here or Max had a *Psycho* fetish. Whichever didn't matter at the moment, her mind focused on the sensual bombardment his body and mouth were delivering. She struggled to offer one last coherent response, "Do you all the share physical characteristics? Your strength? Your incredible…organs?"

"Yes!" His tongue trailed up her neck, and he licked the lobe of her ear.

Her hands clenched the tops of his shoulders. "Then your women are blessed."

"They're too few."

He was telling her something here, but all she could register was the heat of his mouth, gliding back down her neck. "You only need one at a time."

"Huh!" His breath gusted with single laugh. "You're in denial, baby."

"Who's doing the denying?" She was so aroused her skin tingled everywhere they touched, and she wished he'd just stop talking. "I'm getting hornier by the second — *Max*." She pressed her body to his, mashing her breasts against his chest and grinding her sex into his enormous erection.

He let go of her hair and gripped the neck of her shirt. "I need you naked," he said, with a harsh edge to his voice that tightened the coil of sensual tension that curled inside her belly. He ripped her shirt apart.

The bra quickly followed, and Pia reveled in the violence of his act and his hot, hungry stare. Her nipples beaded, hard as pebbles. She gasped when his hands covered her and squeezed.

She shoved down her skirt past her hips, but it bunched where his thighs clasped hers together. "I want to be naked for you, Max."

He spread his thighs, but his mouth never left her skin, sliding over her shoulders.

Pia pushed her skirt lower until it drifted down to puddle around her feet. Then she sought his zipper and opened his pants. His erection fell into her hand, and she wrapped her fingers around him and squeezed.

"Yes," he moaned, and his chest rose and fell faster against hers, further exciting her nipples.

Pia climbed onto his strong, splayed thighs.

His hands sought her buttocks, steadying her as she straddled him.

Then she centered the blunt tip of his cock at the opening of her vagina and sank down. He felt thick as a tree trunk, stretching her inner walls. When at last her pussy met the wiry hair at the base of his cock, she groaned, letting her legs spread and dangle on either side of his widespread thighs.

She wriggled her hips, circling until every last inch of his length lodged deep inside her pussy. "We have a problem now," she said, nuzzling his neck.

"I can't think of one." His hands gripped her ass and pushed her hips forward and back, creating a burning friction.

"But I can't move." She scraped the turgid points of her breasts across his chest. "I need to move."

He raised his head. "But you can," he said, his voice slightly hoarse with strain. His next kiss was straight on, noses touching. His open mouth pressed to hers, then withdrew with a suctioning smack. "Rock on me."

Pia rolled her hips, but the movements weren't the deep, gliding ones she needed. Without something upon which to brace her knees, she couldn't rise. "I need more."

"Is this what you want?" His hands pushed her hips back and forth harder, grinding her pubis into his curly nest.

Nice, but not the sort of sweet violence she needed now. "Not quite."

"I aim to please. How about this?" He raised her by her bottom, then shoved her down again.

She shuddered and moaned, "Closer." Undulating her hips, she scraped her clit into his crisp hairs. A shock of electricity shot straight to her core, and she strained closer. "Do it again."

"No. Too late," he said, his voice raspy. "This isn't about you now."

Pia opened her eyes. "Not fair," she gasped. "I'm not even close."

The hungry, dangerous glint in Max's eyes gave her heart a jolt. Hot arousal gushed from deep inside her while her vagina tightened its grip around his cock.

Max groaned. "*I* need more." He pushed and shoved her hips, grinding deeper, faster. "I've gotta fuck you hard."

Pia sobbed and flung her arms around his neck. "Please, Max. I need that too."

He rose from the chair in one easy, powerful motion.

Pia wrapped her legs around his lean waist to keep him lodged inside her, but he didn't go far. Her back met the cold wood of the door.

He pressed his forehead against hers. "Your ribs—can you take it rough?"

Pia placed her palms on his cheeks, and whispered, "Rattle the door off its hinges, baby." She tilted her head and kissed him, slipping her tongue into his mouth to mate with his.

Max tasted like sin. Lusty, dirty sin.

He dipped his knees and heaved upward. His cock stroked deep inside her cunt. There wasn't time to savor the sensations because he thrust again, hard. The kiss ended when she had to gasp for breath.

He thrust again and again, until Pia calibrated the climb to the summit by the sweat that gathered on his forehead and back, and the excess arousal smearing her thighs. He battered her body against the door, his own breaths becoming labored, harsh, grunting as he drove up inside her.

The door didn't rattle—it thudded loudly. Almost as loudly her moans. This was what she'd needed. A hot, powerful claiming.

Then he changed the length of his thrusts. Angling side to side, pistoning his hips, until the heat deep inside her cunt burned like flickering licks of flame that spread outward, tightening her legs and belly.

"Max! I'm coming, Max!"

"Christ, don't wait. Give it to me."

"Fuck me! *Max!*" Her shouts echoed around the kitchen, punctuated by the pounding on the door. Pia had the fleeting thought that anyone listening might think an earthquake rumbled through the house. But that was her last lucid thought as Max drove her body to climax.

She gasped, arching her back against the door, her pussy convulsing around his cock, squeezing, milking him for the essence of his life force.

How long it lasted, she'd never be sure, for afterward she clung to him like a wilted vine, sobbing.

Max pressed her body to the door and speared his fingers through her hair, lifting her face from the crook of his neck. "Stop crying, Pia. I'm sorry. So sorry."

But she couldn't stop. She clutched him tightly, her legs squeezing around his waist to hold him to her, afraid to break the connection lest she lose the feeling—the glowing one that burst like sun above the rim of the earth at morning. A sight she'd been denied for three quarters of a century.

"I swore I wouldn't hurt you." Max said, stroking her hair. "Didn't mean to. Fuck!"

Finally, she heard what he was saying and opened her eyes. "Baby, you didn't hurt me." She kissed his chin, his jaw.

"I was too rough." His eyes were filled with regret.

She kissed the side of his mouth. "No. You were perfect. Too perfect. I didn't know I could feel so much."

"But—"

She pressed her lips to his—a close-mouthed blessing. "You weren't too rough with me. I promise. Would you be standing in a puddle if I hadn't liked it?"

He blinked and a smug smile tilted the corners of his lips. "I am? Damn, why do I still have my shoes on?"

"I needed your violence every bit as much as you," Pia said, holding his gaze, willing him to understand she'd accept his sensual deflections—*for now*. "Remember, I'm a vamp. I'm not some frail human girl. I can take everything you give me."

His eyelids dropped halfway. She recognized that look. He was considering what she'd just said and wondering what new limits he could push.

Pia felt a smile curve her lips. "Seeing the possibilities, now? Hmmm, lover?"

* * * * *

Max stood back from the window. The blanket he'd hung ought to keep the sun at bay. He grunted. He didn't miss the irony of the care he took with this vampire woman.

He turned to the bed and Pia. She slept curled on her side. Knowing what she was, he still felt uneasy at her stillness. But she definitely needed the rest—she'd fallen asleep before dawn in mid-sentence.

Equally jaded, he smirked, feeling self-satisfied—his balls were drained dry. The woman could fuck. She could take anything he gave her.

He set his alarm, crawled back beneath the covers, and pulled her into his arms, draping her just the way he wanted— her head nestled in the crook of his shoulder, her thigh nudging his spent cock. When they awoke, he wanted her to be right where he needed her to be for a little dusk delight.

Now that she slept and wouldn't attempt to distract him with her sexy demands, his mind was free of the clouding lust that had driven his body the past hours. Free to contemplate the woman lying beside him and the mystery of her sudden appearance in his life.

Her arrival in his life hadn't been a coincidence. That much he was sure of. The male vamps knew her well. He guessed she was an enforcer, of some sort, for the northern council—the one that had spawned the new community of vampire masters here. And her latest assignment had been him. But to what purpose?

His hatred for all vampires wasn't a secret. But he'd done his job, suppressing his natural animosity for their species. If not accepting of them—he'd tolerated them.

And he didn't think he posed any great threat to their organization. He was just one lone werewolf.

So what had changed?

The only thing that came to mind was the woman no one spoke of in "mixed" company — Joe's wife, Lily.

Max had seen her only once on the day Joe returned to Vero after his "sabbatical". Max had known instantly what she was. A breeder in heat. Her scent had been provocative, drugging — an aphrodisiac so potent he'd hardened to oak in seconds.

Others of his kind hadn't missed her arrival either. The male wolves had caught a hint of her tantalizing scent in the air that first day, and they'd been restless ever since to discover her whereabouts.

He wished he hadn't been in the conference room when Joe arrived, looking haunted, bitter. The woman with the cinnamon-colored hair had entered behind him, her pinched, white face betraying how overwhelmed and frightened she felt.

Max's body had stirred at her irresistible allure — but she belonged to Joe. So he fought it, tamped it down viciously. Eventually, her heat had passed and the hormonal dementia it had created dwindled.

He wished now he'd never mentioned her to Alec. Ever since, his brother had reminded him of his duty to his family. Of the possibility that Lily could breed a vampire — the likes of which would be more powerful and horrifying than the creatures born from a vampire's bite.

The kind that had killed their mother.

Max and the other pack members had been raised on tales of the Old Wars. They'd sat fascinated as any child listening to stories of heroic deeds and mythical monsters, little realizing the truth behind the tales.

The stories bred fear of beasts that walked the night, undead bogeymen and women who'd eat a cub if they caught one alone.

That fear became an abiding hatred, reinforced by the training wolves received as they approached their majority. Training that helped them blend among humans, so they might protect themselves and their families from detection. Training that helped them master the monster within and prepared them for The Final Battle for dominion over the Earth.

Max had trained and learned along with the others, but his time living a "blended" life, had taught him how insular his upbringing had been—and how narrow the vision of the clan's future.

Now, he recognized the hatred he was taught for what it really was—prejudice. The woman beside him had changed his heart—opened his mind to the possibility that wolf and vampire could coexist. Her dark passion ignited a sensual storm that paled in comparison to the purely animalistic urges Joe's wife had stirred. He was afraid he might be in love with her.

But what was he to do about his brother? And was it really possible a breeder was going to bear an abomination—a vampire child? As far as he knew, no one in his immediate clan had ever seen one. His mother's death had been attributed to one—but Max wondered how much truth lay in the tale. Had it been embellished to support their fears, to invigorate their fight? There was no living wolf left to corroborate the tale.

The only thing Max could think to do was discover whether Lily truly carried Joe's child. If she didn't, he could put Alec off her scent, and Max wouldn't be forced to make an impossible choice—between killing Joe's wife and offspring or disloyalty to his clan.

But how could he learn the truth when she never set foot outside the Masters' fortress? It was a given *he'd* never be invited inside.

He could think of only one way to get inside The Compound. To accomplish it, he'd have to betray the woman sleeping in his arms. His arms tightened around her as if he should protect her from his intent.

He could tell himself he was laying to rest issues that stood between himself and his vampire teammates—or attempt to justify his actions by claiming Pia and the others hadn't been honest with him about her presence in Vero either. Neither felt honorable, and neither was the truth.

The truth was, he had to know whether a creature like the one who killed his mother grew inside the belly of his best friend's wife. If one did, he'd have to destroy the woman to prevent its birth.

Killing vamps had never been hard—until he'd had to spend time with them. Now they had names and faces he'd remember—soft brown hair and silky skin he'd never tire of touching.

He hoped like hell he found nothing in The Compound. And would never have to make the choice.

Worse, if he was discovered inside the Masters' dwelling, he'd lose Pia and likely his life.

* * * * *

Something wet and slightly rough lapped his balls. Before he even opened his eyes, he pulsed his hips against Pia's mouth.

Seemed Pia was still working on proving a vampire lover's advantages.

Max could definitely attest to the indescribable pleasure her long cat-like tongue was giving him as she rasped his balls and shaft. He groaned and threaded his fingers through her hair, tugging to encourage her to move higher.

A low, throaty laugh vibrated against his flesh. "Sorry. I didn't mean to wake you, but I woke up horny."

"Sorry, my ass," he said, growling with feigned irritation. He peered at her through slitted eyelids.

She sat perpendicular to his body, bent forward so her hair caressed his thighs and groin. Her eyes were closed; her lips glided along his penis until she reached the crown. Then she swallowed him, suctioning strong, her cheeks hollowing as she wrung pleasure from his core. One hand continued to massage his balls, tugging gently, while the other grasped the base of his cock and worked up and down his long shaft. By her expression, she was sucking the most delicious lollipop imaginable.

God, she was beautiful.

Max reached for a breast and plucked a velvety bead. Her hips wriggled and he took the hint, moving his hand to her buttocks. He lifted his hand and smacked her.

She gasped and sucked harder.

Her reaction encouraged him to experiment. He squeezed one cheek, rubbed it in circular strokes until it heated, then slapped her again.

Pia shuddered and her belly lowered, raising her buttocks against his hand. Her teeth grazed the tender flesh of the head of his cock—her tongue fluttered inside the tiny eye.

"Let me suck your cunt, sweetheart," he said, his voice harsh with need.

Without breaking the rhythm of her bobbing head, she crawled over him, centering her pussy above his mouth. She drew back from his cock. "If I have to tell you what to do, I won't be sucking you off," she said, her voice tense.

"Then tell me with your body." His hands reached around her to grasp her buttocks, and he lifted his mouth to her fragrant, moist cunt. One lap of his tongue and he knew she was very close to coming—she dripped creamy excitement. Not one to pass up a gift, Max licked the excess moisture from her thighs, her plump, down-covered lips and finally traced the edges of her delicate folds. The salty taste of her had him growling deep inside his throat.

He decided it was time to show her one of the advantages to be gained from having a lupine lover.

His tongue lapped her flesh, like a dog drinking from a bowl, his tongue caressing the length of her slit in quick strokes.

"Oh my God. Max! That's incredible!"

He grinned and lifted his hips to press his cock against her mouth—a not-so-subtle reminder that she had work to do as well.

She opened her lips and bobbed her head down his cock until he touched the back of her hot throat.

Satisfied she was back on track, he nuzzled between the inner folds of her sex and slid his tongue inside her, licking the inner walls of her vagina as far as his wolf's tongue could reach.

Pia's thighs trembled, but she continued to move on him, her hands and mouth gliding in unison, if perhaps a little jerky now.

Max rolled his day-old beard against her hooded clit and continued to stroke her with his tongue. Then he squeezed the mounds of her buttocks and glided his fingers toward the crevice between them.

Pia's shudder racked her body, and she mewled—the sound making a shivery vibration on his cock that hardened his balls to stones.

Close. She was so close he could feel the slow, building spasms inside her channel and taste her fresh enthusiasm.

He circled a thumb over her anus and observed a marked increase in her quivering. Her breaths came in shallow pants. Feeling powerful, he pressed the blunt, thick ball of his thumb inside, noting the tightness of the orifice. He nearly spilled his seed then and there at the thought of pushing his cock past that tight little ring of muscle.

The warm glove of her mouth lifted. "Oh Max!" Pia gasped. "I'm right there. Please, I'm gonna come."

"Don't stop sucking me, Pia," he said, making his voice low and dangerous. "If you do, I won't give you what you really want." He licked her cunt as a reminder.

She dipped her cunt lower over his mouth. "What if I give you something...unexpected," she said, her voice husky. "Something hotter than you've ever imagined?"

He knew she was talking about the gift of a vampire's bite. Somehow, the thought of Pia drinking his lifeblood wasn't distasteful. If he allowed it, she'd know what he was. Perhaps now was the time to tell her—when she was so wrapped up in her own arousal, she wouldn't be able to stop until she'd fed well. Perhaps when she had the essence of his life warming her belly, she'd be ready to listen…to understand. "Show me, baby."

Her hands stroked his belly and thighs. "I'll be the best you ever had, Max. Promise."

Max turned his head and kissed her inner thigh. "Baby, you already are. Just don't bite my cock."

Chapter Eight

෨

"I promise you'll only feel a prick," Pia said. "You'll love it."

He bit the tender skin of her thigh. "Maybe, but just the thought of…"

Pia laughed, a strangled sound that ended on a groan. "All right. I won't bite your cock."

Max rolled his chin on her pussy. "And what do you want, baby?"

She groaned again. "You're not going to make me say it, are you?"

"Uh-huh." He rubbed her anus with his thumb. "Tell me."

"Oh, do that again." Her hips pulsed back, then forward, until she rocked. Shallow pulses, Max wasn't sure she was even aware she made. "I want…you to fuck my ass with your fingers while you lick me with your incredible tongue," she said, her words coming out in a rush.

"All right. I think I can handle that. You ready?"

"Are you?"

Damn, she sounded sexy. Max didn't answer. Instead he put two fingers in his mouth and wet them. Then he stroked his *incredible* tongue deep inside her body while pushing one finger past the tight ring of her asshole. He rotated his hand, easing her tight muscles before pressing another finger inside.

"Sweet, sweet Jesus!" she moaned. "Oh, that hurts so good." Her body told him how much she approved when her cunt tightened rhythmically around his tongue. Pia went to work, gliding her tongue up and down his cock, lubricating it so her hands glided easily along his shaft. Then she licked his balls.

At first, Max felt only the rasp of her wet tongue, and then he noticed a slight, burning that turned to a tingling sensation. He recognized the cause—she'd released the enzymes in her mouth, the ones that numbed the flesh of her hosts. *Christ*, she was going to bite his balls!

Max's thighs tightened, his cock felt ready to explode—if she bit him there, he wouldn't last a second. He had to distract her.

With his tongue stroking her vagina and the fingers of one hand pumping inside her ass, he brought his free hand to the top of her pussy and pushed back the skin covering her clitoris. He found the hard, slick knot and touched it with the pad of his finger.

Pia widened her stance, bringing her cunt lower still. Her belly quivered now against his. Then he felt her mouth close around his balls, and he tensed.

There, where his sac snuggled against his groin, he felt the prick of her teeth. She hadn't lied—the pain was slight and he relaxed a fraction. Then she drew blood, and he heard her gasp.

He didn't give her time to think about what her tongue tasted—about the undeniable fact his wolf's blood revealed. He rubbed her clit, working his fingers back and forth, faster, as he finger-fucked her ass and laved her juicy channel.

Pia shuddered and drew again, sucking hard, pulling blood from his extremities in a rush of cold-hot sensation that brought him to the brink, but held him there. His cock was so hard the skin that clothed his shaft felt tight enough to burst. His balls, nestled in the cavern of her mouth, grew hot and impossibly harder, but she controlled his release, keeping him at the brink until he thought his heart would explode in his chest it beat so fast.

Then she moaned and her hips rocked, and he was flying, his cock erupting in a geyser of cum that never seemed to end.

Pia's cunt convulsed and she cried out, the spasms stroking his tongue. Until they both slowed their rhythmic shudders.

She licked the punctures closed and let go of his cock, laying her head on his thigh as she dragged air into her lungs.

Max eased his fingers from her ass and gave her one last soothing lap of his tongue and then swept his arms around her hips, holding her tightly for a long moment. Giving her time. Time he knew she used to gather herself, to consider what she'd just learned.

Then she tensed and struggled against his hold.

He let his arms fall to his side and lay on the bed while he watched her climb off him and turn.

Her expression was wary, then her eyes widened. "It was you on the beach!"

Max nodded, waiting to see what she'd do next.

"I didn't want to believe…" Her lips twisted in self-disgust. "I smelled wolf all over you. I just wanted to think you'd rolled on the ground with one of those monsters—but I *knew* better when I cleaned your wounds."

"I wondered how long it would be before you pieced it together," he said softly.

Pia's cheeks grew red as her anger built. "I didn't want to believe what my brain was telling me all along. But you knew what you were doing—deflecting me with sex. You must have thought I was incredibly stupid. Probably laughed at me the entire time."

Max kept his face solemn and he shook his head. "Never."

But she acted like she hadn't heard him, lashing out at him. "I should have known. You're stronger than any human I've ever encountered. And your tongue! No human has a tongue like that."

He gave her a crooked smile. "There are advantages to having a werewolf lover."

Pia's eyes narrowed. "I would never have fucked you that first time if I'd known."

"Well, now you can't deny it." He kept his voice deliberately mild. He needed her to let loose all over him, so he prodded. "What are you going to do about it, sweetheart?"

Pia launched herself at him, her hands curved into claws, her mouth open, teeth protracted to slash at his flesh.

He caught her and rolled, pinning her to the bed.

She bucked, nearly unseating him, but he straddled her body at the tops of her thighs to keep her legs in check, and held her arms above her head. "Listen to me."

"No! You're a goddamn werewolf. I knew it! You were too good to be human."

"You knew it all along. Don't pretend otherwise." He pressed her hands into the mattress. "In the back of your mind you had to know. Did it excite you? Having an animal between your legs?"

"Bastard!" She bucked harder, panting with exertion.

Max felt his belly tighten in renewed arousal. "Did you like what my tongue did to you? Would you like a wolf's cock fucking you?"

"Get...off...me!" she said between gritted teeth. "We don't mix. It's impossible. We're mortal enemies, and it's my duty to kill you."

Max held her, not an easy task since she was strong and writhed like a snake. He ignored his arousal stirring between his legs. "Mine too, love. But I saved your ass. Doesn't that tell you something?"

Her eyes blazed with anger and betrayal. "It only tells me you're more devious than the hounds who slaughtered those vampires." She lifted her head and banged her forehead hard against his chin.

Max tasted blood from his split lip. "Pia, stop fighting me. I'm not going to hurt you."

"And I should believe you?" she yelled. "You lied to me."

Max heard the hurt and confusion in her voice. "I never lied."

"Then you should have told me."

"I just did. I let you bite me for fucksake!"

She halted her struggles. "You should have told me," she repeated, this time her voice broke on a whimper.

"Like you told me you're a vampire?" he asked softly.

"That's not the same!"

"But it is, baby. What was I supposed to say? 'Hey, Pia. I'm a werewolf.' Could I trust you not to tell the others? I work surrounded by your kind. How long do you think they would have let me live?"

"They aren't monsters!"

"And I am?"

Her eyes filled with tears. "Damn you!"

"Sweetheart." He sighed and let go of her hands.

She didn't fly at him. She covered her face and sobbed.

Max climbed off her and gathered her into his arms.

"Wh-what are we going to do?" she asked, burrowing her head into the crook of his shoulder.

He stroked her hair and her back. He didn't know what to say.

* * * * *

From a distance, Max heard the muffled rattle of his garage door opening and the roar of a motor. Alec was back. He glanced at the clock. It was nearly dusk.

With Pia sleeping like the de—well, like a vampire, Max decided not to join his brother in the kitchen. Alec could eat his way through the groceries for all he cared. He had more important things to consider—like the woman lying in his arms and his future, now that he'd been outed.

He wouldn't ask Pia to keep his secret. Too many weighed on his conscience as it was. Besides, an idea had planted a seed. One that could potentially grow to bridge their worlds.

The garage door closed and Max heard a car engine rev. Alec was in a hurry. Max settled his head in his pillow, ready to return to sleep, and then a niggling thought brought him wide awake.

The golden wolf. Not so unusual a shade. But he remembered something—something masked by his transformation the evening before. A scent. One *familiar*.

Max rolled out of the bed and quickly donned a pair of sweatpants. Then he headed to the garage. He flicked on the light switch. As usual, Alec hadn't bothered to give the bike a wash before returning it. As meticulous as he was about his appearance and his own belongings, he wasn't careful with Max's things.

Max knelt beside the bike and sniffed. Above the scent of gasoline, rubber, and oil he smelled traces of wolf. And on the seat, beneath a leather strap, he found a tuft of hair—from a golden wolf's coat—and a smear of blood.

A cold knot of anger settled in his belly. Damn Alec!

* * * * *

Max quietly entered Alec's apartment and followed rustling sounds down the hallway to his bedroom. He eased open the door to see Alec slinging clothing into a duffel. "Little brother, what have you done?"

Alec froze, but kept his back to him. "What you should have been doing. Killing vamps."

"If your cause is so righteous, why are you sneaking away?"

"Because you'd never approve. You always follow some rulebook the rest of us haven't read and don't understand."

"You killed humans. What do you think our pack will think about that?"

Alec's broad shoulders tensed. "They'll understand. Those humans were garbage. They fed vampires, willingly. Besides, I didn't kill them. I just couldn't stop—"

"You couldn't control those mindless beasts you made. Could you, brother?"

"No." Alec turned, his gaze was fevered. "I didn't intend for it to happen. We talked about it beforehand, but they seemed crazed by bloodlust."

"It was you at that bar last night, too. You knew how unstable your cubs were, but you brought them there anyway."

"Yeah, and we would have killed every last vamp in that bar." Alec picked up a shirt, wadded it into a messy bundle and stuffed it into his bag. "What of it? You stopped me from killing your girlfriend. Your *vamp* girlfriend." He tossed the duffel aside and turned, his fists clenched at his sides. "She had your scent all over her. Can you imagine how sickening it was to discover you'd fucked one of those creatures? You! My own brother?"

Max felt his body go cold. "Go home, Alec. Don't come back. If you do, I'll have to kill you." He turned on his heel and walked away.

"You'd kill your own?" Alec screamed after him. "For what? That bitch? That fucking vampire whore?"

Max left the apartment, climbed on his bike, and sped to the station. He needed to see Pia. Needed to hold her and remind himself why he was turning his back on his own kind.

* * * * *

Pia slid the keys to the sedan across the conference table.

Joe raised an eyebrow. "What's this? Max still not feeling well? He didn't drive you?"

She shook her head. "No, he left me a note to say he'd meet me here."

The conference room grew still. Pia glanced around the table and noted for the first time that only vamps were in the room—Dylan, Quentin, and Joe.

"He was on his bike then?"

Pia wondered at Joe's pointed question. His gaze was too alert for it to be a casual inquiry. "I'm not sure. I haven't seen a bike. Why? What's going on?"

"The team ran a check on all the vehicles parked along the boardwalk last night," Dylan said, his voice even—a little too controlled. "Max's motorbike was among them."

"I don't understand."

"Neither do we," Dylan said. "That's why we asked."

"But he didn't drive there on a bike. He arrived with Joe and me."

"What do we really know about Max?" Quentin asked.

Pia turned to Joe. "He was your friend before you turned."

"We drank beer," Joe said, his eyes narrowing, "and watched each other's asses on the job, but I wouldn't say we were ever bosom buddies. I didn't even know he had a brother in town."

That caught her short. "A brother?"

"We ran some checks on my old buddy. Max has some deep, dark secrets."

"We're thinking he has some big hairy ones actually," Quentin said.

Pia blushed guiltily.

"You know, don't you?" Quentin asked softly.

She raised her head reluctantly, afraid they'd read Max's secret in her eyes.

Quentin's narrowed gaze pinned her to the spot. "He's a fucking werewolf, isn't he?"

Fear for Max instantly dried her mouth. Her heart pounded in her chest.

Joe rose from his seat and grabbed her upper arms. "Pia! This is important. Is Max a werewolf?"

Tears pooled in her eyes and trickled down her face. "He's not dangerous to us."

His face grew red, his mouth twisted with anger. "Goddamn! Fuck!"

"Where is he?" Quentin asked, rising from his seat.

"H-he's supposed to be here," she whispered.

"All of us are supposed to be here," he said, his voice deadly calm.

"Lily! He's going after Lily!" Joe released her. "We've got to get back to The Compound."

"He's not like that," Pia cried out. "He wouldn't hurt her. Why would you think he'd hurt her?"

"If he finds out she's carrying vamp kits, he'll fucking kill her!" Joe shouted.

"She is?" Pia grew cold. "I wondered, but the women were so tight-lipped."

"She's having my babies—and if anything happens to her, I'll kill anyone responsible."

"Let's go," Dylan said. "Call the women on your cell, Quentin. Let them know we're on the way."

A phone. Shocked and feeling like events were whirling out of her control, Pia could only think that she needed to get to a phone. The second part of her mission was accomplished. Navarro needed to know his hunch was right, a breeder was pregnant by a vampire.

Instead, she let the men herd her outside the station and into the sedan. As the tires spit gravel, she wondered where the hell Max was and hoped he'd gone to ground. If the vampires found him, he was a dead man.

* * * * *

Finally, the sedan came to a screeching halt. Max waited long heart-stopping minutes before he opened the trunk latch and climbed out onto the driveway inside The Compound.

His impulsive action to hide inside the sedan had paid off. Although their voices were muffled, he'd discovered they were on to him. His life in Vero was forfeit. After he learned the truth for himself about Joe's wife, he would disappear. He couldn't return to the clan. He couldn't remain in his "blended" world either.

He couldn't have Pia.

Her tearful comments to the rest of the SU vamps had tugged at his heart. He was warmed by her defense.

"He wouldn't hurt us," she'd said. "He saved my life last night."

"I don't know what Max's game is," Dylan had said. "But there's a reason he's still hanging around. I just hope it's not the one I'm thinking. If it is, we have to hope like hell he hasn't had time to tell others of his kind."

What had they been talking about? They were speeding toward The Compound. He knew because Quentin called the women to tell them to make sure the place was locked up tight. The only reason Max could think for their desperation was that he'd been right about the woman, Lily.

But he had to know for sure.

Max kept to the bushes next to the house, looking for an unguarded entrance. Finally, he spied one, fifteen feet above him—a balcony. He stripped in the darkness and shifted into werewolf form, telling himself to follow the scent of the breeder. Hoping he'd remember his purpose once he'd changed.

The wolf backed up several feet from the wall and ran at it, leaping into the air to catch the railing above with his paws. Then he was over it, standing on the balcony. He heard voices within, raised in shouts. A woman—his woman—crying. His hackles rose on his shoulders and back. He lowered the door latch with his nose and crept inside the darkened room.

The room held faint traces of popcorn and beer. He rushed past sofas redolent with human and vampire scent to the door, which stood open. The light from a hallway shone like a beacon. He peered around the door into the hallway, raising his nose to catch scents in the air.

He smelled a woman with a muddied aroma—human-vampire-*breeder*. He knew he should follow it, but the other scent, his mate's, was the one that pulled him down the hallway to an open area.

A railing stood between him and the large, hollow-sounding room below. The voices came from there. The overriding odor of several vampires set his heart beating faster—he peered between the rails and found his woman surrounded by large male vampires. They emanated anger and spoke harshly to his woman. Two human women, pregnant by their scent, and a vamp female hovered around the edges of the circle.

Then the male with hair the color of sunlight, lifted his face, his nose twitching. His gaze rose. He'd caught the wolf's scent.

Letting a warning growl build in his throat, the wolf leapt over the railing to land at the feet of the woman.

Pia screamed as a large black beast leapt into their midst. He whirled in front of her to face the group closing in around them, snarling, his long fangs bared in a feral grimace.

Weapons were drawn and aimed directly at his broad chest.

Oh God, Max! She threw herself over him, clasping her arms around his neck. "Don't shoot him!"

"Stand away from him," Joe yelled.

She held on to the bristling male wolf whose deep-throated growl raised goose bumps on her flesh. "You can't shoot him. I won't let you hurt him."

"He's here for Lily," Joe said, his face darkening, his face transforming into a vampire's mask.

Joe's leer was every bit as frightening to Pia as the rumble emanating from the wolf's chest. Still, she clung to Max.

"Damn you! He'll kill her. Step aside, or I'll shoot you both."

"Joe, please," Lily said, clutching his sleeve. "He's surrounded anyway. Think!"

Joe hesitated. "Stand behind me, Lily. He'll have to come through me."

"Fine," she said, slipping behind him. "Be a hero. Just hold your fire."

Pia leaned close to Max's twitching ears. "Please baby. Come back to me. I need you to change now."

The wolf shuddered beneath her. The rumbling didn't lessen.

"Max! I love you. If you don't change, they'll kill you. They'll kill both of us. You'll leave them no choice." She hugged him hard. "Please, baby. Come back to me."

The wolf grew silent, his body tensing at every restless movement made by the men, but Pia sensed he listened. Some part of his animal brain heard her.

"I love you, Max. I trust you."

From one moment to the next, the wolf shuddered and fell to his haunches. He whimpered as he curled on his side, then the hair covering his body seemed to melt away, his body grew broader, his legs straightened. Pia let go of his neck and watched as his face morphed into the one she loved.

"Max," she sighed and threw herself against his bare chest.

He rolled to his back taking her with him. "Pia." His fingers swept away the tears she hadn't known were on her cheeks. "I heard you crying," he said, his voice sounding rough and husky. "Did I also hear you say you love me?"

Pia gave him a smile, knowing her lips trembled, but not caring he saw how much he meant to her. "Yeah. I'm crazy in love with you."

His hand cupped the back of her head and forced her down. His lips captured hers with a "Max" kiss—hard, forceful, passionate.

Pia opened her mouth and groaned, taking his incredible tongue into her mouth. Her hands smoothed over his bare chest and upward to cup his face.

"This opens a whole new avenue for my research," Lily said. "And I'm never going to take a vamp's word for a wolf's attributes again."

"Lily! Just keep that damn tape measure in your pocket," Joe grumbled.

"Joe, you're such a spoilsport," Emmy murmured.

Chapter Nine

಄

"This isn't over," Quentin said, his narrowed eyes telegraphing his deadly intent.

Max gently set Pia aside and sat up, leaning back on his hands so they could see they were occupied holding him up. "You're right. I'm only the beginning of your problems."

Joe stepped forward, his fists curled, but halted when his woman grabbed his sleeve. "And you're going to tell us what they are?"

"I don't blame you for thinking the worst," Max said. "Yesterday, if I'd happened upon Lily, I might have killed her."

Joe shook off Lily's hand and took another step.

"He said might," Pia interjected, scrambling to kneel at his side.

"What's so different about today?" Dylan asked, his quiet tone not fooling Max a bit. His body was tensed, ready to spring into action.

Max held himself perfectly still. No use exciting the men into opening fire. "I've had time to think about things—about what all this means."

"What? You found God?" Joe snorted. "Gimme a break."

Max stared at his old friend. "Something like that. I found love. And it didn't matter if it would be returned. I knew despite what I'd been taught all my life, I couldn't let Pia be harmed last night."

Pia's gasp drew his gaze. Her face was pale, and her eyes glistened with tears. "Max, you don't have to say it."

He gave her a crooked smile. "I do. I'm naked—"

"Mmm-hmm."

All eyes turned to Emmy O'Hara.

Her blue eyes widened, and she lifted her hands in mock-surrender. "I'm just agreeing. I can't help looking. The man's made of muscle. Hell, he's got muscles on his muscle."

Dylan's glare would have quieted a hard man, but Emmy just grinned.

Max ignored her, staring instead at Pia whose cheeks reddened. "What I mean is I've got nothing to hide behind, sweetheart. I'm in love with you. You're my match in every way. You're a vampire and I'm a werewolf, but we're more alike than any two people I know."

"Did you join the force just to kill vampires?" Quentin asked.

Max didn't try to hide a smirk—the man got on every last one of his nerves. "Mostly."

"Well at least he's honest," Quentin murmured. "Stupid, considering who has a bead on him, but honest."

"Still doesn't explain what he's doing here," Joe said.

"We all know why I came." Max nodded beyond Joe's shoulder at Lily. "Your wife, Joe, is a magnet for werewolves."

"And vampires," Pia whispered.

Everyone turned to stare at Pia now.

"I have a secret of my own to share. When you called asking for help with Max," she said, avoiding his gaze, "you played right into Navarro's hands. He'd heard things—about a breeder who might be carrying a vampire's children."

"And what were your orders, Pia?" Dylan asked.

Max heard the steel edge in Dylan's voice.

Pia must have too because she shivered. "Just to report what I learned on the ground here."

"Navarro's one devious bastard," Quentin said.

Joe cursed. "That caps it. We're leaving, Lily. We have to hide."

"Lily needs the strength of our numbers," Dylan said. "She's safer staying here, even if her existence isn't a secret."

"Besides, who's going to watch over her during the day, Joe?" Darcy asked. "I may be pregnant now, but I'll pop in a few weeks. Remember, I'm the day shift."

"I don't fry in the sunshine either," Max said.

Laser-hot glares met his suggestion.

"Isn't that like leaving the fox to watch over the hens?" Joe asked, sneering. "You'd like that, wouldn't you?"

"Hens!" Emmy spluttered.

Joe rolled his eyes. "Sorry, ladies."

"As I told you before Joe, I've changed my thinking about this war between our species."

"Because you love Pia?" Joe's eyebrows rose. "We're supposed to believe that? Just days ago, you aimed an arrow at Dylan's back."

"You son of a bitch!" Emmy shouted and lunged toward him.

Without dropping his aim, Dylan snaked an arm around her waist and pulled her back.

Emmy's fists rose. "What are you waiting for? Kill him!"

"I'm sorry for that," Max said. "I blamed you, all of your kind really, for the horror I saw in that house."

"But your kind committed those crimes," Quentin said.

Max shook his head. "Not my kind. That's the point. I'm not like that. You're not like that. I didn't see that then."

"You do now?" Pia asked, sliding her hand over his shoulder.

His heart felt squeezed in a tight fist at the look of love and trust in her misty eyes. "I thought there was a *good* reason werewolves and vampires were enemies. But I fell in love with you, knowing what you were, and I can't think of one goddamn reason why it's wrong."

"Whoa, *everyone* can see how much you love Pia," Emmy said, her anger of a moment ago replaced with a hint of wonder in her voice.

Max smirked, unashamed his cock reacted so fiercely to Pia's presence beside him.

"Get him a blanket," Dylan said, his voice filled with disgust.

"I think he needs a room," Quentin murmured.

"He can't stay here," Joe said flatly.

"No, he can't." Dylan finally lowered his weapon and sighed. "You are a problem. Our wives won't let us kill you, but we can't trust you."

Still leaning back on his hands, Max drew a sigh of relief when the others put away their weapons. "I understand it'll take time."

Dylan released Emmy and sat on the edge of a nearby sofa. His expression was troubled. "Why are you willing to help us? And leave Pia out of the equation."

Max thought that last command was unreasonable. Pia was the end of his resistance to all things vampire. "I was raised on stories of the Old Wars between our species. I stayed on with the SU when you came aboard, because I waited for you to show your true colors. I expected you to grow in strength and take over. But it didn't happen.

"I envied how strong you were—how organized. My kin are surviving at the brink of extinction. We talk about building our numbers to face you, but it never happens. We live in isolated communities—we haven't learned to blend well with humans."

Max felt his face tighten. "We don't police ourselves. I think that's our greatest failure. I'd like to learn from you."

"Why?" Dylan asked. "So you can take the knowledge back and teach them how to defeat us?"

"No, so I can teach them how to get along with you so that we don't have to live on the fringes."

Dylan stared at him. "I think we have a lot to talk about, Max, but we can't build trust in a night."

Max nodded. He had his life still. One step at a time.

"We have a special room here—it's contained."

Max stiffened. "A holding cell?"

"It has a few more comforts than that." Dylan gave Pia a wink. "You'll stay the night. We'll talk more tomorrow."

"What about work?"

"We still have patrol, but we'll be keeping you covered tonight."

"I don't suppose you can tell us about the werewolves?" Joe asked. For the first time this evening, his tone was a shade less than hostile.

Max drew a deep breath. "My brother was responsible. He left for New Orleans today. He's gone home."

"Did he leave any nasty reminders behind?" Quentin asked, flexing his shoulders and looking as though he halfway hoped he had.

"I don't know," Max said. "But I believe his remaining wolves were killed last night."

"Damn." Joe's face reflected disappointment. "It could be a really boring night."

Dylan rose and kissed Emmy on the lips then he turned to the men. "Let's head out."

Max rose slowly to his feet, happy to be included, even if the vamps would be watching him as closely as the criminals. He gave Pia a quick kiss and indicated to Joe to precede him. "After you."

Joe's eyes narrowed. "No, after you."

Max lifted an eyebrow and led the way out of the room. "Didn't know you had a thing for my ass, Garcia," he said, over his shoulder.

"Just don't drop the soap when you hit the showers."

* * * * *

The women had gathered once again around the kitchen table for a little late night gossip. Waiting for the men to come back and see whether they'd killed Max had taken the toll on their patience. At least two of the women were well into their cups.

"Max-sh has an amazing body," Emmy said, tilting the last of the whiskey to spill into Pia's glass. "I couldn't help noticing that."

"I think everyone noticed you noticing," Darcy said dryly.

"Yeah, he does," Pia replied dreamily. "And an incredible tongue."

Darcy blinked. "A doggie tongue?"

Pia waggled her eyebrows. "Oh, yeah."

"So, what else does a werewolf have that's different from the average vamp?" Darcy asked, leaning as far forward as her round belly would allow.

"I don't know. He's never…you know…" Pia blushed. "…um…transformed while we…"

"Never?" Emmy giggled. "Looks like you have lots-sh more surprises coming."

"Max is surprising even when he's in purely human form."

"It seems like it might be a little weird, making love when he's in his wolf's clothes," Lily said. "All that hair, and all. But I wonder if his cock is like a dog's." Her eyes brightened with intellectual curiosity.

"Lily!" Darcy gave her a playful slap, then turned to Pia. "Do you think?"

Pia shrugged. "I'm not sure what you mean."

Darcy held up her hands, formed a circle with two fingers and poked another finger through the middle, and then cinched the "O" tight. "Well, when dogs mate, they kind of 'lock' together," she said, emphasizing her point by trying to pull her finger free. "But his penis swells inside the bitch."

"Swells? Like what, a balloon?" The thought was vaguely alarming, but the Jack Daniels kept her from worrying too much about it. Pia downed the last sip of her drink.

"I don't know, I've never really been *that* into canine sex," Darcy said, wrinkling her nose. "Thought you might know something."

"I still can't get past the 'bitch' part," Emmy shook her head sadly.

"You'll tell us, won't you?" Darcy asked. "What it's like, I mean."

"Darcy!" This time Emmy swatted at Darcy's arm, but missed and almost unseated herself.

"I have to live vicariously these days," Darcy said, scowling. "I'd love to learn what sort of 'nip and tuck' games werewolves play."

"Nip and tuck? I take it we're not talking plastic surgery."

"If I have to explain it—"

Emmy bounced on her seat. "Oh, I get it!"

Pia grinned at the two, her heart warming at the friendship they'd extended her. She truly felt like "one of the girls" tonight. "Sure, we women have to share information, otherwise we'd be totally left in the dark."

Lily cleared her throat. "Speaking of locks, do you think Dylan was serious about keeping you guys confined?"

"I'm sure he was," Pia said. "But I'm thinking that won't be so bad."

Emmy raised her glass. "I imagine not—all that muscle on his muscle has to be...filling!"

Dylan turned from the monitor trained on the kitchen.

"I can't believe you spy on them," Max said, a smile still stretching his lips at the women's ridiculous conversation.

"It's the only way to stay one step in front of them," Quentin said, with a desperate note in his voice.

"Aye, they're a devious lot." Nodding toward Quentin, Dylan said, "You wouldn't believe the plots we've had to squash. Quentin here can attest to that."

Quentin's narrowed eyes promised retribution. "Dylan, stuff it."

"That's precisely what Darcy did, wasn't it?" Dylan's dry wit had every male in the room, save Quentin, grinning. "But fortunately, we stopped the proliferation of that particular weapon in their arsenal of tricks."

Thinking the men exaggerated the threat, Max turned back to the monitor.

Darcy was leaning over the table. "So what's so special about his tongue?"

"Fuck, we need to get in there quick and break this up. She has that look in her eye." Quentin turned the monitor off with the remote. "They'll be sharing techniques next."

"And that's bad?" Max asked.

"It is when Darcy gets around to describing her finger method." Dylan looked worried.

"Finger method?" Curiosity had him trailing the men to the kitchen. In their rush, they spilled inside the room.

The women turned at the noise.

Emmy shot to her feet. "What the hell? What happened to your faces?"

"Were you fighting?" Darcy's hands were on her hips. "I thought you'd put that discussion aside until tomorrow. You were supposed to be working."

"We were. We suffered these injuries in the line of duty." Quentin looked to Max.

Max nodded, even though it was a blatant lie.

"What was-sh it?" Emmy asked. "Vampires? Werewolves?"

"No, honey." Dylan stepped close to his wife and steadied her with an arm around her waist. "Just a bit of a barroom brawl. We finished it."

Emmy's snort conveyed her disgust. "Just like men! You're not happy unless you're bangin' on something."

Everyone turned to Emmy and stared.

Her face blushed an unattractive shade of embarrassed. "I'll just shut up."

"That'll never happen," Max said.

Joe's eyebrows rose. "Did you just make a joke?"

Max trained his expression into a fierce scowl. "I was dead serious."

The men laughed.

The women faced off, hands on their hips.

Joe raised his hand to his mouth to cover a cough. "I think those of us who still have a sex life ought to hit the sack."

"Ladies, remember the details," Darcy said.

Quentin slung his arm around her shoulder. "Sweetheart, you don't think you're going to be left out, do you hon?"

"Quentin, I'm as big as a house now."

"And your point is?"

Darcy's eyes grew misty. "Oh, Quentin."

Dylan pulled Emmy back to his side. "Love, do you want to play a little 'hide the sausage'?"

"Ooh, my favorite." She let him lead her from the room without ever looking back. "You know how much I love organ meat."

Joe nodded toward the door. "Lily? You coming?"

"I just thought of a few questions I'd like to ask Max. I hate to waste an opportunity to interview—"

"Lily! You're coming to bed with me, just as soon as I lock these two in."

"Unfortunate choice of words, don't you think?" Darcy said, her lips stretching into a wide smile.

Lily nodded emphatically. "He said 'locked'."

"Yes, he did."

Pia swung toward Max, a frown marring the lovely curve of her brows. "Were you guys eavesdropping?"

"Love, would we do anything so unethical?" Max felt sweat pop on his forehead. He hadn't *exactly* told a lie.

Joe's eyes widened. "We need to get you put away for the night." He nodded toward the door. "After you."

Max rubbed the edge of his tender jaw, a reminder of the trouble he could cause if he spilled the beans about the true nature of their evening. "No, after you."

* * * * *

"What were you ladies talking about downstairs?" Max asked, as he threaded his fingers through Pia's dark mane. "We heard you laughing when we walked in."

Pia pulled away from sucking his cock and tilted her head. "Um…we were just talking about the latest surgical techniques."

Max tugged her hair, bringing her lips back into contact with his aching sex. "You're a terrible liar. But you're entitled to your secrets."

Peering up from the floor where she knelt in front of him, Pia's expression grew solemn. "I don't want any more secrets between us."

Max could think of one he'd never tell. His brothers in the spy trade would carve out his innards if he ever let it slip. "Have I told you how beautiful you are?"

Her lips pouted. "You're changing the subject. If I could remember what I just said, I might figure out why."

He pressed his cock to those pursed lips, and she opened her mouth to swallow him.

She moaned deep in her throat as she rocked forward and back, suctioning him to within a heartbeat of orgasm.

"Like my cock, do you?" He peeked down through slitted eyes. "Baby, there's so much more I have to show you."

Pia grew still and reared back. "Um...Max?"

"Yes, love?" He hid his grin. He knew what was coming. Pia's curiosity had been aroused by the women's conversation.

"Is there anything different about the way you have sex when you're...transformed?"

He helped her to her feet, and then swung her up into his arms. Two steps and he deposited her in the center of the mattress. "It's a matter of degrees," he said, sliding over her. He sucked a turgid nipple into his mouth and groaned.

"Degrees of what?" she asked, excitement making her breathless.

"Transformation, love. But as a vampire, I'm sure you wouldn't be interested." He plucked the dampened nipple and switched to the neglected breast, tonguing the tip. "And I'm plenty satisfied with the sex we have. Don't worry about it."

"I would hate for you to feel the need to stifle any part of you."

The earnestness of her comment had him hiding another grin. "I'm not sacrificing love. Is that what you think?" After schooling his expression into one of concern, he crawled up her body. "Let me prove it to you."

She pressed her hands against his chest, holding him off. Her eyes glinted with a touch of irritation. "You know damn well what I'm talking about, don't you?"

A smile won out. "You're going to have to spell it out. I can't make any mistakes."

"You said the same thing that first night."

"I still mean it. I don't want to frighten you or disgust you. And I never want to hurt you."

Her gaze fell away. "Max, would you teach me about some of those...degrees?"

He leaned down and nuzzled her neck. "Tell me, what you want," he whispered next to her ear.

"How can I, when I don't know what you offer?"

He raised his head, his nose an inch from hers as he stared into her wide eyes. "Well, I could transform into a wolf and lick you from your eyebrows to your toes. After your arousal reached fever-pitch, I'd nudge you with my snout until you rolled over, onto your knees, and then I'd mount you—doggie-style—from behind."

Pia gulped and her heart hammered against her chest so hard, his changed rhythm to match.

"There'd be hair all over my body, and I'd rub all over you before catching your shoulder between my teeth. I'd need to hold you still to drive my cock deep inside—deeper than you've ever experienced. But we'd need a lot of time, because something special happens when I mate as a full wolf."

Pia's breath caught and her chest expanded.

Max leaned back and cupped her breast tenderly. "Or I could transform partway, just enough to give me added strength—"

"More muscle?" she asked, her voice scratchy.

"More muscles on my muscle—and fine, downy hairs to rub all over your body."

Pia's belly quivered against his.

He slid between her legs and nudged his sex against her portal. "But I'd still have fingers to tease these luscious nipples and a mouth to kiss yours. So what's it to be?" He squeezed her breast. "You have to be specific."

"I want you to fuck me, Max. Fuck me like an animal."

Pressing a kiss on the tip of her nose, he said, "Baby, it's the only way I know."

About the Author

&

Delilah Devlin dated a Samoan, a Venezuelan, a Turk, a Cuban, and was engaged to a Greek before marrying her Irishman. She's lived in Saudi Arabia, Germany, and Ireland, but calls Texas home for now. Ever a risk taker, she lived in the Saudi Peninsula during the Gulf War, thwarted an attempted abduction by white slave traders, and survived her children's juvenile delinquency.

Creating alter egos for herself in the pages of her books enables her to live new adventures. Since discovering the sinful pleasure of erotica, she writes to satisfy her need for variety--it keeps her from running away with the Indian working in the cubicle beside her!

In addition to writing erotica, she enjoys creating romantic comedies and suspense novels.

Delilah welcomes comments from readers. You can find her website and email address on her author bio page at www.ellorascave.com.

Why an electronic book?

We live in the Information Age—an exciting time in the history of human civilization, in which technology rules supreme and continues to progress in leaps and bounds every minute of every day. For a multitude of reasons, more and more avid literary fans are opting to purchase e-books instead of paper books. The question from those not yet initiated into the world of electronic reading is simply: *Why?*

1. ***Price.*** An electronic title at Ellora's Cave Publishing and Cerridwen Press runs anywhere from 40% to 75% less than the cover price of the exact same title in paperback format. Why? Basic mathematics and cost. It is less expensive to publish an e-book (no paper and printing, no warehousing and shipping) than it is to publish a paperback, so the savings are passed along to the consumer.

2. ***Space.*** Running out of room in your house for your books? That is one worry you will never have with electronic books. For a low one-time cost, you can purchase a handheld device specifically designed for e-reading. Many e-readers have large, convenient screens for viewing. Better yet, hundreds of titles can be stored within your new library—on a single microchip. There are a variety of e-readers from different manufacturers. You can also read e-books on your PC or laptop computer. (Please note that Ellora's

Cave does not endorse any specific brands. You can check our websites at www.ellorascave.com or www.cerridwenpress.com for information we make available to new consumers.)

3. *Mobility.* Because your new e-library consists of only a microchip within a small, easily transportable e-reader, your entire cache of books can be taken with you wherever you go.

4. *Personal Viewing Preferences.* Are the words you are currently reading too small? Too large? Too… ANNOYING? Paperback books cannot be modified according to personal preferences, but e-books can.

5. *Instant Gratification.* Is it the middle of the night and all the bookstores near you are closed? Are you tired of waiting days, sometimes weeks, for bookstores to ship the novels you bought? Ellora's Cave Publishing sells instantaneous downloads twenty-four hours a day, seven days a week, every day of the year. Our webstore is never closed. Our e-book delivery system is 100% automated, meaning your order is filled as soon as you pay for it.

Those are a few of the top reasons why electronic books are replacing paperbacks for many avid readers.

As always, Ellora's Cave and Cerridwen Press welcome your questions and comments. We invite you to email us at Comments@ellorascave.com or write to us directly at Ellora's Cave Publishing Inc., 1056 Home Avenue, Akron, OH 44310-3502.

THE
✞ ELLORA'S CAVE ✞
LIBRARY

Stay up to date with Ellora's Cave Titles in
Print with our Quarterly Catalog.

To recieve a catalog,
send an email with your name
and mailing address to:

CATALOG@ELLORASCAVE.COM

or send a letter or postcard
with your mailing address to:

Catalog Request
c/o Ellora's Cave Publishing, Inc.
1056 Home Avenue
Akron, Ohio 44310-3502

Cerridwen, the Celtic Goddess of wisdom, was the muse who brought inspiration to storytellers and those in the creative arts. Cerridwen Press encompasses the best and most innovative stories in all genres of today's fiction. Visit our site and discover the newest titles by talented authors who still get inspired - much like the ancient storytellers did, once upon a time.

CERRIDWEN PRESS

www.cerridwenpress.com

Discover for yourself why readers can't get enough of the multiple award-winning publisher

Ellora's Cave.

Whether you prefer e-books or paperbacks,

be sure to visit EC on the web at
www.ellorascave.com

for an erotic reading experience that will leave you breathless.